YESTERDAY

YESTERDAY

c. k. kelly martin

RANDOM HOUSE NEW YORK

Text copyright © 2012 by C. K. Kelly Martin

Jacket art: photograph of cityscape © Konishkichen Artwork/Flickr Select/ Getty Images; photograph of girl © Rich Legg/Vetta/Getty Images

All rights reserved. Published in the United States by Random House Children's Books, a division of Random House, Inc., New York.

Random House and the colophon are registered trademarks of Random House, Inc.

Visit us on the Web! randomhouse.com/teens

Educators and librarians, for a variety of teaching tools, visit us at randomhouse.com/teachers

Library of Congress Cataloging-in-Publication Data
Martin, C. K. Kelly.
Yesterday / C. K. Kelly Martin. — 1st ed.
p. cm.
Summary: After the mysterious death of her father and a sudden move back to her native Canada in 1985, sixteen-year-old Freya feels distant and disoriented until she meets Garren and begins remembering their shared past, despite the efforts of some powerful people to keep them from learning the truth.
ISBN 978-0-375-86650-0 (trade) — ISBN 978-0-375-96650-7 (lib. bdg.) — ISBN 978-0-375-89644-6 (ebook)
[1. Science fiction. 2. Identity—Fiction. 3. Memory—Fiction.
4. High schools—Fiction. 5. Schools—Fiction. 6. Family life—Canada—Fiction.
7. Canada—History—20th century—Fiction.] I. Title.
PZ7.M3567758Yes 2012 [Fic]—dc23 2011023994

Printed in the United States of America

10 9 8 7 6 5 4 3 2 1

First Edition

For my mom and dad, who took my brother and me down to Philadelphia for Live Aid in 1985 because they knew how important the music was to us. Thanks for always getting it!

Rage on

YESTERDAY

I dreamt about you last night and I fell out of bed twice.
—The Smiths, "Reel Around the Fountain"

He who controls the present controls the past.
He who controls the past controls the future.
—George Orwell

PROLOGUE

When I've wailed for so long and so hard that my throat is in shreds and my fingernails ripped and fingertips bloody from clawing at the door, I collapse in front of it curled up like a dead cat I saw on an otherwise spotless sidewalk as a child once. The cat's fur was matted with dried streaks of deep red but mercifully its eyes were shut. Its fetal position posture looked like a cruel joke—a feeble attempt to shield itself from a threat it couldn't outrun and couldn't fight.

I'd never seen anything as grisly in real life, and Joanna, my minder and my parents' house servant, pulled me swiftly away from it with one hand, her other cupped to the side of my face in an attempt to obscure my view. But you can't unsee something once you've seen it. Not without a memory wipe anyway.

Joanna wouldn't remember that dead cat anymore but I haven't forgotten. I remember more than most people, it seems. Like that Latham hasn't stopped being my brother just because he's sick. The biologists will find a cure for him and the others any day now, and I can't believe my father, with all his power and influence, could allow his only son to be taken from him—*from us*—to be extinguished forever.

Latham was right. My father isn't any good. He only pretended and I was too naive and weak to want to see through his act. Until now.

The anger churning inside me raises me to my knees again, my fingers scraping the bloodied door of my bedroom as I shout, in a voice as hoarse and unforgiving as your worst memory, "Murderer. Latham's blood is on your hands."

I tried begging my father for hours before this. *Daddy, don't let them do it. Make them hold on to Latham until there's a cure.*

There's always a cure. . . .

You said you wouldn't ever let anything hurt us. You boasted that this was the best country in the world and that you were almost as powerful as the president herself.

But no matter how I pleaded or railed, my father and mother stayed mute downstairs. Their silence was deafening. It screamed that I was the only one who believes there's nothing more important than saving Latham. The one who doesn't merely *remember* more than most people, but *knows* more than the majority of them too.

Sometimes I know things before they happen. For all the biologists' knowledge, that's something they can't fully explain, and as I sink to the ground again, shrieking that I hate my father and mother with all my heart and that they should hate themselves for this too, I see, in a secret sliver of my mind, the SecRos coming for me, dispassionate and unrelenting.

My parents must have sent for them and they'll be here soon.

Any minute now.

I scramble to my feet, exhausted but frantic, and scan the room for some means of escape or at least something to defend myself with. There's nothing . . . nothing. My parents already have me on lockdown, a force field encasing my bedroom. I might as well be trapped inside a steel box with only my bare fists to defend myself against unyielding machines.

I was never someone who worried about the SecRos' strength and what it can steal from those of us who are flesh and blood; I believed they existed to keep us safe and were only following orders that someone else would have to obey in their place. It turns out that I've been wrong about a lot of things, but not about Latham. How can he and the others possibly be any threat if they're locked away? He only needs more time. Surely an antidote must be nearly within reach.

But there's no time for my conjecture now either. I do the only thing I can think of to conceal myself—I tear one of the sheets from my bed and fix the quilt over it. Then I slide underneath my bed clutching the sheet and wait for the SecRos to arrive.

First, there's a knock. From the other side of the door my father says in a reedy voice, "This is for your own good,

Freya. No one's going to hurt you, I promise. Please trust me on that much."

I don't reply. The time of talking things over was finished the second he let them take my brother.

I hear the door swing open and see my father's shoes from my place under the bed, then the black boots of the SecRos entering my bedroom. I don't have the luxury of a moment's hesitation, I'm hauling myself forward in a flash, out from under the bed, my wounded fingers gripping the sheet. I toss it out ahead of me, unfurling it like a picnic blanket in an old-time movie, only higher and more furiously.

The SecRos are fast but they've probably never had anyone throw anything as ridiculous as a sheet at them before, and while the two of them are untangling themselves, as my father numbly watches, I sprint out the open doorway and into the arms of a third SecRo. His hands clamp on to my arms; he swings me into the air like I'm no heavier than the sheet his fellow Ros had to fight their way out from under. My fists pound at his arms, my fingers scraping at his sleeves and underneath to the flesh that isn't really flesh. I kick his pelvis—hard enough, I'm sure, to bring a human male to his knees. The SecRo feels no pain. He stares blankly into my eyes and then past me, to my father.

"Instructions, sir?" the SecRo asks as my limbs flail.

"Just go," my father commands. "Take them now. Escorting them to the destination is your highest priority, you understand?"

"We understand," the SecRos reply in unison.

The SecRo who has ahold of me marches through the upper hallway, flanked by the other two SecRos, one ahead of us now and one behind. Downstairs my mother joins us, her face waxy and her hair lank. "Where are they taking me?" I ask, ready to beg one last time. "Don't let them take me, Mom."

"Us," my mother corrects. "They're taking us."

Us?

"Evacuation," she continues as the SecRo carts me outdoors into the rain, my mother a step behind us. "Stop struggling and save your energy, Freya."

I watch her climb willingly into the military vehicle parked in front of the 152-year-old house she has always professed to love but doesn't stop to look back at. The first SecRo climbs in after her, and the one holding me passes me inside, where the waiting SecRo grips my arms. They ache in a way that tells me the SecRos' tenacious hold is leaving bruises, not that they'd care about that—bruises heal quickly, and they're under orders.

"What do you mean?" I ask my mother.

"The Toxo," she says listlessly. "They expect it to spread quickly."

Then they aren't close to a cure after all. There's no chance for Latham. Maybe what was left of him has already been extinguished. I begin to cry again, silently this time, as we pull away from the house. I stare at the upper window that was Latham's for our whole lives and suddenly I spy something else in that secret sliver of my brain, something my mother hasn't told me yet. A dark void that stretches beyond the edges of my existence.

"Where are they taking us?" I ask, my voice breaking in exhaustion. Dread erupts onto my skin in the form of goose bumps. "What's happening?"

Too late. It's already done. I didn't see the needle coming and now the SecRo is pulling it out of my arm, its former contents swimming into my bloodstream.

Tired.

No. Hold up your head. Don't give in.

So tired.

Latham's swimming inside my head now too. *Remember me,* he whispers, his voice strangled but his eyes still his own.

I will, Latham. I promise.

I close my eyes, unable to feel my body any longer. There's nothing but the two of us, Latham and me, and the promise I make him again and again as I slip away from consciousness and towards the void that will seek to strip me of everything I am in the name of salvation.

ONE

When I wake up I have a pounding headache behind my eyes just like I've had every morning lately. At first my eyelids refuse to open fully, and when they do the weak winter light wafting through my window burns my retinas. My brain feels sluggish and confused as I take in my surroundings: the white chest of drawers and matching mirror across from my bed; a collection of freshly laundered clothes folded neatly on top of the dresser, waiting for me to put them away; and a wooden desk with an open fashion magazine lying across it. Sometimes it takes me ten seconds or so to remember where I am and what's brought me here . . . and as soon as I remember I want to forget again.

My mom says the headache's probably a remnant from the bad flu we all caught flying back from New Zealand, but the other day I overheard her friend Nancy whisper, as the two of them peeled potatoes in the kitchen, that it could be a grief headache. The kind that strikes when you suddenly lose your father to a gas explosion and the three-quarters of you left in the family have to move back to a place you barely remember.

Today is unlike the other days since we've been back because today I start school here. A Canadian high school with regular Canadian kids whose fathers didn't die in explosions in a foreign country.

I've gone to school in Hong Kong, Argentina, Spain and most recently New Zealand, but Canada—the country where I was born—is the one that feels alien. When my grandfather hugged us each in turn at the airport, murmuring "Welcome home," I felt as though I was in the arms of a stranger. His watery blue eyes, hawklike nose and lined forehead looked just how I remembered, yet he was different in a way I couldn't pinpoint. And it wasn't only him. *Everything* was different—more dynamic and distinct than the images in my head. Crisp. Limitless.

The shock, probably. The shock and the grief. I'm not myself.

I squint as I kick off the bedcovers, knowing that the headache will dull once I've eaten something. While I'm dragging myself down to the kitchen, the voices of my mother and ten-year-old sister flit towards me.

"I feel hot," Olivia complains. "Maybe I shouldn't go today. What if I'm still contagious?"

My mother humors Olivia and stretches her palm along her forehead as I shuffle into the kitchen. "You're not hot," she replies, her gaze flicking over to me. "You'll be fine. It's probably just new-school jitters."

Olivia glances my way too, her spoon poised to slip back into her cereal. Her top teeth scrape over her bottom lip as she dips her spoon into her cornflakes and slowly stirs. "I'm not nervous. I just don't want to go."

I don't want to go either.

I want to devour last night's cold pizza leftovers and then lie in front of the TV watching *Three's Company, Leave It to Beaver* or whatever dumb repeat I can find. All day long. Repeat. Repeat. Repeat.

"Morning, Freya," my mother says.

I squeeze past her and dig into the fridge for last night's dinner. "Morning," I mumble to the refrigerator shelves.

"They're behind the margarine and under the bacon," my mother advises.

And they are. I pinch the Saran Wrap–covered slices between my fingers and let the fridge door swing shut. Then I plop myself into the seat next to Olivia's, although she's junked up my table space with her pencil case and assorted school stuff. I could sit in my father's place, which is junk-free, but nobody except Nancy or my grandfather has used his seat since he died. This isn't even the same table that we had in New Zealand, but still Olivia, Mom and I always leave a chair for my dad.

If he were here now he'd be rushing around with a mug of coffee, looking for his car keys and throwing on his blazer.

You'd think a diplomat would be more organized but my father was always in danger of being late. He was brilliant, though. One of the smartest people you'd ever meet. Everyone said so.

I shove Olivia's school junk aside and cram cold pizza into my mouth with the speed of someone who expects to have it snatched from her hand. My mother shakes her head at me and says, "You're going to choke on that if you don't slow down."

I thought sadness normally killed appetite but for me it's been the opposite. There are three things I can't get enough of lately: sleep, food, television.

I roll my eyes at my mother and chew noisily but with forced slowness. Today's also a first for her—her first day at the new administrative job Nancy fixed her up with at Sheridan College—but my mother doesn't seem nervous, only muted, like a washed-out version of the person she was when my father was alive. That's the grief too, and one of the most unsettling things about it is that it drags you into a fog that makes the past seem like something you saw in a movie and the present nearly as fictional.

I don't feel like I belong in my own life. Not the one here with Olivia and my mom but not the old one in New Zealand either. My father's death has hollowed me out inside.

No matter how I happen to feel about things, though, I have to go to school. After breakfast Mom drives Olivia to hers on the way to work but since mine is only a couple of blocks away and begins fifteen minutes later I have to walk.

Fresh snow is falling as I trek away from my house and it makes the otherwise bland suburban neighborhood look almost pretty. I guess I should be cold, jumping from New Zealand summer to Canadian winter, but I really don't mind. My lungs like the cool air. It feels clean.

In minutes I'm at Sir John A. MacDonald High School, stalling at the main entrance with a single snowy binder under my arm because I still don't want to go in. If I thought I'd get away with it I'd double back to the house, root through the kitchen cupboards for something else to eat and then lie on the couch for so long that I'd begin to grow moss. It's not that I don't want to go to school specifically; it's that I don't want to have to do much of anything.

As I'm hesitating at the door, watching bored-looking teenagers file inside, a blond boy in a blue coat and red winter hat does a double take and stops next to me. "Are you coming in?" he asks with a smile that reveals his braces.

I shrug and trail him to the door. He goes first but holds it open for me. "Thanks," I tell him, and I guess I must look disoriented because he says, "So, new student?"

"That obvious, huh?" I pull off my gloves and try to smile.

The boy cocks his head. "Do you know what room you're heading to?"

"One fourteen."

"Easy," he proclaims, yanking off his hat. "It's right beside the music room. I can show you."

I follow the boy down the hall, around the corner and up

a second hallway and when we arrive at 114 I stare down at my boots and coat realizing I should've stopped to put them in the locker they assigned me when my mother got me signed up for school last week.

I tell the boy this, frustration rolling around in the back of my throat, but he patiently offers to take me to my locker too. The narrow sameness of the hallways (off-white walls punctuated by row after row of faded green lockers) makes me feel vaguely claustrophobic—I preferred it outside in the open air, though I guess I'll get used to it. School is school. At my locker (which is midway between the gymnasium and the guidance office) I thank the boy again and he says, "No problem" and then, "What grade are you in anyway?"

"Ten," I tell him.

The boy runs one of his hands through his blond hair. "Too bad."

"Why's that?"

"Because I'm in eleven. But hey, at least I know where to find you." He taps my locker with two of his knuckles. "See you around." He flashes me one last grin before disappearing into the crowd.

By the time I've stuffed my coat into my locker, shaken my binder and boots off (having forgotten to bring a pair of shoes to change into) and retraced my steps back to room 114 I'm late for homeroom. Mrs. Snyder seems like the cranky type but because I'm new she cuts me a break. She's written today's date—Monday, February 4, 1985—on the blackboard and I stifle a yawn as I weave my way over to an empty seat in the second row. We have to stand for the national anthem and then listen to a series of announcements that most of the other students seem to sleep through. I would probably sleep through them too but I don't feel at ease enough for that.

The discomfort clings to me like a second skin as I move from homeroom to math to English. Being the new kid is never good but I don't think I've ever had people stare at me this much and it makes me paranoid. Like I'm never going to fit in here because no one except the teachers and the blond guy from earlier will ever say anything to me; they'll just keep sneaking peeks at me from across the room like I'm seven feet tall or my skin is purple.

At lunch I don't know where to sit without making it look obvious that I'm alone and I pause just a few feet inside the cafeteria door, scanning the tables as though I'll magically spy someone I know. Just as I'm resolving to stride boldly forward a girl I recognize from math class appears at my side. She has wavy black hair that you can tell was dyed and is wearing equally dark clothing but her makeup (except for her paint-thick black eyeliner) is as pale as death. "Freya, right?" she says.

She doesn't allow time for me to answer or maybe I'm just too slow, neck-deep in that fog I can't escape. "You can sit with me if you want," she says, pointing to a table on our left. "Derrick and I usually sit over there."

"Thanks." I step forward to trail the girl from my math class to her table. Her friend Derrick is already seated.

He's black and skinny and his clothes are as decisively dark as hers. His hair, however, is the exact same color as a bumblebee—wide, alternating strips of black and yellow. I can't work out why everyone's staring at me when his head doesn't seem to be scoring the slightest bit of attention.

"This is Derrick," the girl tells me as we sit down across from him.

"Hi," I say.

"Freya's in my math class," she explains. "Is it your first day here?" she asks, turning towards me. "I don't remember you from last semester."

"First day," I confirm.

Derrick rests his sandwich on his lunch bag. "So what other classes do you have?"

He brightens when I run through the names of my teachers. "You have bio with me last period," he notes. "Believe me, Payne is the nicer tenth-grade biology teacher, despite his name. We lucked out."

"Cool," I murmur. I need all the luck I can get. I've already forgotten virtually everything my math and English teachers said this morning and I doubt my afternoon concentration levels will be much of an improvement.

My stomach roars like a wildcat as I head over to buy my lunch (chili with a bread roll), but I'm relieved that I don't have to sit alone and now know people in half of my classes. Once I return to the table, Derrick and the girl, who I learn is named Christine, are bad-mouthing a French teacher and discussing bands I've never heard of. It's like eavesdropping on two people speaking a secret language and after I've polished off my lunch and have essentially been staring into space for a few minutes, Derrick notices that I've tuned out. He wags a finger at me as he remarks, "We're losing her."

Christine scrapes at one of her cuticles and switches her attention to me. "So, who do you listen to?"

I shrug. "Whatever's on the radio. I'm not big into music."

Christine's chin dips like I've given the wrong answer and, not wanting to be a disappointment, I rack my brain for band/musical artist names to give her. Coming up with any is surprisingly difficult. "Wham's okay," I offer at last. "And, like, Prince and Van Halen. The Police. Cyndi Lauper."

Christine's and Derrick's twin expressions reveal that these, too, are the wrong answers. Then Derrick shrugs with his elbows and says, in what I think is meant to be a charitable tone, "Music's a really personal thing. Everyone's taste is different."

Christine scrunches up her face. "Van Halen, though, seriously? David Lee Roth is such a joke."

I mean . . . I don't know. Why does it even matter?

"Whatever," I say, her disapproval beginning to grate on me. "I told you I wasn't really into music." I can't remember a single person asking me about bands at my old school, not one, and I struggle to recall who my best friend Alison's favorite band or musical artist was but the information's not there. I see us riding horses together and laughing about boys. She'd land herself in trouble with teachers more than I would but never about anything serious, just stuff like talking and passing notes in class.

Last July she convinced me to walk to the supermarket three blocks from my house and finally speak to the cute stock boy I liked to stealthily stare at. His name was Shane and he kissed me by the bike rack behind the grocery store three days later. In another week and a half he was my boyfriend and two months after that we were breaking up.

Suddenly I can't stop thinking. About him. Alison. Everyone. Everything. My mind's racing with thoughts of life in New Zealand and all the other places I've lived in the past sixteen years. Teachers I liked. The gerbils my mother let me keep as pets in Hong Kong. My father building a network of elaborate sand castles with me on a Spanish beach. My parents coming home from the hospital with my sister days after she was born. Dates, names, geographic locations and cultural events flood my brain, making my head throb like I've just gulped down a frostbitten scoop of ice cream.

December 8, 1980: John Lennon was shot and killed by Mark David Chapman in New York City.

January 20, 1981: After fourteen months, fifty-two American hostages were released, ending the Iran hostage crisis.

July 29, 1981: Prince Charles and Lady Diana Spencer were married at St. Paul's Cathedral in London, England.

November 30, 1982: Michael Jackson's *Thriller* album was released.

March 23, 1983: U.S. president Ronald Reagan announced a defense plan popularly known as Star Wars.

April 23, 1984: The discovery of the virus that causes AIDS was announced.

I'm a human encyclopedia, pictures, concepts and people flashing behind my eyes: Macintosh personal computers. Pac-Man. Cabbage Patch Kids. "Do They Know It's Christmas?" Compact discs. MTV. Mount Saint Helens. *E.T.* Rubik's Cube. Duran Duran. Madonna. Space Shuttle *Discovery*. Atari. Margaret Thatcher. Pope John Paul II. James Bond. Blondie. Trivial Pursuit. Darth Vader. VCRs. Oreos. *Playboy* magazine. Tylenol. Touch-tone telephones. Big Macs. Easy-Bake Ovens. Kool-Aid.

Remembering, remembering. Lost in an avalanche of information . . .

"Hey!" Christine snaps, waving her hand in front of my face. "Earth to Freya."

I hurtle back into the present, my fingers massaging my forehead and the pain beginning to subside. I shouldn't have come today; I should've tried Olivia's line about still being sick. I'm not ready to be around people. Not *right*.

I could beg off sick after lunch. Postpone my first full day at school until tomorrow or the next day. But will being here feel any more natural then? I doubt it.

When the bell rings I stick with Derrick and head for bio, feeling quiet and tired (and already hungry again, always hungry). Because this is the first day of second semester

Derrick and I are able to grab seats together and as I slip into mine I notice what I've been noticing all day—furtive eyes on me. I try to let it slide, act like I don't notice, but thirty minutes into the period my resolve cracks and I lean close to Derrick and whisper, "Why does everyone keep looking at me?"

Derrick's expression shifts from slightly sheepish to incredulous. "Have you looked in a mirror lately, Freya?"

My eyes dart to my cable-knit sweater and then my jeans and casual winter boots. Is there something wrong with what I'm wearing?

"You look like a model," he adds. "You must get guys staring wherever you go."

Derrick's not kidding but his explanation comes as a shock. I know Shane considered me pretty but it's not like I had guys lining up at my door to ask me out in New Zealand. I've always been the kind of girl who blended into the crowd.

I take a sweeping look around the room, eyeing up the other girls in my class. Maybe I'm better looking than a few of them—I don't have braces, acne, or frizzy hair—but I'm nothing special. As I'm scanning the room, thinking this over, my gaze collides with a dark-haired guy's in the row ahead of me. Caught, he fixates on Mr. Payne talking about worksheets and quizzes at the front of the room.

A similar scene plays out during history class last period. Guys staring. Some girls too. Most of them avoid my eyes when I zero in on theirs but a couple of the boys are bold enough to smile at me. It's bizarre to have this attention out of nowhere; I'd feel out of place enough without it but now, more than anything, I don't want to stand out.

I look exactly the same as I did when we left New Zealand two and a half weeks ago—it doesn't make sense for people to see me differently—and as soon as I'm home again I track snow into the hallway, tugging off my coat, gloves and scarf as I approach the mirrored sliding closet door. Olivia, already back from school, has the TV on in the other room and I hear a siren wailing and pretend cops shouting as I focus on the image in the mirror.

Of course I know what I look like. Slim. Just shy of five foot nine. Dirty-blond hair. Fair skin. Straight teeth. No scars. The mirror doesn't reflect anything other than my usual self.

"What're you doing?" my sister asks, coming up behind me.

"Nothing. I thought I had something in my eye." I lean closer to the closet, pulling one of my eyelids down and scrutinizing my eyeball like I'm searching for a stray lash or speck of dust. "It must be gone."

I twirl around to study Olivia. I never noticed how flawless she is compared to other people, like she won the genetic lottery. Symmetrical, blemish-free, each part of her body in perfect proportion to the rest. Her hair's dark and curly where mine is light and straight and her skin tone's closer to olive than ivory. Even her eyes are darker than mine—navy blue to my pale aqua. You probably wouldn't guess we were sisters if you didn't know us. We really don't resemble each other much.

I don't know why it should come as a surprise to me that Olivia and I don't have the same hair or eyes. Why does my entire life suddenly feel so alien to me? Can my father's death really account for all of that?

"*Laverne and Shirley*'s going to start in a second," Olivia says, like she's offering the best news either of us will hear today.

A smile jumps to my lips, despite my confusion. My sister and I have both transformed into absolute TV addicts since being back in North America. But that's one thing I'm actually not worried about. The television stops me from thinking, blocks out my sadness and the feelings of strangeness that cling to this new life in Canada. Could it be that I need to stop fighting the strangeness and simply surrender? What would my father advise if he were here?

I know the answer to that one as well my own name.

He'd say, "Trust me, Freya. This is for the best."

And maybe being home is what's right, even if I don't feel that yet. *Give it time,* I tell myself. *You just lost your father and moved across the globe. Disorientation is normal. Stop thinking so much and just let things be.* I'm not as convinced by my own words as I want to be but I follow my little sister into the family room, curl up in an armchair and give in to the higher power of television.

TWO

By Tuesday my teachers are already assigning hours of homework and by Wednesday I half expect to find myself sitting alone at lunch because while Christine and Derrick are two of a kind I'm more like an unnecessary third (and broken) wheel. But they're too nice to try to get rid of me, despite our pronounced differences. Maybe they sense that although I don't fit in with them I don't really fit in with anyone else at school either. Not the preppy kids, not the jocks, not the metalheads (Derrick's word), not the honor-roll kids and not even the nerds.

As I approach the cafeteria I wonder if I should plop myself down at some other random table and release Christine and Derrick from what they likely see as an obligation, but that would feel like giving up. As if I'm prepared to spend every lunch hour of the semester alone, no one to gossip with or bitch about my classes to. Just sitting hunched over my food solo, the object of silent stares.

In some ways that would be easier. I wouldn't have to pretend to anyone at school that I don't feel like I'm in the wrong place. But what's the point of being here if I don't speak to anyone? In the end I think it would just make me feel even more lost.

Listening to Christine try to educate me on the merits of new wave music is better than sitting across from an empty chair and I gladly take the handful of tapes (by The Cure, The Smiths and Depeche Mode) she lends me in the hopes that they'll improve my musical taste. As I'm shoving her tapes into my purse with one hand and holding my chicken burger with the other, Derrick asks where I lived before. I guess he's trying to get to know me, find some common frame of reference, but it's not a good subject for me and I give him a severely condensed account of my family history. "We were in Auckland, New Zealand, where my dad was working. He was killed in a gas explosion on the way home from work."

The story's more involved than that but the more I say the greater the likelihood that my throat will close up around the words. A somewhat longer version of events goes like this: A woman my father worked with was having car trouble that afternoon and my father helped her out by dropping her off at home. It was my dad's tragic luck to be pulling into her driveway when a gas leak inside her house caused an explosion. The newspaper said the sky lit up and the whole house collapsed in the blink of an eye. The car was destroyed in the blast too, my father and the woman from his office along with it.

The bottom line is that my dad went to work one morning as usual but never came back and for several seconds Christine and Derrick are too stunned to say anything. I can't stop blinking into the silence, my mind hanging on those golden days at the beach in Valencia with my father years ago: swimming on my dad's back, building worlds in the sand with him and stopping for gelato breaks to help fight the heat. I'd never seen ice cream melt so fast. It poured down between my fingers like a glass of milk. My father's too. Watching the ice cream landslide made us laugh as we lapped at our gelatos, struggling to beat the sun.

The sense of loss drills deeper inside me. I can't believe I'll never see him again.

"I'm so sorry," Christine says finally, her lips twitching as she frowns. "I had no idea."

"No one does." I put down my chicken burger and fiddle with the zipper on my purse. "And I don't really want to talk about it."

"*Of course*," Derrick murmurs with such sympathy that I'm afraid he might tear up. "Changing topics—uh . . . what's with the tenth-grade field trip to the museum next week? The museum's something you do in fifth grade."

"Better than spending the day here, though, isn't it?" Christine says. "I'd rather stare at dinosaur bones and mummies than sit in math class."

I nod in agreement. My diminished attention span won't matter on a field trip.

After wolfing down the rest of my chicken burger and

fries I have to go back to the lunch counter to buy chocolate chip cookies to carry me through the next couple of hours. Christine, who is on the pudgy side, shakes her head at me when I return to the table with the cookies. "How can you stuff your face like that all the time and stay as skinny as you are?"

Even with Derrick having mentioned my appearance two days ago, I'm taken aback by her comment. "Bulimia," I quip after a brief pause.

Christine's eyes pop like I've dropped a second dark surprise in her lap. She tosses her head back, relieved laughter spilling from her lips as she realizes I'm not serious. It's just then that the blond guy who showed me to my homeroom and locker on Monday grazes my shoulder. "Hey, can I talk to you a second?" he asks.

My eyes seek out Christine's—she looks as quizzical as I feel—before I face the guy again and tell him yes. I can't imagine what we have to talk about but I squeeze out from my space at the table and follow him to the noisiest corner of the cafeteria where Derrick and Christine have told me that the jocks sit. I already recognize some key members of the different cliques thanks to Derrick and Christine. They're not the only tenth-grade new wavers at school but for some reason they don't seem to speak to most of the others.

The blond guy stops and stands with one arm against the wall, smiling at me. I guess Derrick and Christine would characterize him as a jock but I don't even know whether he plays sports.

"I stopped by your locker this morning but you weren't around," he says, right hand slipping casually into the front pocket of his jeans. "So, how's it going?" He stares at the spot we left behind, Derrick and Christine's location across the room. "What are they like?"

I shrug, thinking about my cookies, wishing I'd brought them with me. "What are *you* like?" I ask, meaning who is he to question me about Derrick and Christine when I hardly know him but he takes it in a different way, like I'm flirting.

"We should hang out sometime so you can find out." His blond bangs flop forward as he tilts his head. "There's this party thing my friend Corey's having on Saturday night." He pushes off the wall and taps a finger to his lips. "Want to go with me?" He squints at me with his mouth closed and in that second he does look sort of interesting—kind of intense.

"You don't even know my name," I say.

He blinks, reclining back against the wall. "Of course I know your name, Freya."

I wasn't the one to tell him and the mix of uncertainty and curiosity I'm feeling comes out sounding blunter than I mean it to. "Well, I don't know yours."

The guy's mouth falls open for a split second before he clamps it shut again. "Okay, it looks like I'm doing this really badly," he says. "I'm Seth—Seth Hardy. If you talk to Nicolette in your history class she'll tell you I'm an okay guy. She's Corey's girlfriend. Anyway, I've been trying to find a way to talk to you and I thought the party could be a good place for us to get to know each other better."

I exhale slowly, multiple thoughts coursing through my brain at the same time. My father's gone forever. I don't understand this place. I'm starving. Something's missing here . . . something aside from my dad, something I can't put my finger on. And do I actually want to go to this party with Seth or not? From my place in the fog I can't tell, but he was the first person at school who was nice to me. It could be that going to a party with him would be like watching TV—a decent way of distracting myself.

"I have to ask my mom," I tell him.

"Cool." Seth nods, his grin returning and his hazel eyes twinkling. "Tell her you're going with a bunch of people if that helps. I can bring Nicolette with me when I pick you up."

He says that like I've already agreed, which irritates me a bit, but I walk back to Derrick and Christine without contradicting him. The two of them glance guiltily up at me as though they've been talking about me behind my back since the moment I disappeared. "Seth Hardy likes you," Christine intones. *"Prepare to be popular."*

I roll my eyes at her and chomp into one of my cookies. Who says I want to be popular? I just don't want to sit alone in the cafeteria.

It's not long before lunch is over but two periods later Christine and I have math together. I get there first and snag the desk next to hers just like I did yesterday so it looks like it's mine for the duration of the semester. Our teacher, Ms. Megeney, has feathered Princess Diana hair and is wearing a blouse with an ultra-ruffled collar that flaps like a wing whenever she moves. The second I see it I know Christine will have something funny to say about the blouse. I keep watching the door, expecting her to zoom into class with her head down at any minute, but it never happens. The entire period goes by and Christine never shows.

I feel a momentary buzz of concern in my stomach that I can't explain (she's probably just cutting class and forgot to mention it). Since I don't have Christine's phone number there's no way for me to check on her or pass on the math homework. I don't see her again until the next morning on my way to homeroom—a vision in black elbowing her way through a group of slow-moving students in the hallway.

"Hey," she says tonelessly as she emerges from the crowd.

"Hi." I balance my books against my hip. "You missed Ms. Megeney's blouse yesterday. It was the star of math class."

Christine nods vacantly, like she'd completely forgotten about the existence of math class. "Sorry I missed it." I watch her jaw harden and it's the strangest thing but I feel as if I know approximately what she's going to say before her mouth can form the words. "The guidance counselor, um, pulled me out of history class to tell me my mom was in the hospital."

"The hospital?" I repeat. Although logically I couldn't have had any inkling, I'd swear the idea was already in my head. "Is she okay?"

Christine nods but her eyes are anxious. "Yeah, she's

fine. It was nothing serious. She's already back at home." Maybe it's Christine's tone that suggests the final part of her answer is true, at least. Though I've never been to her house I can vaguely imagine her mother there, like the pictures you form in your head when you read a novel. Not a face or anything, just a bathrobe and slippers, a hazy image of feet moving slowly across a carpeted floor.

I hover around for another few seconds to see whether Christine's going to tell me more. At the very last second, as I'm turning on my heel to leave, she calls, "Wait. Maybe we should swap phone numbers, in case we ever need them."

We print out our respective numbers on paper Christine tears from her binder. She tucks mine into her pencil case before turning her back on me.

Clearly Christine's done talking and as I walk away I'm back to wondering how I knew she'd say her mom had been in the hospital. It has to be some kind of brain hiccup, like déjà vu. I couldn't have really known beforehand. My brain must've only tricked itself into believing it did for a moment. The more I think about it the more absurd the idea that my mind could've raced ahead of Christine's words seems.

The main thing is that her mom's okay and by lunch Christine seems back to her regular self. She and Derrick bug me about the party (which I still haven't asked my mom about) but pretend they're joking. I act disinterested, which isn't hard, but when I slide Christine's Smiths tape into my stereo later that night and lie on my bed listening to lead singer Morrissey's special brand of acute misery, my head hurts with such a vengeance that I think I'm going to be sick.

I roll onto my back, hanging my head over the side of the bed as Morrissey sings, "So you go, and you stand on your own and you leave on your own. . . ."

On your own.

Alone. It's how I always feel lately. Alone or out of place. And now it seems a song understands me better than anyone on the planet does. "How Soon Is Now?" is the saddest, most painful thing I've heard. Worse than the day my father died. Like an infection that will never heal.

Crippling loneliness. The certainty that you don't belong. The suspicion that maybe you never will. I hang my head and wait for a stream of sickness that doesn't come, feeling ancient as I listen to the rest of "How Soon Is Now?"—ancient and empty—and then I slink downstairs and bury my head in my mother's shoulder as she stands at the kitchen counter chopping carrots. She swivels to fold me into her arms, rocking me wordlessly for what could never be long enough.

I pull away first. Both our eyes are a messy pink because she misses my father too. Only whatever's wrong with me isn't just about my father. My tears now aren't solely for him but I can't say that to my mother.

"Your grandfather's coming for dinner on Saturday," my mom says, sniffling back the rest of her sadness.

Saturday. The night of Corey's party. I'd nearly forgotten to talk to my mom about it for the second night in a row and when I open my mouth to ask if she's okay with me going I'm honestly not sure whether I want her to say yes or not.

Just before dinner on Saturday my grandfather asks many of the questions about the party that my mom forgot to pin me down on earlier and I have to call Seth to get Corey's phone number and address to hand over to her. "What class did you say you share with the girl you're going to the party with tonight?" my grandfather pries as we sit at the kitchen table, him occupying my father's spot.

This is another detail my mother may have honed in on if she were feeling better but there's a lot on her mind. Sometimes I think the constant support of her friend Nancy and my grandfather are the only things really holding her together. That should make me more patient with my grandfather's questions and it probably would if I'd grown up around him, but aside from the last few weeks my memories of him are sparse.

I frown at my mom directly across from me, wishing she'd make him stop, and then plunge my fork into my lasagna. "History," I mumble. If my mom knew there was a guy involved she might have wanted to meet him. I made things easy for all of us by leaving that part out.

My grandfather scratches the end of his nose and scrunches up his eyebrows. "Do you know many of the other kids who will be there?" he cross-examines.

Mom lays her right hand on her father's arm. "It's okay, Dad. Freya will be fine. She knows she can call me if she needs to and you'll be home by midnight, right?" Midnight was my party curfew in Auckland and Mom turns to me for confirmation.

"For sure." I bob my head, grateful for her intervention. "If not earlier."

"I don't think I want to go to parties when I'm older," my sister claims, her eyes sullen and both her elbows on the table exactly like they're not supposed to be. "Teenage parties always look dumb."

"That's just from the movies and TV you've seen." Annoyance creeps into my voice because Olivia has a habit of saying stupid things just to get a reaction. "You've never been to a real teenage party so how can you have a clue what they're like?"

My grandfather laughs and when I shift my gaze to him to figure out why, he remarks, "Typical sibling rivalry—one says left and the other says right."

My head twinges right behind my eyes and I set down my fork and rub my forehead with two fingers. I haven't woken up with a headache since Wednesday but the pains still come and go. They make me want to shut my eyes and hide out in the dark. Crawl backwards out of existence to whatever came before.

Crazy, Freya. Who the hell thinks things like that? Only people who need to be on serious amounts of medication.

"You still getting those headaches, Freya?" my grandfather

asks. "Maybe Doctor Byrne should have another look at you."

Doctor Byrne is the Toronto physician my grandfather set my family up with when the three of us came home with a nasty flu. He drove out to suburban Brampton to make a house call for us because he's also a close friend of my grandfather. My grandfather wants us to become Doctor Byrne's permanent patients, despite him working out of the city. Ever since we got back he's been stressing that he has absolute faith in Doctor Byrne and that we'd never find a better physician.

"You okay, hon?" my mom asks, worry in her eyes.

The pain's disappeared with the same swiftness it arrived and I let my hand fall away from my forehead. "I'm all right. It's probably just a little eyestrain. They dumped a lot of homework on us this week." I shovel another forkful of lasagna between my lips because the hunger, like the headaches, is a constant in my life. The tip of an iceberg that I'm trying to ignore.

After dinner Olivia and I do the dishes and then I go upstairs to shower and get ready for the party. It's almost nine-thirty when Nicolette knocks at my front door. I drag her inside to introduce her to my mother and soon we're hurrying out to Seth's car, Nicolette climbing into the backseat so I can sit next to Seth.

They have two bottles of rum in the trunk and when the three of us get out of the car at Corey's house Seth lights a cigarette and hands me one of the bottles to carry. Then he opens Corey's front door without knocking and Nicolette strides past us into the house, looking for her boyfriend. Some kids I vaguely recognize from school, and many I don't, are sprawled out on the living room furniture while a swarm of others dance in the middle of the room to the sounds of Prince's "1999." Seth leads me along the hall and into the kitchen where a second crowd is standing around drinking out of paper cups. We deposit the rum on the kitchen counter and then Seth cups his hand around my ear so I can hear him over the sound of the music. "I forgot to tell you to bring your skates," he says. "Corey's got a rink out back."

"A rink?" I repeat.

"Yeah." Seth points to the sliding door at the back of the kitchen. I lope over to it, Seth a step behind me, and peer into the backyard, which, sure enough, sports an ice rink of about thirty-by-forty feet. Six guys are playing hockey in their jeans and coats, flying over the ice. Several summer folding chairs (three of them occupied by girls cheering on the game and another few empty) wind around the rink.

I haven't been skating since I can't remember when and I turn my back to the sliding door and say, "That's okay. I don't think I know how to skate anyway."

"Don't *think* you know, huh?" Seth smiles wide enough for me to see his braces. "You'd think that'd be the kind of thing you'd know about yourself."

He's teasing, trying to be cute, but he's also right. I

should know whether I can skate and I don't. There's a blank space in my mind where that info should be, just like the blank about Alison's favorite band.

Seth and I are standing close together so we don't have to shout to compete against the music and he plants a hand on my waist and leans in nearer still to kiss me. He tastes like spearmint gum and smoke and the feel of his mouth on mine is warm but unfamiliar. For the life of me I can't compare Seth's kiss to Shane's. Tonight feels like the very first time I was ever kissed.

How can that be? Shane and I kissed tons of times during our two months together. At the local swimming pool, crammed in the backseat of his car, curled up on my parents' couch. Not to mention the few stray kisses I had with other boys at parties before I met Shane and after we split up.

As Seth and I ease apart, Nicolette interrupts my thoughts by approaching with Corey in tow to introduce him. Before I know it she's leading me around to meet people with names like Sheri, Lisa, Denise, Tonya, Ron, Mike, Terry, Jennifer and Justin and shortly after that I'm sipping rum and Coke from a paper cup and standing behind Nicolette in the line for the upstairs bathroom, with no clue what's become of Seth.

"I think he's playing hockey," Nicolette tells me, which makes me grin dazedly because I hadn't realized that I'd wondered about him out loud.

"Wow," she says, giggling, "your alcohol tolerance is worse than mine."

I don't remember drinking before.

I don't remember skating.

I don't remember my best friend's favorite band.

I don't remember what it felt like to kiss my ex-boyfriend on the mouth.

And I'm still smiling at Nicolette because it's so stupidly ridiculous, trying to lose myself in sitcoms, paper cups and a jock guy with braces. As though any of those things can really help me. If it was that easy to make me feel normal again I wouldn't need to be here.

Once I get out of the bathroom Nicolette's gone. I spend a couple of minutes searching for her and then another couple of minutes staring out the sliding glass door at Seth charging around the ice in pursuit of the puck. A tower of paper cups is stacked on the kitchen counter next to the alcohol and I pour myself another rum and Coke (is it my third or fourth?) and wander into the living room. Paul Young's singing "Everything Must Change." I sway to the music, fighting the sadness welling up inside me.

Why does everything have to change? And when was the last time I felt connected to the things around me?

"Hey, gorgeous," a voice sings into my right ear. I swivel towards the voice, expecting to stare into Seth's hazel eyes.

But there's some other guy standing next to me, eyeing me up from head to toe. He's taller than Seth and wearing a T-shirt that shows off sizeable biceps. "I'm Matt," he says. "What's your name?"

"Freya," I drawl, the alcohol in partial control of my voice.

"Fray-ya," he pronounces, nodding after the fact. "Do you want to dance with me, Fray-ya? It looks like you like this song." Matt steps closer to me, sliding his hand around my waist to guide me into the middle of the room, where the other dancers are.

I take a single step forward, my defense mechanisms working slower than usual because of the alcohol too, before stopping to pry his hand from my waist. "I'm here with someone," I tell him.

"Figures." Matt frowns, his arms dangling awkwardly at his sides. "You can't blame a guy for trying."

I guess not. Truthfully, if I didn't feel so adrift maybe I'd be sort of flattered. While it's weird to have people I don't know staring at me in class it pumps up my ego to have guys chase after me for a change. I don't know how to account for it, but maybe I don't one hundred percent hate it all the time.

I spot Nicolette edging her way through the crowd towards me as Matt's slinking away. She bumps my hip and exclaims, "There you are! Come dance with us." By "us" she means herself and three of the girls she introduced me to earlier.

We whirl in time to the music, our arms in the air and the crowd feeling like they're closing in on us, making me hot and a little dizzy until the other strange feelings catch up with me and begin to take over. I consider weaving through the crowd and out to the rink to make Seth kiss me again, just to stop them. But it doesn't matter how much I dance or how many times I kiss Seth Hardy—I know the feelings will always catch up.

I don't belong here. I'm not like the people around me. Each and every memory I have of dancing with friends in muggy rooms, giggling as we point out cute boys, flirting in dark corners with the ones we might like enough to kiss, is paper-thin, with no emotional weight or dimension to it. Strip back the surface and I'm a blank slate. It's as though I've never in my whole life felt at home *anywhere*.

I take an unsteady step back, easing my way out of the circle of dancers and into the front hall where I spy two girls in bright eye shadow and skintight jeans making a beeline for the door. One of them has bloodshot eyes, like she's recovering from a crying jag. "Dave's an asshole," the other girl claims with a vehemence that sends a globule of spit soaring from her mouth. "We should key his car."

"Wait!" I call, striding forward to intercept them. "Are you leaving? Can you give me a ride home?"

The sad girl's chin wobbles. It's her friend who answers me. "We can give you a ride—as long as you don't care if we key the shit out of someone's car first."

I don't care at all. This place and every person in it feel twenty times realer than the majority of my memories but regardless, nothing that happens here tonight feels as though it has anything to do with me.

THREE

arrive home early, with the taste of bubblegum in my mouth (the sad girl gave me a piece to hide alcohol breath). My mom's lying on the couch waiting for me and wanting to talk about the party. I mention the dancing and the guys playing hockey on the ice rink and say it was okay but that I miss my old friends.

This feels like what I should say. I can't tell her how most of the things that happened before we returned to Canada feel hazy and that the things that have happened since don't seem right either. I don't want that to be true.

My father doesn't feel vague or blurry the way New Zealand, Alison and Shane do. His image is as vivid in my mind as my mother's is. He has the kind of face that turns to stone when he's angry, thinking that he's not betraying any sign of emotion. When I was younger I used to hate seeing that blank expression aimed at me because I knew it meant he was supremely displeased. He wasn't the type to shout—he rarely raised his voice—but having my father mad at you felt a little like losing a sunny day. And when my dad was happy the world seemed like a better place. If he were here with us now, would I still feel lost? Would I remember everything the way I should?

There's no one I can ask, no one I can really talk to, and I don't call Seth to explain my disappearance the next day. He doesn't call me either so he's maybe written me off, which is for the best. It's not right to use someone as a distraction and besides, it didn't work.

Monday at lunch I pretend all over again, for Christine and Derrick, that I had an all right time at Corey's party. There's a blend of contempt and curiosity, with an overlay of forced casualness, buried in their questions about the party. They know I don't belong with them but maybe they don't want to lose me to the jock table either.

As we're leaving the cafeteria afterwards, Christine pulls me aside and says, "Aren't you going to tell me how things went with Seth? You hardly mentioned him."

I drag my fingers through my hair and bite down on my molars, silently debating how much I can share without sounding like a weirdo. Since Christine and Derrick are outsiders themselves, I feel closer to them than I do to anyone else at school, but I don't want to scare them off. "I thought you didn't like Seth," I say, stalling.

Christine folds her arms tightly across her long black sweater. "There are people *like him* who I don't like very much but I don't know enough about Seth Hardy personally to have a specific opinion on him." She digs her black nails into her arms. "But that's not the point—you like him, right?"

I pull my chin in under my turtleneck. "He's okay."

Christine's eyes roll back in her skull. "God, Freya, don't you trust me at all? I just thought you might want to talk about it because it's not like you have many other people to talk to around here yet but, okay, you're all right." She throws a helping of exasperation on the words "all right" before adding, "You don't *need* to talk."

"Christine!" I erupt in frustration. The two lanky freshman guys in front of us turn at the sound of my voice and then quickly look away. My cheeks are warm as I bend my head and whisper, "Did it ever occur to you that maybe it's not about trusting you and that I'm just a private person?

"Okay, I sit with you and Derrick at lunch but I've known you, like, a week," I continue as we hurtle up the hall. "And you're not exactly a warm and fuzzy person, you know. I don't necessarily want to spill about what did or didn't happen just to have you crap on it."

Even as I'm saying it—angry that Christine doesn't feel like she can talk about things going on in her own life but expects me to blab about my own—I only feel half in the moment and half like I'm looking at myself from a distance, surprised that I care enough to react this way.

Christine hasn't looked at me once since I began my rant but when I fall silent she sneaks a peek and I imagine that I see a hint of red in her cheeks bleed through the pale makeup. "I wasn't going to crap on anything," she says. Her voice gets smaller as she goes on. "Really . . . but I get it. I get why you don't want to say anything. I mean, I never really tell anyone anything either."

"What about Derrick?"

"Some things," she says, her gaze fixed stubbornly on the sea of moving bodies ahead of us. "Some things I just don't tell anyone."

I think about her mom being in the hospital last week and the other new wavers she never talks to and I feel bad for the two of us believing we have to keep our secrets to ourselves. Still, that feeling isn't enough to change my mind about confiding in her on the most important things—the crazy things inside my head.

I sigh into my palm and say, "To tell you the truth, the party felt kind of weird. I just wasn't on the same wavelength with most of the people there." I figure I'm safe to admit that much to Christine, who wouldn't have felt in tune with Corey's party either. Because she's still staring at me, her face returning to its earlier state of paler than pale, I add, "I actually left early, without telling Seth. I bummed a ride home from two girls and haven't spoken to him since. He's probably mad."

Christine smoothes her lips together like someone who's just applied lip gloss. "He probably is. But hey, it's not like he could've gotten terminally attached to you this quickly. He'll get over it."

I'm sure he will. I just feel guilty for using him. I'd have been better off staying home and watching *Family Ties* and music videos, not in danger of hurting anyone's feelings and not trying to pretend I fit somewhere that I don't.

"If you're not feeling it, you're not feeling it," Christine adds helpfully.

That could apply to either Seth or the party in general and I say, "You're right. Thanks." I wish all my problems could be resolved as easily. It's on the tip of my tongue to add that Christine can talk to me sometime too, if she wants, but then the second bell goes and we have to rush the rest of the way to math class.

Seth calls me on Monday night demanding to know why I took off on him on Saturday, never called to explain and didn't search him out at school today to talk about it either. I guess I let him down three times and I have nothing to say for myself. The longer I fail to provide an explanation the angrier he gets until I finally mumble that it's not a good time for me to start seeing anyone and he hangs up on me.

I can't blame him.

With that out of the way, I feel marginally better and magically ace a multiple-choice biology quiz on Tuesday afternoon and then argue with my sister over TV access on Tuesday night (I want to watch videos on MuchMusic and Olivia wants to see *The A-Team*). On Wednesday morning the entire tenth grade is assigned a bus to the museum according to their homeroom. This means that I'm not on the same bus as Christine or Derrick and I end up sitting in the third row from the front with a girl named Tracy who's in my homeroom but I've never spoken to.

She sticks on earphones, closes her eyes and promptly falls asleep. I have the window seat and watch highway traffic. As we approach Toronto I find myself getting mildly excited. The skyscrapers and level of activity feel invigorating compared to life in the suburbs. My grandfather lives downtown, near the Davisville subway station. Maybe we would've been better off moving closer to him rather than situating ourselves in the burbs.

Forty minutes later I'm loitering among a mob of tenth graders in front of the Royal Ontario Museum, looking for Christine and Derrick. The first person I find is actually Nicolette who is standing around with a couple of other girls who qualify as popular and pretty. Standing together as a trio they remind me of the women on *Charlie's Angels,* only younger. I met one of them at Corey's party on the weekend and they all act really nice to me, despite what happened with Seth. They even say I can stick with them today, if I want.

Meanwhile Derrick's fighting his way through the crowd towards me and one of Nicolette's angels sees him and points him out to me. "What's with his hair anyway?" she asks snidely. "Does he think he's that guy from General Public?" Nicolette levels an icy look at her friend on my behalf. Because I've been paying more attention to music lately I get the reference and Derrick's hair is, in fact, exactly like the guy's from British band General Public but that's no reason for Nicolette's friend to be bitchy. Especially when she happens to style her hair and dress exactly like her friends do.

I wave at Derrick and step away from Nicolette. Derrick hasn't found Christine yet either but we're all being corralled towards the front entrance. Derrick and I both have homework questions to fill in during our stint at the museum—me for history class and him for geography. The kids who have both classes this semester must be pissed off at facing double the work but I doubt that any of the museum homework really matters.

As Derrick and I head inside we overhear that a busload of tenth graders from our school arrived ahead of us and have gotten started, which means we might not be able to catch up with Christine right away. Tons of people are scrambling off in the direction of the dinosaur exhibit so Derrick and I decide to check out geology first. While Derrick's scrawling out an answer to a question about metamorphic rock I wander around staring at weirdly beautiful minerals and rocks.

I stare at them for such a long time, being sure to read every inch of the text that goes along with the exhibits, that Derrick gets bored and has to hurry me up. It's the same when we're staring at gorgeous Greek statues, ancient hieroglyphs and ugly insects. I can't get enough of any of it and Derrick jokes about what a geek I've turned into when we finally do stumble across Christine in the museum cafeteria at lunchtime.

Since we sit together in bio, Derrick's well aware that I'm not normally so raptly interested in things that feel like homework. This is different. This building holds the knowledge of our past—humanity's past and the planet's past.

Who wouldn't find that interesting?

Most of my classmates, I guess, but I don't understand that. They're so stuck in the moment that you'd think history had disappeared and that the future will never arrive: 1985 forever.

I buy gloopy macaroni and cheese and salad for lunch and then finish Derrick's hamburger (which isn't as bad as he says it is), wishing that I could come to the museum every day instead of going to school. I don't feel out of place here. Do I need to become an archaeologist to successfully fit into my own life?

After lunch Christine, Derrick and I hit the dinosaur exhibit, which seems to turn everyone (because I can see it in other tenth-grade faces too) into awed children. It's strange to conceive of a time that dinosaurs roamed the earth—that they were here before we were. The perspective sends my head spinning. Will we have as long as they did or will nuclear arms wipe us off the face of the planet?

"You're quiet," Derrick observes as I stare up at a cast of *Tyrannosaurus rex,* one of the last dinosaurs to walk the earth before mass extinction approximately 65 million years ago.

Mass extinction. I can't wrap my head around the concept.

"Do you think we're doomed?" I ask. "Humanity."

Derrick nods readily. "Absolutely. Everything dies—and look how destructive we are as a species." He shrugs and folds his crumpled geography homework pages in two. "But it would happen anyway. Everything ends."

I can't argue with that.

I'm not even sure how I feel about it.

How can *anything* matter from a perspective of probable mass extinction? Is it better to live like it will always be 1985?

Beads of sweat are gathering on my upper lip. It's too hot in here. I'm burning up. No headache yet, though, thank God.

"You don't look so good," Christine tells me. "Are you feeling okay?"

"Warm." I smooth my palm across my face to soak up the sweat. "I think I'm getting dehydrated. I'm going to head back to the cafeteria for another drink."

"We'll come with you," Christine offers.

"No, stay." I point to Derrick's crumpled sheets. "You guys still have blanks to fill in."

"So do you," Derrick says.

Yeah, but I don't care. Derrick may think we're ultimately headed for mass extinction but he's still the kind of person who likes to have his homework done on time. He's not just going through the motions like I am.

I tell Christine and Derrick I'm fine, wave them both away and say I'll catch up with them in the next gallery. It's what I fully intend to do but then I get to thinking that the fastest way to cool down is to step outside into February.

Canadians complain about the weather nonstop but I don't mind the cold. I retrieve my coat from the museum coat check and step out onto the heavily salted city sidewalk. There's no question that it's better out here. The air inside is stale and warm in comparison. I stretch my legs and walk to the corner, enjoying the feel of the breeze on my face. I still love the museum—I just wish they'd lower the temperature, not that it seems to bother anyone else.

I smell hotdogs cooking before I see them and my first thought is that if I hadn't eaten lunch less than an hour ago I'd be reaching into my pocket to pay for one with everything on it—heaps of peppers, relish, mustard, ketchup, onions—but there's a first time for everything and I'm not hungry. However, my craving for ice-cold soda (like they're advertising on the front of the hotdog cart) is something fierce and pushes me into line behind a teenage guy only a couple of years older than me. In the beginning I don't bother to look at him closely, just catch a glimpse of his profile and black winter coat, which is hanging open the same way mine is.

Then I notice him licking his lips as the vendor hands him a sizzling hotdog loaded with the works. He bites into it, ingesting nearly half the hotdog in a single bite and I stifle a laugh but the guy's too busy eating to notice me anyway. I watch him stroll away as I order a Coke. My eyes can't tear themselves from his form.

For a start, he's the best-looking guy I've laid eyes on since I landed back in Canada, maybe even the best-looking guy I've *ever* seen, and secondly, I know I've seen him before. I don't know that with my mind the way you're supposed to know things. It's an instinct or at least something deeper than my consciousness and that thing, whatever it is, is drawn to him with a strength that would be frightening if I could think about this rationally . . . which I can't.

It's like hunger or needing oxygen. It's not something you can make up your mind to quit craving. It just *is*. And then I'm taking my change from the hotdog vendor and trailing after the guy, like a spy or private detective, only they'd have a logical motive and I just have . . . a hunger, a need.

Not something sexual, although that's there too because he's breathtaking to look at. From my place about thirty feet behind him, all I can see is his close-cropped dark hair (any darker and it would be jet black) and his six-foot-something medium-build frame sauntering west along the sidewalk. But for a moment before he turned to walk away I had an unobstructed view of his face and it was like staring into a living, breathing version of one of those Greek statues from the museum: high cheekbones, smooth skin, a perfectly straight nose and what looked like an unbreakable jawline. Examined alone none of those things would be extraordinarily impressive—it's the way they work together that's acting on me like a drug—and not even quite that, but the absolute certainty that I've felt this way about him before.

I can't remember him.

But I know.

In my mind I see his eyes, as clear green as a tropical ocean. I see him staring at me. Smiling for me. Being the person he is, the one I should remember in full, not in this hazy, unformed manner.

Random people in winter jackets, gloves and hats flow between us but I keep my eyes on the guy in the distance, only shifting my gaze for a split second to read a street sign and find we're on Bloor Street. I'm afraid to get closer and risk him seeing me but I don't want to lose him either. None of this adds up. If I *know* him, he should know me. But I was standing right next to him on the corner by the museum. . . .

I was as good as invisible to him.

It doesn't matter that this is insane; I can't let him get away. I follow him along Bloor Street until he turns north onto Spadina. The streets are less crowded there and I have to hang back farther to avoid being conspicuous. Soon he's turning again, left this time, and I'm surrounded by houses, their front yards covered in graying snow. A blue van pulls into a driveway ahead of me and I jump at the break in concentration, afraid he'll evaporate into thin air.

He doesn't, of course. No matter how improbable this seems so far, it's still the real world.

No, he's striding easily along the residential street, his arms swaying at his sides like he doesn't have a clue he's being followed and that there's no problem on the planet he couldn't handle.

The gap between us is so large that it makes me ache and I can't stop searching my mind for the missing information—who this boy is to me and why neither of us remember. I pull my arms tight around my waist, fighting an overwhelming feeling of withdrawal when the inevitable happens and he turns up a pathway, steps onto a pale blue fenced porch and disappears inside the front door.

Slowly, I approach what I assume to be his house. It's semi-detached and old but in good repair. Its other half sports beige trim and fencing, making the homes look like a pair of mismatched socks. Both residences feature second-floor bay windows and porches nearly as big as the ones on ground level. The third-floor windows are smaller and I wonder where the boy sleeps and whether he has brothers and sisters. The driveway's empty, as is the curb space directly in front of his house, meaning his parents are probably at work.

Is he alone inside?

I stare at the door he retreated through. It's closed and the ground-floor window merely offers me a reflection of the street. *Damn.* My heart's racing like I'm running a marathon. How do I stop this insanity? How do I let go of him?

The can of Coke I've been holding all along is freezing in my naked hand. I pop it open and gulp down sugary liquid caffeine, hoping the normalcy of the action will help calm me down. Then I continue forward at a snail's pace, past the boy's property, ogling a street sign as I go: Walmer Road. At the next cross street I stalk across the road and double back towards the guy's house, still guzzling Coca-Cola and hoping he'll emerge again, although I have no idea what I'll do if he does.

For the next while I patrol the street in this way. Drifting up one side of the road and then coasting down the other, avoiding the eyes of the pedestrians who stroll past but keeping a vigilant watch on the mystery guy's house. Only when two red-haired children, a skinny boy and rosy-cheeked girl who must be walking home from school, zip past me do I think about the time and where I'm supposed to be.

It's ten minutes to three and the Sir John A. MacDonald buses were scheduled to leave the museum at 2:30. I've missed my ride home.

I've missed the bus to Brampton *and* I've been trekking around Toronto with a raging case of temporary insanity. No, temporary would mean it was over with, and I still don't want to leave Walmer Road. I've pulled just far enough out from the spell I've been under to realize I have to go. No matter what I *think* I know, I can't pace the sidewalk outside his door forever.

I point one final stare at the boy's house before retracing my steps back to Spadina and then Bloor Street. The museum hasn't gone anywhere. Neither has the hotdog vendor. However, the school buses are nowhere in sight.

I slink guiltily into the museum lobby, pondering my situation. I'm too old to embarrass myself by approaching the museum staff like a lost seven-year-old but there's only one location I know how to find from here and that knowledge won't help me now.

My fingers fumble for a quarter in my pocket. Then I scan the lobby for a pay phone and dial home. Olivia's usually only in the house alone for about fifteen minutes after school and I hope she doesn't freak out when she hears I won't be there soon.

Initially I figure my mom will have to pick me up once she's finished work but by the time Olivia picks up on the third ring I have a better idea and after explaining about missing the bus I ask her for my grandfather's phone number. His and Nancy's numbers are both stuck to the front of our refrigerator and when Olivia comes back on the line to recite his number I tell her to make sure the front door's locked and not to open it for anyone.

"I won't," she says. "Do you have Mom's work number in case Grandpa isn't home?"

She gives me that number too. I scribble it down but it turns out I don't need it; my grandfather's at the museum to pick me up within twenty minutes. He smiles at me, making his wrinkles pop, as he ambles into the lobby with a long red scarf wrapped around his neck and says, "You're lucky you caught me at home. I just got in from Cooke's place."

His friend Cooke is in bad health and so is Cooke's wife. My grandfather spends lots of time helping them out—running them over to church, doctor's visits and the grocery store. Nearly every time we see my grandfather he makes some mention of Cooke.

"Thanks for coming to get me," I tell him. "I thought I might have to wait for Mom."

"Glad to do it," my grandfather says heartily. "But how'd you manage to miss the bus? Isn't the school supposed to keep track of you while you're on a field trip?"

"I was in the bathroom," I lie. "I wasn't feeling well. I guess someone screwed up the head count."

My grandfather purses his lips, his eyebrows pointy with suspicion. "Are you having more of those headaches?"

I'm a step ahead of my grandfather, ready with another lie. "No—not that. Women's stuff."

This is a surefire way to steer my grandfather away from the topic of headaches and another visit to Doctor Byrne. Men my grandfather's age generally don't like to hear about periods.

A quizzical look, which I interpret as discomfort, clouds his face. "Let's get you home before it snows again, Freya," he declares. "The forecast says there'll be quite a bit of it tonight."

We trudge out of the lobby together and towards my grandfather's car nestled at the curbside, my thoughts back on Walmer Road with the boy who's a complete stranger to me yet feels so much more familiar than my flesh-and-blood grandfather.

FOUR

What I want to do is sit quietly by myself and churn it all over in my mind until I figure it out. Peel back the layers and unravel the core mystery of what happened today. The dark-haired boy haunts me in the car trip with my grandfather and once we're home he haunts me throughout my mom's rant about the school being neglectful and irresponsible in abandoning me at the museum. When my mother says she'll call tomorrow and let them know leaving me in Toronto to fend for myself was totally unacceptable, I don't argue. It would've been worse if one of the trip supervisors had noticed my absence on the bus, begun a search (how would I account for leaving the museum?) and raised the alarm. If any of that had happened they'd have alerted my mother, so it seems I fell through the cracks. Their neglect was my good fortune.

My grandfather leaves before dinner, wanting to beat the

snow, and when my mother, Olivia and I are eating lamb at the table later, the phone rings, breaking the silence. My mom reaches for it, her cheeks flaring as if she's expecting to hear a school official on the other end and is eager to tear a strip off them. Mom's anger is usually subtler than my father's but I instinctively suck in my cheeks, like I've tasted something sour. Tension prickles under my skin.

Then my mother presses the receiver to her ear and I begin to relax as I watch her face soften. "I'll have her call you back if that's all right," she says into the phone. "We're just in the middle of dinner."

She hangs up, announcing, "That was Christine for you, Freya."

I thank her as the boy from earlier keeps blinking his green eyes inside my head, trying to tell me something I should already know.

I envision him in the old brick house with the pale blue trim and try to imagine what he might be doing there this very second. His parents could be home from work now. He might be eating dinner with them. Will he be hungry despite the hotdog he inhaled, practically in one piece, earlier? Is he in high school like me or has he already graduated? What does he do with his spare time? What does he want to be? Does he ever think about mass extinction?

Do I know him like I think I do? How is that possible?

Nothing concrete happened today—I didn't even speak to the boy—but just seeing him has changed things and

I'm so swept up in him that I almost forget about returning Christine's call. It's my mother who reminds me when I pass her in the upstairs hallway just before eight o'clock.

"What happened to you at the museum?" Christine wants to know once I have her on the phone. "You never came back. Are you ditching us like you ditched Seth?"

"Of course not." It never occurred to me that she and Derrick might think I didn't want to hang out with them at the museum. Since the three of us were assigned different buses I guess they didn't have a clue I wasn't on mine when it left.

"Just kidding," Christine claims. "So what *did* happen?"

I tell her that I fell asleep in the cafeteria and that I must have some kind of twenty-four-hour bug because I still feel sort of groggy. As I'm explaining about missing the bus I hear a female voice in the background mumble something about popcorn. "In a few minutes, Mom," Christine replies. "I'm on the phone."

"How is your mom anyway?" I'm glad to have the focus off me but that's not the only reason I'm asking. I really do want Christine to feel like we can talk. Behind those concerns a large portion of my brain is still obsessing about the guy on Walmer Road and I tighten my grip on the phone and begin pacing my room, restless like a caged thing.

Christine hesitates. "She's okay." Christine drops her voice to a feathery whisper. "She . . . it was just a panic attack. She's been under a lot of stress because she . . ."

I stop walking and give Christine my full attention.

"She . . . lost her job last summer."

People never know the right thing to say when they hear I lost my father and I don't know the right thing now but at least Christine's mother is still around. "I'm glad she's all right," I venture. "So . . . you two are watching a movie? I heard her say something about popcorn." From what I *do* know of Christine she wouldn't want me to feel sorry for her.

Christine's tone brightens. "She's a total popcorn nut. If she has to go more than two nights in a row without it she has to rush out to the supermarket. But anyway, we were just going to watch *MacGyver*."

That sounds nice and I smile into the phone. "Okay, well, I don't want to make you miss it."

"See you tomorrow, then?" Christine asks, because after all, I'm supposed to be sick.

"*Oh.* Yeah. I think I'll be better by then. See you tomorrow."

As I hang up I feel an odd flutter of satisfaction in the pit of my stomach. *Christine trusts me.* But it's not long before I'm lost in thoughts of the boy on Walmer Road again. If anyone could read my mind I'd be embarrassed. To have trailed a strange boy home and then prowled around his street is beyond simple crush behavior. The rational side of me knows that as well as anyone else would but the other side won't give way—today it's in charge.

As the night wears on I climb into bed where I toss and turn for hours, sleepless, before opening my drapes to stare at the moon overhead. The very same moon that presided over rampaging dinosaurs millions of years ago.

My mind begins to melt with thoughts of mass extinction, just as it did at the museum earlier. I sweat through my pajama top and have to change into a T-shirt.

When I curl up in a ball under the covers again, the image of the green-eyed boy feels like comfort. *Like home.* Calmed, I drift into a dream that feels every bit as real as the majority of my waking life.

In the dream the world is a different place but the moon is the same, as close to eternal as any of us can comprehend.

In the dream I live in an old house—a mansion filled with unexplainable objects that I don't question. Not all of the people within my dreamworld are human. But everywhere, the air is rife with fear and uncertainty.

In this dream place, which is here but not here, I stare through a looking glass at a tall boy with dirty-blond hair. He's a close friend or maybe even family, someone I've always known. He's protected me, consoled me. He's someone I can't do without but I can't reach him. The looking glass serves as a fence—it keeps us apart.

He's not himself. He snarls at me through the glass, gnashing his teeth as he lunges.

He detests me. The fire inside him wants to destroy everything. It hates without end and that should scare me but it only makes me sad.

I'm inconsolable at the thought of living in the world without him. I need him back.

When I wake up I'm crying like a child. Sobs rack my body and I can't catch my breath. The noise is loud enough that I'm afraid it will wake my mother or Olivia and I grab my pillow and weep into it. For the blond boy from my dream. For everything my heart feels it's lost.

The pain seems bottomless and in my mind, like a looping sound track, I hear the words of Winston Churchill: "You ask, what is our aim? I can answer with one word: Victory—victory at all costs, victory in spite of all terror, victory however long and hard the road may be; for without victory there is no survival."

On Thursday morning I'm exhausted and my mother has to wake me up three times. On the third occasion she has a glass of orange juice with her and sits on the side of my bed watching me drink it to be sure I'm really getting up.

My stomach hurts with last night's sadness but the intensity of feeling that the dream prompted in me is a mystery like so many other things are lately. I'm no longer heartsick, only tired and achy the way children get when they're coming down from a tantrum or crying jag.

Downstairs, Olivia stares at me from behind a box of Cocoa Puffs. "They plowed the road already so we have to go to school after all," she complains.

"That sucks," I mumble, although I'd forgotten that last night my mother mentioned classes might be canceled.

In the light of day my rational side has grown marginally

stronger, or maybe it's only that I'm too sleepy to cling to thoughts of the green-eyed boy with the same tenacity that I did last night. If it was thoughts of him that made me dream the frighteningly vivid way I did, then I need to find a way to mentally put him aside.

I don't want to land in that dark place again. The sense of loss was too much to take. It didn't feel like a dream.

The blond boy was as familiar to me in my dreamworld as the green-eyed guy seemed to me downtown yesterday but what am I supposed to do with that kind of craziness? Is it the kind of break with reality that could've been caused by the shock of my father's death? Or could a brain tumor be loosening my grip on the real world and dragging me into fantasy?

I swallow cold cereal and stare blearily at my sister who seems to be adjusting to life in Canada with much more ease than I am. I wait until my mother's left the kitchen before asking, "Olivia, do you like it here?"

"It's okay," my sister replies with her mouth full. "Do you like it?"

"I don't know. It feels different . . . strange."

"Because we were away for so long," Olivia says sensibly. She brushes her dark bangs off her face and picks up her cereal bowl to drink down the leftover milk. Since Olivia's six years younger than me we're not as close as we might have been otherwise but aside from my mother, she's the only one who's been through these changes along with me and I don't want to worry my mom by bringing any of this up to her.

"I know," I begin. "But it doesn't feel as if it's only because we've been living in other countries. Does it ever sort of seem like . . ." I search for the right words. "Like what's happening now is more *authentic* than the way our lives used to be?"

Olivia sets down her bowl, her eyes sparking with confusion. "What do you mean?"

My toes jerk against the floor beneath my feet. "Say with Grandpa, right? We saw him on visits home and he came to see us in Auckland but when you think of that—your New Zealand memories of him—does he feel like the same person?"

Olivia gapes at me as if I've either lost my mind or she's hopelessly misunderstood me but I've gone too far to back down. "And your friends in Auckland," I continue, "the kids you went to school with there—do they seem as complicated and"—I flex the fingers of my right hand, grasping for an idea just beyond reach—"genuine as the kids you go to school with now?"

Olivia swats at her bangs again and pokes her tongue inside her cheek. "Canadian kids are just different," she says slowly. "We're not used to them yet." She pushes her empty cereal bowl forward a couple of inches and then slides it back towards her. "But Grandpa is the same as he always was. Remember the time he let me drive the boat?" She smiles brightly.

"I do," I say. It was just over a year ago but it feels like longer. My dad was busy with work and my grandfather had rented a boat and taken my mom, Olivia and me for a day trip.

We were out on the water, about a half hour away from the ramp at Kawakawa Bay, and Olivia was so excited by the speed and the sight of the frothy waves the boat was leaving in its wake that my grandfather asked my mother whether it would be all right to let Olivia take the wheel for a while. Surprisingly, my mother agreed and Olivia turned solemn at the helm, steering good and straight, like she'd done it countless times before. My grandfather let her remain at the helm for at least ten minutes before taking over again.

I see the pride Olivia felt that day reflected in her face now. "Maybe we can get Grandpa to rent a boat here sometime this summer," I suggest. "Explore Lake Ontario."

I wish I could remember that day in the same way that Olivia's eyes tell me she can. I remember the fact of it but the memory itself is sterile. Just images, sounds and a transcript of events that didn't leave any deeper an imprint on me than the latest episode of *Knots Landing*.

"Don't you like Grandpa?" Olivia asks, unwilling to be distracted from my original questions.

"Of course I do. I think . . . nothing feels the same after Dad. I can't explain it."

Olivia sets both her hands on the table, wriggles her fingers and peers worriedly down at them.

I clear my throat and say, "I miss him. I miss New Zealand. I miss the way everything used to be." This is far from the whole truth but I don't want to make my sister anxious. If she's doing okay, I'm glad for it. "I think it's just going to take some time for me to settle in here."

I yawn like I'm bored with the topic and ready to put it behind us. Then I take our dirty dishes over to the sink and wash them so my mother won't have to, as if that will make up for the weird things going on inside my head. I wipe down the kitchen counter too and even make my bed, which is something I rarely do, if I can trust my memory at all.

As pointless as it seems, at school I try to keep my mind on what my various teachers are jotting sloppily down on their blackboards but during English there's a knock at the classroom door and the vice principal's standing there in a white shirt and blue tie, asking to speak to me. He apologizes for "what transpired at the museum" as I think to myself that he doesn't know the half of it.

At lunch Christine and Derrick want to know if I'm feeling better. I say I'm back to normal but I end up listening to them more than I talk and as the three of us are streaming out of the cafeteria at the end of the period, I find myself within arm's length of Seth. He pretends I'm invisible and speeds up, breaking away from me.

It's how I'd probably act if our situations were reversed so it doesn't come as a shock but what *does* surprise me is that at the end of the day one of the guys Nicolette introduced me to at Corey's party is leaning against my locker scratching at the knee of his black jeans.

"Hey you," he says as though we know each other much better than we actually do. "How's it going?"

"Hey," I say guardedly.

"I was just wondering if you needed a ride home?" he asks, straightening. "I know you're new here and all so . . ."

I narrow my eyes and point to my locker so he'll stand aside and let me open it.

"Sorry." He laughs and shifts his weight to the locker next to mine.

My hair falls forward so that I can only make out thin strips of him through my curtain of dirty-blond strands. I enter my locker combo and slide the lock open. "The thing is, I don't live that far," I say, more to my locker than to him.

"That doesn't matter," he tells me, all perfect teeth and quarterback shoulders. "I'm sure you could still use a ride. It's real windy out there today." His name comes to me as he's trying to sell me on a ride home: Terry. The guys he was hanging out with at the party were calling him something else, a jock nickname I've forgotten, but Nicolette introduced him as Terry.

"The cold doesn't get to me," I say, because Terry isn't my type in the first place and in the second, I really don't want to repeat what happened with Seth.

"So you're saying you'd rather walk home in the cold than take a ride from me?" Terry recaps like the concept of a girl not being interested in him is a completely foreign one.

"I just don't want you to get the wrong idea." I turn to stare Terry straight in the eye. Distracting myself with a guy from school isn't a workable concept and if it was, I would've chosen Seth. Meanwhile, the boy I won't let myself actively think about is still blinking his green eyes inside my head.

"How do you know it's the wrong idea if you haven't given me a chance?" Terry quips, a smarmy grin taking over his face.

My eyebrows slant together in aggravation. "I guess you just have to trust me on that."

Terry flinches and focuses on the floor. "Wow," he mutters. "You're pretty hostile. I think I'm starting to get why Seth dumped you."

A startled laugh chokes up from my diaphragm. "Is that what he told you?" I smother the impulse to set Terry straight. Who cares what someone I met *once* and have never had a conversation with thinks?

I need to keep my head on straight. I need to keep my problems to myself and not let them bleed into my mother's and sister's lives. I need to cement myself in strength and logic, lock my brain into the here and now and forget about dreams and visions. Someone like Terry, I don't need.

Having made that decision so resolutely, it's doubly annoying to face a similar situation the very next day with a guy I get paired up with in English class for a short assignment on Greek myths. Kyle's not a jock or any other obvious thing and I like the sound of his laugh as we joke together about King Minos, Prince Theseus and Princess Ariadne but then he spoils it by telling me how cute I am when I smile. "Well, you're cute all the time," he says. "But especially when you smile." Then he pauses, slouches down in his chair and adds, "Maybe I shouldn't say this but I was glad when I heard you weren't with Seth anymore."

"I was never with Seth," I correct. Not that it's anybody's business.

The guy nods slowly. "Better still."

I bite down on my pen cap and scan the story of Theseus and the Minotaur as Kyle, in his long-winded and self-deprecating way, proceeds to ask me out. There's a part in Theseus and the Minotaur where Princess Ariadne writes to Prince Theseus. Her letter begins, "I am a beautiful princess as you probably noticed the minute you saw me." A couple of minutes ago Kyle and I were kidding around about how conceited Princess Ariadne was to note her own beauty but from my first day at school so many people seemed to have judged me by my appearance.

I've gone from being unnerved by it to slightly flattered (on occasion) to feeling straitjacketed by it and when the final bell rings on Friday afternoon I dash for Christine's locker with a special request. If people can't get past how I look without a shove, I'll give them the push they need. Maybe Princess Ariadne was cool with guys fawning over her for the wrong reason but I'm tired of it.

Christine's head is down and she's yanking on tall boots with a zillion chunky straps down the front. Her black top hangs on her like a piece of drapery, cinched at the waist and then falling in pleats halfway down her thighs. She doesn't notice me until I'm right next to her. "Oh, hey, Freya," she says, glancing up at me. Her shock of heavy black eyeliner highlights the stunning light blue, nearly violet, of her irises in a way that makes my breath catch when I stare at them straight on.

"I was wondering if I could ask you a favor," I say. "Do you think you could help me dye my hair?"

"Are you serious?" Christine's fingers tug at her own black locks as she stands up next to me. "Why do you want to do that?"

"Because"—I ball up a fistful of blond hair in my right hand—"this doesn't feel like who I am."

Christine tilts her head to one side and says, "So how do you want to look?"

"More like you," I admit. "I want to change my image." I want the people who only talk to me because of how I look to leave me alone. I want my outsides to match the prickly, shady, mysterious way I feel on the inside.

Christine's lips curve into a small smile. "That sounds radical. Are you sure?"

As sure as I've been about anything lately. I don't have any control over what's going on inside me but buying a tube of hair dye and some new clothes is definitely within my power.

"Positive," I tell her. "The sooner the better. When do you think you could do it?"

"Um . . . tonight," Christine says, smiling harder. "If that's good with you."

Tonight is excellent.

FIVE

As soon as my mom's home from work I ask her if she can drop me off at the mall after dinner to meet a friend from school. In Auckland I had a restricted driver's license that allowed me to drive around by myself during the day, which usually only happened on weekends when I had access to one of my parents' cars. We moved back here before I was old enough to get a full driver's license in New Zealand and now I'll have to start over from the beginning—qualify for a learner's permit and take driver's ed.

My mom looks as tired as I felt after my bad dream the other night but she chauffeurs me to the mall later anyway. Christine and I hit the store where she usually buys her hair dye and the girl at the cash register gives me a discount because she knows Christine. Afterwards we pick out the palest pressed powder we can find in the department store makeup counter along with a brand of eyeliner Christine recommends and I tell her what Terry said about Seth dumping me. "I guess that's him trying to preserve his reputation or something," I add.

Christine bares her teeth like she's about to growl. "You shouldn't let him get away with that shit."

I shrug. "I don't care what he says. It's not worth worrying about."

"I knew he was an asshole," Christine says, almost to herself.

"You told me you didn't know him well enough to have an opinion about him," I remind her.

Christine smiles slyly. "I lied. Not about knowing him but about having an opinion. What can I say? I have finely tuned asshole radar."

We catch a bus back to Christine's house with the stuff I bought (the clothes shopping will have to wait for another day) and hole up in the upstairs bathroom where she puts on rubber gloves and parts my hair four ways so she can get at my roots. She starts squeezing the dye onto the back of my head and by the time she's gotten to the front the chemical smell's making my eyes water. Christine says it stinks but that it's never really bothered her eyes. She advises me to tough it out for the next thirty minutes and then we'll be able to wash the dye out and meet a whole new me. In the meantime she sits on the toilet lid and I balance myself on the side of the bathtub.

Because I'm already technically crying and I'm sort of in the middle of becoming someone else and Christine's the only person for thousands of miles that I've spoken to about guys even a little, I impulsively ask her if she's ever had a déjà vu about a person she's never met.

"I get déjà vu all the time," Christine says, "but not usually about people, more about things I'm doing."

That sounds normal and I stretch my legs out in front of me as I think about the guy on Walmer Road and what he could be doing with his Friday night. He didn't recognize me before and he'll be even less likely to recognize me when Christine and I are done here.

The problem with knowing where he lives is that I can go back anytime I want to. I'm trying not to do that but I'm fighting with myself on so many fronts lately that I'm afraid I might give in. I'm almost equally afraid I won't, that I'll stop trying to figure out what really matters and why and end up just like everyone else.

"Did *you* have a déjà vu about someone you've never met?" Christine asks pointedly.

A pause to a question like that is as good as an affirmative response and after a couple of seconds I drag my teeth across my bottom lip and say, "A guy I passed in the street." I can't tell her about following him home from the hotdog stand outside the museum—that would sound psycho, even to someone who's trying to be my friend. "It was such a strong feeling that I can't stop thinking about it."

"About *him*," Christine qualifies, not looking fazed so far.

"About him, yeah, but also about the situation in general—how someone who I've never met could feel that familiar to me." My ears are beginning to warm and I pinch my left earlobe, causing Christine to reach down for a wad of toilet paper.

She hands it to me so I can wipe the dye from my left hand. Then she says, "Maybe you did meet him before, a really long time ago and your subconscious remembers it even if you don't."

"Maybe." I get up to run my hand under the water and then sit myself back down on the tub again. "It just seems weird."

"What's weird about it?" Christine's black-rimmed eyes study me.

"Well, if I *did* meet him a long, long time ago, how come I can't stop thinking about him? You'd think he'd have to have been someone important, in which case I should remember and so should he."

Christine stares contemplatively at the matching purple hand towels hanging beside me, next to the bath. "Past life," she offers.

Her tone gives no clue whether she's kidding or not and I say, "Do you believe in that?"

"Not really. But what do I know?" She tucks her hands into her lap and leans forward. "Maybe you should've tried to say something to him. Where did you see him?"

"On the way home from school earlier this week," I lie. "But he doesn't go to school with us—I mean he looked like he could be a high school student but not at Sir John A. Macdonald. I would've noticed."

"Maybe not. You've only been going there two weeks. There must be a lot of students you haven't seen yet."

I raise my eyebrows as if to say she could be right but my mouth is downcast, like I'm not convinced.

"If you see him again you have to say something," Christine coaches.

She has no idea that she's making it harder for me to resist temptation. I blink back another chemical-induced tear as I picture the boy's arresting eyes and perfect mouth. I'm driven restless by the thought that I don't know what he's doing at this very second, that I don't know the tiniest thing about him except where he lives and that he likes hotdogs. It doesn't seem right not to know.

I have to change that.

Soon Christine's washing the excess dye from my hair and spraying on a leave-in conditioner. The dark hair framing my face makes my blue eyes stand out more. I was afraid my blond eyebrows would look stupid with black hair (Christine was afraid to blind me so left my eyebrows alone) but even that contrast looks sort of cool and once I'm finished with Christine's hairdryer I stare into the mirror, feeling infinitely more like the external me matches the shadowy person inside.

When I thank Christine she says that if I get some of my hair chopped off, tease it like crazy and then we do my makeup right I'll be pure Siouxsie Sioux. Having been impressed with the Siouxsie and the Banshees's video for "Dear Prudence" I saw the other night, the suggestion makes me smile.

"I like it long, though, so I'm not going to cut it," I tell her, running my hand down a newly darkened strand. I brush it forward, flopping it over my eyes so I can hide behind it. "But we can work on the makeup a little bit and pick out some new clothes."

"Oh, definitely new clothes," Christine says emphatically. "Otherwise there's not much point in changing your hair—you'd still look part preppy."

Christine's dad drives me home when we're done experimenting with makeup (which mostly translates into pale skin and kind of scary eyes) and I hesitate before stepping inside my house, afraid my mom won't be happy about the new look. But the first person who lays eyes on me is Olivia, who wrinkles her nose as I step into the kitchen. "You smell like chemicals," she complains from her spot at the refrigerator.

"I know." I move in close to her to peek into the fridge. My appetite's been under control during the last couple of days—this feels more like a run-of-the-mill snack craving.

"And you look like an evil twin of yourself," Olivia adds, reaching past me for the carton of orange juice.

"Thanks," I say, sarcasm pooling on my tongue. "That's exactly the look I was going for." With no interesting leftovers to munch on, I close the fridge and seek out my mother. She's up in her bedroom with the door ajar so it doesn't occur to me to knock but as I swing through the doorway I see that she's sitting on the double bed, her feet curled up beside her and a family photo in her lap. I recognize the photograph from across the room. It was one that was taken of all of us in an Auckland portrait studio just before Christmas. There's a snowy backdrop and the four of us are wearing Santa hats with fake fur cuffs and a fluffy white ball dangling from the end of them.

We were happy then, I guess. I wish I could feel that way when I remember it instead of being broken the way I am. When I look at old photos of myself, it's like I never really existed.

I take a step back, sure I'm interrupting my mother's memories. The floor creaks underfoot, giving me away.

"Freya!" my mother exclaims, her jaw tightening as she takes in my image. "What have you done to your hair?"

I clasp my hands behind my back and frown. "A girl from school helped me dye it. I wanted a change."

My mother has set down the family photo and she straightens her legs, throwing them over the side of the bed. "It's pretty drastic. Why didn't you say anything when I was dropping you off?"

I shrug. "It's not that big a deal and it's my hair."

My mother grimaces as she casts an eye back at the family photo. "But your real color is so lovely."

My real color is something I'm not. If my mother and I have had a conversation like this before, I don't remember it, yet the resentment rising up inside me is so familiar that it feels like second nature. I knew she wouldn't approve.

"Ordinary," I counter, my brain beginning to simmer at the thought of what my mother will say next, how she'll make me feel like I've done something stupid or selfish. "And what's wrong with wanting a change? Everything else has changed lately. What's the matter with me taking charge of something that *I* can control?"

My mother raises her eyes to meet mine again. "What's done is done. It's just so"—she squints as she examines my hair—"so dark. And your makeup . . . Did you think I would've tried to stop you? Is that why you didn't say anything?"

"I don't know." She seems more surprised than angry and I push aside my instinct to fight with her. Why did I suspect her reaction would be worse? "I guess I didn't want to have to stop and talk about it."

I begin to explain to my mom, as best I can without giving some of my darker feelings away, how things here are different from New Zealand. I tell her I don't want to look like the preppy/jock kids who listen to bad music, can't think for themselves and tend to treat the less-popular kids like they're invisible or worse. The bottom line is that I'm hoping she'll give me money for new clothes to complete my transformation.

My mother listens with her head cocked. "If it'll make you feel better, you can buy some new things," she says eventually. "I guess I should consider myself lucky if your teenage rebellion amounts to some hair dye and dark clothing, huh?" She ventures a smile.

The smile I return is wider and warmer. "Very true," I say, plucking the family photo from the bed and staring down into my own eyes. They're sort of like my dad's but the rest of my face is more like my mom's. My parents are what you would call attractive people—tall, thin and youthful for their age. Olivia seems to have a general predisposition towards good looks in common with them but not much else and as that occurs to me, a wave of heat washes over my body from head to toe, just like the one that overwhelmed me at the dinosaur exhibit in the museum. My head swirls with dizziness and I clutch my elbows and exhale slowly, fighting for control over my body.

"I find it hard to look at photographs of him too," my mother says as she peers sympathetically up at me. "Difficult but comforting at the same time."

I hand her back the photo, feeling, for the zillionth time, like a phony.

I do miss him. I'd give anything to have him back. But I can't shake the feeling that my dad's absence isn't the only thing that's the matter, that it's not even the worst thing. It's as if I'm . . . *infected* by some quicksand type of suspicion.

I don't know who I am anymore.

This moment. Here and now in my mother's bedroom. That's real. Christine dyeing my hair earlier. My sister down-stairs . . . my *sister* . . .

I sit down on the bed next to my mom to stop myself from collapsing. Sweat dampens my forehead. I press my palms into my eyes and then drag my hands out to my hair-line, counting in multiples of three to stop the panic racing through me.

Three. Six. Nine. Twelve. Fifteen. Eighteen.

Stop thinking, Freya. Just count.

Twenty-one. Twenty-four. Twenty-seven. Thirty. Thirty-three.

This is all the reality you need. Here and now.

Thirty-six. Thirty-nine. Forty-two. Forty-five.

My mother's rubbing my back, drawing me to her, and I rest my head on her shoulder, breathe measured breaths and count all the way to ninety-nine before I'm okay enough to stand again. Then I kiss her cheek and plod into my bedroom where I open the window to let in winter air. It's a long time until I'm calm and cool enough to quit counting entirely and when I reach that place, the blond boy from my dream is there too. He looks okay. Normal. Not furious and feral like the last time. He knocks his arm affectionately against mine and says, "You're *all right*, Freya. You're *okay*. Everything's going to be all right, you'll see."

I want to believe him.

The boy's lips form a goofy, lopsided grin, like he's aiming to make me laugh. I recognize the funny expression just like I recognize him. He makes me feel better and it's not the first time.

When I wake up—from a dream I didn't realize I was having—I'm smiling into my pillow. My bedroom's freezing and I tug a sweater over my head and pull the window shut. I climb under the covers and quickly shut my eyes, trying to find the place I left the boy. Trying to find the Freya I was in my dream.

SIX

The boy eludes me. My dreams are of other things. Standing silently next to my mom on an ice rink in my bare feet, my entire body numb. Christine lopping off my hair as Seth watches, telling me I should get to know him better. My father yelling at me that I'm selfish.

I shout back that he's the selfish one. Too selfish to really be dead.

When I wake up again I feel terrible for screaming at someone I miss so much. I'm so fucked up inside that maybe it would be better if I were the one who'd died instead.

But I can't even feel that properly because as fucked up as I am, scrambling after delusions and dreams while distrusting what's as plain as day in front of me, I know I want to live. I just want living to feel the way it should.

I spend the conscious hours of my weekend trying not to think because it seems really letting myself go—allowing my mind to wander beyond the boundaries of everyday

·life—risks loosening my grip on reality to a point that scares me stiff. I can't handle one more doubt or feeling of suspicion.

On Saturday night and Sunday afternoon I shove all my brightly colored clothes into a garbage bag that I hurl into the back of my closet. Then Mom, Olivia and I go out for a late lunch with Nancy, who acts as if I look the same as ever but then asks if I've been having any more headaches lately.

"Nope," I say truthfully over my buffet plate. "They must have been a flu leftover." I resist the urge to tell her she sounds like my grandfather. Why do the two of them keep going on about my head when I haven't said a thing about headaches lately?

According to my mom a guy named Frank broke Nancy's heart years ago and she hasn't been interested in anyone since. Her nearest family is down in Kansas and my mom also says that Nancy spends a lot of time alone, which makes Nancy sound like a sad person but as far as I can tell, she's not. If anything she's perky but with a propensity to want to fix other people's problems.

I listen to Nancy and my mother chat about work and then toss around the idea of renting a cottage up north this summer for a couple of weeks so that we'll all have the chance to soak up some scenery. "And make the most of the hot weather, right, Leila?" Nancy adds, staring first at my mother and then at Olivia and me. "How are you readjusting to Canadian winter?"

My mom replies that she feels as if she's forgotten the

knack of driving in snow but I say, "I sort of like the cold. It's not as bad as people say. It makes me feel . . ." I catch myself before blurting out something weird about how it stops me from overheating when my mind's spinning, roots me in the present.

"How does it make you feel?" Nancy presses.

"Like I'm really home," I reply, spearing salad with my fork. "It's Canada. It's supposed to be cold."

Nancy smiles but her stare feels like a microscope, as if she senses I'm editing myself and would like to stare through the façade to the real me. Maybe her real calling was to be a therapist.

"How about school?" she continues. "Is it a repeat of things you already learned in New Zealand or do you feel like you're ahead of the game?"

With my mouth full of salad, Olivia answers. "All the geometry stuff I already know but French is hard. It's funny, they call them grades at school here instead of years. I think 'year' sounds better."

I was in year eleven in Auckland but now I'm in tenth grade. It sounds like going backwards but I don't feel like it's a repeat. I'm behind the kids in my classes in some things and ahead of them in others, which is what I tell Nancy when she asks me directly.

She doesn't give me the microscope look from before but nods thoughtfully like this is precisely the reply she wants to hear. Maybe my mom is right about Nancy spending too much time alone after all. It's nice of her to take an interest and everything but I don't want to be analyzed.

I get quiet and stare around the restaurant at the other diners—an old couple eating steaks in silence, a rowdy group of about ten people who appear to be celebrating some kind of occasion, and a lone woman puffing furiously on a cigarette. As I'm watching the woman give herself lung cancer I spot a familiar face in the booth behind her, my biology teacher, Mr. Payne. He notices me looking over at him but doesn't wave. I bet he doesn't know it's me.

This is my life now, I tell myself. Being new wave Freya with the black hair and scary eyes and recognizing my biology teacher in a restaurant. *There's nothing but this moment.*

If a person tells themselves something often enough, will they begin to believe it?

Back at home after dinner, my mom and Nancy sit in the kitchen drinking tea while I return to my closet to pick out an outfit to wear to school tomorrow—a hunter-green top and black pants. Somber but not that different to what I'd normally wear. The main thing is to avoid anything that looks remotely cheerful.

At school on Monday morning Christine agrees to head straight for the mall with me after class to replenish my wardrobe with similarly somber and androgynous attire. Derrick approves of my new look and I notice some of the other new wavers checking me out at lunch and in the halls (especially a tall guy with a Flock of Seagulls–inspired haircut that completely obscures one of his eyes, so technically I can only see *one* eye checking me out). Surprise registers in several other faces, including Seth's and Terry's, but the only other person who really says anything to me about my appearance is Kyle from my English class who, despite me turning him down last week, tells me he likes my hair.

I could be imagining it (I've been imagining so many things lately that one more would hardly be a surprise) but for the most part it seems as if people—the guys especially—have pretty much quit staring at me by Wednesday. I make it through the first part of Wednesday feeling okay, successfully pushing thoughts of the green-eyed boy from Walmer Road to the back of my mind. But it's impossible to avoid the fact that it was a week ago today that I trailed him home. Would he follow the same schedule and route today?

At the end of math class, I edge over to Christine and ask whether she still thinks I should talk to the guy from my déjà vu if I see him again. She raises one eyebrow and asks, "Is that a hypothetical question or have you already seen him again?"

I pick at my thumbnail and glance down at the Doc Martens boots Christine helped me pick out on Monday night. "I haven't seen him but I think I know where to find him."

Christine frowns, her eyes flashing in alarm or surprise—I can't tell which. She must've just been humoring me the other day when she mentioned past lives and told me that I should try to make contact with the guy if I see him again.

"Okay," I say quietly. "You think I'm being crazy." I know I am. I just can't seem to help it.

"I don't think you're crazy," Christine says as we troop out of math class together and forge a path through the hallway. "It's just a"—she sighs lightly as she searches for a more sympathetic word—"kind of an obsessive thing. Like, you've gotten this idea in your head and are running wild with it."

I continue my assault on my fingernail. "No. It's crazy." Crazy is when your past doesn't feel real. Your grandfather doesn't feel like your grandfather but you dream of a boy you don't know and follow another home in the street. Crazy is thinking your sister isn't your . . .

Stop it, Freya. Don't think. You'll burn out.

Christine knocks her elbow against my arm. The action reminds me of the boy from my dream. She says, "Let's think it through. If you *do* approach him, what are you going to say? And if he tells you that you've never met, where are you going to take it from there? If you're really going to do this you have to be prepared for anything."

I'm so not. Obviously.

Christine's eyes bug out. "He could be mental for all you know and see this as a good opportunity to take someone home and chop them up into little pieces."

"Jesus, Christine," I mutter.

Christine tosses her head back. "Okay, so he's probably

not psychotic but I'm just saying, be smart about this. Don't rush up to him in some lonely place and don't freak him out by saying anything weird. You have to be cool and matter-of-fact if you talk to him."

"I know that. I need to play it casual." I don't want to freak him out and I certainly don't want to be chopped into little pieces. If I had my head on straight I'd forget about him entirely.

I've been trying to forget for a whole week but he's still in my head. If I could just talk to him maybe it would break whatever spell he has over me—prove he's not the person I think he is, just another average teenage guy who happens to have the face of a Greek statue. . . .

There's nothing but this moment, but for a minute he could be in the moment with me. My brain threatens to overheat as I ponder that: standing in front of him, his green eyes taking me in as I ask him where I know him from.

No, I snap at myself. *Don't think, Freya. Just do it.*

I can't tell whether my decision means I'm losing a battle or winning it. Either way, it feels inevitable.

Once Christine and I have parted ways I duck into the nearest bathroom, slip a sheet of loose-leaf paper out of my binder and write a note excusing Freya from afternoon classes in my neatest impersonation of my mother's handwriting. I take the note to the school secretary who smiles as though she doesn't suspect a thing and points at the school attendance book where I have to sign out.

The note says that I have a doctor's appointment but I

catch a bus to the mall and then hustle over to the information stand where I question the lady behind the counter about the fastest way to get to Toronto. As it turns out there's no rapid way to reach the city by public transportation. I take a commuter bus (which only leaves once an hour) to Yorkdale Shopping Center and then catch the subway from there. The entire time I'm trying not to think too hard, staring fixedly out the bus window and then at the subway map, repeating Depeche Mode and Smiths lyrics in my head (Christine would be so proud of herself for transforming my musical taste) to distract myself so that I don't lose it entirely.

By the time I reach the museum subway stop it's a few minutes later than when I saw the green-eyed boy last Wednesday, but I buy a hotdog from the vendor in front of the museum and hover around the cart for a few minutes anyway. It would seem less ridiculous to speak to him in public, as if I just happened to be here like I was last week. Unfortunately, that's clearly not going to happen.

My feet carry me to Walmer Road. I'm jittery in my skin. Blinking in double time. There's a moving truck parked down the road from the boy's house and a series of men in scruffy blue jeans are lugging hefty boxes out to the truck. None of them notice me as I pass but closer to the boy's house, where three children are making a snowman in their front yard, a little girl in an orange snowsuit stops to stare at me.

It's the scary eyes, I bet.

I smile and wave—most people, unless they're genuinely

psycho, look less scary when they smile. The two older kids wave back at me but the little girl only continues to stare.

Soon I've passed them too. Soon I'm eyeing the boy's house from the sidewalk, hoping he'll saunter out his front door, walk directly towards me and explain the mystery. That doesn't happen either. It's up to me to continue heading for his door, up the steps of his front porch, my gloved finger pressing his doorbell. Because I haven't let my mind focus on my actions, it's a complete blank as I wait on the boy's doorstep, listening for any sound of movement from within.

My heart thumps erratically in my chest as I force myself to ring the bell a second time. Fifteen seconds or so later the door pulls open and I jump like it's a surprise.

The green-eyed boy is standing in the doorway, pulling his sweatshirt down over his waist as though I've interrupted him at something. His shoulders relax as he looks at me but I hunch over like I've taken a punch to the stomach. It seems impossible to stare back at him and manage to breathe at the same time. He runs a hand quickly over his short dark hair and says, "So, are you selling something or what?"

I shiver at the sound of his voice. It's as familiar as the rest of him.

I do know him. I'm sure of it. I shouldn't have waited to come see him; I should've come before I asked Christine to dye my hair. Maybe he would've recognized me then.

"No," I tell him in an unnaturally high voice. "I'm looking for someone." Since I haven't allowed myself to contemplate the meeting in any depth, I'm improvising as best I can. "My friend Alison. Alison Leighland." My old Auckland friend is the first person who springs to mind. "This is the address she gave me."

"There's no Alison here," the boy tells me. Then he turns to shout over his shoulder, "It's just some girl with the wrong address."

I hear someone bound downstairs behind him as I mumble something about this being the address Alison gave me and then ask the boy how long he's lived here. A pretty girl with strawberry-blond hair spilling halfway down her back runs up behind the boy and locks her arms around his waist. She whispers into his ear, making him laugh at words I can't hear.

"In a second," he tells her before refocusing his attention on me. "I've been here for just over a month but I have no idea who lived here before. Sorry."

I stare blankly at the boy and the strawberry-blond girl now standing next to him like they've been surgically fused at the hip. I want to grab the boy's hand and force him to look at me more carefully. Instead I'm glued to the spot, speechless. How come he can't sense even a fraction of the familiarity that I do?

Awkwardness infuses the air between the three of us. I watch the boy and girl exchange a look that translates as: *Why's this creepy girl congealing on the doorstep when she's been told that her friend doesn't live here?*

"Do you have a phone number for your friend?" the guy asks. "Can you call her up and check the address?"

"Um." I tap the toe of my Doc Martens gingerly against his doorstep. "Could I use your phone? It's a local call—it won't cost anything." I don't know where I'm going with this—only that I'm not ready to give up but I don't want to breathe a word of what I came to say in front of his girlfriend.

"Go ahead," the guy says, opening the door wider and stepping aside to allow me entry. There's snow on my Docs and I bend to begin unlacing them so I won't drag it inside. "Don't worry about it," he tells me. "I'll show you where the phone is."

The girl's forehead creases as I straighten to follow them. They lead me into the kitchen where the guy indicates the telephone hanging on the wall near a circular yellow table. I pick up the phone and randomly dial seven numbers while they watch. As I listen to the telephone receiver ring into my ear, I overhear the girl say, "Garren, I should get going now. I'm supposed to be at work in fifteen minutes."

The boy's name sends a shiver up my spine. I couldn't have guessed it five seconds earlier but it sounds right. *Garren.* At first his name makes me feel hopeful and warm, like I've won a secret prize. Then an avalanche of loss and longing that has nothing to do with my father rumbles inside me. It scares me to feel that lost and scares me even more to feel that someone else, *Garren,* is part of a cure for the hole inside me.

Before Garren can reply to his girlfriend, the doorbell rings and he stalks off to answer it. I've allowed the phone to ring enough times (and been lucky that no one's answered) to hang up without looking like I'm giving up prematurely. With only the girl and me left in the kitchen, I coat my voice in frustration and say, "There's no one there."

Seconds later Garren reappears in the kitchen with a middle-aged handyman in tow. "I'll need you to go to the fuse box and cut the power to the refrigerator for me," the handyman instructs, paying no attention to me or the girlfriend.

Garren's girlfriend leans in to kiss him goodbye and tells him she'll see him soon. She stares expectantly in my direction, no doubt waiting for me to announce that I'm leaving too. "Would you mind if I wait another ten minutes and try again?" I ask. "No one picked up and I came all the way from Brampton on the bus."

"Okay," Garren says after a two-second pause. "Have a seat. I have to deal with the fuse box."

Garren and his girlfriend vacate the kitchen while I pull a chair out from the table and slip into it. The handyman's busy tugging the fridge away from the wall, whistling to himself, and with Garren gone I take the opportunity to scan the room for clues about his life. The kitchen's been painted a pastel green and there's a collection of small houseplants growing on the windowsill. A thick cookbook is sandwiched between a jar of dried pasta noodles and a cookie tin. Aside from the table, the only piece of furniture in the room is a wooden stool that stands flush against the counter. Overall the kitchen looks like a tidy, welcoming place but reveals very little about the people who eat inside it.

My stomach flips over as Garren steps back into the room with me. This would be challenging enough without him looking like a sculpture come to life. My fingers tingle as I glance up at him and make myself say, "Can I talk to you for a minute?"

A thinly veiled wariness seeps into Garren's pupils. He leans against the door frame and beckons me forward with his hand. I follow him out of the kitchen and into the living room. The wall opposite us is populated with crammed bookshelves. In the corner of the room nearest the TV, I spy a family photo of what looks like a typical 1970s scene—a man in polyester pants positioned in front of a barbecue, holding a spatula in one hand. His other hand rests on the shoulder of the young boy standing in front of him. In the background, behind the two of them, a woman with a nightmare of a perm stares dreamily off camera.

"What's going on?" Garren demands. He stops next to the couch and folds his arms in front of him but doesn't sit down. He's already out of patience with me; I'm running out of time.

I pull my hair back to give him an unobstructed view of my face. My voice is wispy as I spit out, "My name's Freya Kallas and my hair's normally blond. I moved back here from New Zealand with my family just over a month ago but I . . ." The next part is the toughest and I clench the fingers of my right hand as I continue. "I *know* that I know you somehow and if you could just have a good look at me maybe you'd remember me and remember how we know each other."

Garren's already-wary eyes darken. His head jerks on his shoulders. "What was that with the phone? I thought this was about your friend."

"I know." I release my hair and fight the impulse to look away. "I'm sorry. I know it probably sounds mental. It's just that I'm sure I know you and I need to remember how. I don't know what it means. Just that this is important."

"I don't get it," Garren says, spiky with annoyance. "I have no idea who you are. I've never seen you before in my life. You just show up here, looking for someone and ask to use my phone but you're . . ." He shakes his head, his left hand slicing through the air in aggravation. "Now you think you know me or something?"

I know how this looks and sounds and that I should feel pathetic and maybe sprint out into the street and never come back but I can't. *I can't.*

The angry Garren in front of me isn't the only one I've met. Behind my eyes another Garren is smiling and saying my name like we're friends or . . . something. We've been something. Sometime and somewhere.

"I don't seem familiar at all?" I ask. "Take a good look."

"Yeah," he snaps. "I can see you fine and like I said, we've never met."

If I were to hold my hands out in front of me I know they'd shake but I can't back down now. I plunge my fists into my coat pockets and stare at my feet. "Look, my dad was a diplomat. We've lived all over—New Zealand, Spain, Hong Kong, Argentina. Have you been any of those places?"

I see Garren's resolve flicker. He bows his head, lost in thought.

"What?" I nearly trip over my tongue with excitement. "You've been to one of those places?"

"No." Garren's eyes are quizzical. "Not any of those places but my dad was a diplomat too."

"*Was?*" I repeat.

"He died in December." Another flash of anger bursts onto Garren's face, like he's mad at me for making him say it.

The shock of what he's just revealed renders me speechless. It's as though we've been living flip sides of the same life. What does it mean?

Before my brain can begin to process the information, the fever and head-rush strike full-on. I hold a hand to my forehead and sip oxygen into my lungs, like I'm drinking it through a straw. "My dad . . . died too," I stammer, pushing the words out despite the dizziness taking me over. "December seventeenth. Back in Auckland."

"Don't mess with me," Garren warns. With my head in my left hand I can't see him and he sounds fuzzy, like either his mouth or my ears are full of cotton balls.

"I'm not messing with you. *I'm not.* I saw you walking in the street last week and—"

"Last week?" Garren cuts in. "Where?"

I lift my head from my hand to look at him. Garren's glaring at me like he doesn't trust a word of what I'm telling him but is helplessly curious just the same.

"Outside the museum. Last Wednesday." I rub my

temples and swallow air. Hold it deep in my lungs before releasing. I can't believe we're finally having this conversation.

"And you what . . . you followed me?" Garren says, almost shouting.

"Because I knew there was *something*. I don't know how I knew but when I saw you, something hit me."

"The feeling that you know me," Garren says with a sneer in his voice. "Look, I don't know who the fuck you are or what you think you're doing but you need to go."

"No!" I protest. "This isn't a joke. I'm telling you the truth. My father died two months ago in an accident—a gas explosion. You can look it up."

"An accident?" Garren barrels over to me and closes his fingers roughly around my left arm. "*Fuck you.* Get out of my house." He frog marches me out of the living room and towards the front door.

"Garren, listen to me. It can't be a coincidence about our dads." I struggle against him but he's stronger. "There's something going on. We need to figure out what it is."

Garren freezes behind me, his hand tightening its grip on my arm. "How do you know my name?"

"I didn't until a couple of minutes ago. I overheard your girlfriend say it in the kitchen. I didn't know anything about you, I swear. I saw you in the street last week and followed you home but I didn't have the guts to say anything." I turn my neck to look at him over my shoulder. "I had to come back. Please, just give me a chance so that we can—"

"Shut up," Garren snaps. We're standing directly in front of the door and he has to release me to open it. When he does, I swivel to face him.

"Please," I repeat. "I'm telling you the truth."

Garren's green eyes are livid, his body taut with tension. "You need to get out." He steps back and points to the open door. "Now."

I do as he says, afraid of what will happen otherwise. Out on Garren's porch I spin back towards him, legs quivering underneath me, and ask, "How did your father die?"

Garren glares at me with more concentrated rage than I've ever felt pointed in my direction. He slams the door in my face. It rattles on its hinges as I feel my heart pound in my chest. I stare at the closed door, out of breath and burning up. My mind's somersaulting with conspiracy theories. Two dead Canadian diplomats in the same month. Who would benefit from that? And why is my memory of Garren still only a shadow thing now that I've spoken to him? Why doesn't he know me? If it weren't for the February air breathing cold life into me, I'd be falling to my knees with the weight of wondering.

I'm hot but upright. Hot but thinking, thinking, thinking as I retrace my steps through the city streets, moving ever farther from the place I want to be most because the one person who I'm sure is caught up in this mystery with me never wants to see me again.

SEVEN

Soon the sky is violet and as I hit Spadina, I realize that I've left my sister hanging for the second time in a week. It's not that I forgot about her exactly but I lapsed in remembering my responsibility towards her. I call Olivia from the first pay phone I find and tell her I'm sitting in at a yearbook meeting at school and won't be home for a while yet. Two hours, one subway train and two buses later I'm trudging into my house, throwing off my winter clothes and yanking off my salt-stained boots. My mother meets me at the door and complains, in a voice like a jagged line, that I shouldn't have left my sister alone after school without warning.

At first I apologize, my mind still too busy trying to wrap itself around what happened earlier with Garren to pay much attention to anything else, and then I begin to argue with her. My frustration with Garren (how he shut me out and wouldn't listen) fuels my anger and I tell my mother I shouldn't be expected to babysit every single afternoon, that things happen after school that I want to be a part of.

My mother counters that she doesn't expect me to be a full-time babysitter, that she's only talking about a couple of hours after school and suggesting that I tell her ahead of time if I can't be here so that she can make alternate arrangements.

In the middle of our disagreement I realize that I don't care about what either of us is saying. It's not important.

I stomp away from my mother and up the stairs to my bedroom where I fling myself onto the bed, thinking about how I need to convince Garren to give me another chance. I was wrong to talk my way into his house with a lie. Maybe I would've been less threatening if I'd told him the truth from his doorstep.

I thought we'd have some kind of breakthrough once I spoke to him. That he'd know me. But the information about his father's a start. I need a plan for the next time I see Garren. Something to say that will make him stop resisting me and listen.

Just then my mother hurls my door open and charges into the room, hands on her hips. "I know none of us have had it easy lately," she begins, "but I don't like what's been happening to your attitude, Freya. First changing your appearance drastically without warning and now acting like it doesn't matter if Olivia is left alone. This isn't like you."

I fold my hands under my head as I meet my mother's

gaze. "No? What am I like, Mom?" Because I honestly don't know anymore. I don't know what any of us are like.

A lie gets halfway around the world before the truth has a chance to get its pants on. Winston Churchill's making pronouncements in my head again, like when I woke up from my first dream about the blond boy.

And what Churchill said fits. The majority of my life feels as though it's been some kind of lie. I don't know where I've picked up his words—they seem to have always been with me, a kernel of authenticity in a web of falsehoods. Is my mother in on the pretense? What does she know that I don't?

"Freya," my mother warns, like I'm goading her for fun. Her form appears to shrink from me, her gaze coldly retreating as though she's already tired of this but won't let me win. The moment echoes inside me, a dripping tap that will never stop. It feels like we've faced off against each other a hundred times before, each instance as aggravating as the last.

Only we haven't. Not like that. We don't fight any worse than your typical mother and daughter. It just *feels* that way. Another lie in my life.

I smother the urge to shout at her. "Mom." I soften my tone, regretting that I pushed her because it might make her more reluctant to answer my next question. "Is there any reason to think that what happened to Dad wasn't an accident?"

I remember the many black-suited men and somber women at my father's funeral, pumping my hand as they told me how sorry they were. The minister had only met my father a few times and the sermon he gave could've been for just about anyone, except for the words about my father's service to his country. Shortly afterwards, the investigation into the accident was concluded and the findings printed in the *Herald*: "A failed transition fitting that connects the gas line from the street to the house's gas system was the source of the gas that fueled the explosion."

But governments can cover things up. They do it with such frequency it's like a compulsion. How do I know the official version of the accident is what really happened?

My mom stands at the edge of my bed, blinking as if she misheard me. "Why would you say that?" she asks, a lump of wet sadness in her throat.

I prop myself casually up on my elbows. "No specific reason. It's just that we left only a month after. I wondered if any other information had come up. Have you heard from anyone at the consulate?"

"Neil Kingsley's written to see how we're doing," she says.

Neil Kingsley was my father's closest friend in New Zealand, one of the men in black suits with a strong handshake. The only thing I can really remember about him is that he always smelled sort of like ginger and grapefruit.

My mother stares at the floral pattern on my bedspread and adds, "But there's no news about the accident and there won't be. The investigation's long finished. *It was an accident.* You know that, Freya."

I hang my head and bite my lip. She thinks I haven't accepted my father's death.

I don't know what else to say to her. Either she doesn't know anything or doesn't want to tell me.

"Come downstairs and help me make dinner," my mom says. "Your sister's been asking for Hamburger Helper." The sudden warmth in her eyes puts a lump in my throat too. I don't want to be angry with my mother; I don't want things to change for the worse between us.

We go down to the kitchen together, me remarking how hooked my sister is on Hamburger Helper. Ever since the first package Nancy picked up for us along with a bunch of other groceries when my mom was too sick to go shopping. Olivia ate so much of it that she nearly made herself sick again, something I teased her about once she was feeling better.

When I realized I'd left Olivia alone after school again today I felt guilty but the other feelings I have about her, the ones that make me dizzy and feverish, haven't left me either and at the end of the night—hours after I've helped my mom with the Hamburger Helper and the three of us have watched *Magnum P.I.* together—I dream about Olivia.

A slightly smaller Olivia on a path to a stately Victorian building. I'm several feet away but can see her clearly from my spot on the path. She's flanked by two things that look almost like men but aren't. Inside, the building is filled with children and teenagers—all of them attractive, whole, healthy and intelligent.

I know that because I know exactly where we are. The place is a school, our school. In another time and another place. I catch a glimpse of Garren as I wander through the hallway to my classroom, my clothes feeling weightless like a second skin.

The sight of Garren, his dark hair wavy and nearly wild, makes my breath catch in my throat. He's talking to four other teenagers in a cluster in the middle of the hall and I stop to watch him like I've done so many times before. Sometimes I think he knows that I watch him.

I've never felt this way about anyone else. It seems a little like insanity.

Garren's the kind of person who says what he thinks and that makes some people angry and draws others to him like honey. He doesn't like the way things are and that's not something you're supposed to say, although this is a free country.

I should stop staring before he catches me at it, but he's smiling and that makes it tougher to look away and then . . . then his gaze flicks over to me and it's already too late.

In the morning I feel gloomy and weak and lie on my side with the covers pulled up over my chin wishing that I were someone else. My dreams mock me. I don't know which parts of them point to a deeper truth and which are only a kaleidoscope of images from my everyday life. What will happen to me if I can't filter out the truth? I have the terrible feeling that leaving the truth buried will poison me in one way or another and when Olivia—sent upstairs by my mom—tells me that if I don't get out of bed soon I'll be late for school, I burrow into my pillow.

I don't want my feelings about Olivia to be true but the creeping doubts won't leave me alone. I listen to Olivia pad out of my room and shout from the top of the stairs, "Mom, she won't get up!"

I throw back the covers and yell after her, "I'm up! I'm *up*."

"You better be!" my mother hollers from downstairs.

I change out of my pajamas and into clothes. My hair's kind of grimy but there's no time to wash it; there's barely enough time to do my makeup. I fly through the process and then dash downstairs to gulp down cold cereal.

Less than thirty minutes later I'm standing at my open locker, pulling out the textbooks and notebooks I need for my morning classes. Having to deal with such mundane things when I don't know what happened to my father and why a boy who should be a stranger to me isn't, seems ludicrous and just like that, the energy it took for me to get out of bed fizzles and dissipates. Misery descends with a vengeance and I freeze in front of my locker with my bio textbook in one arm.

Time stops.

For a while—who knows how long—I'm not sure where I am, the Victorian school from my dream or Sir John A. MacDonald. The realities merge unevenly in my head and the pieces that don't fit make my head ache.

I could stay this way forever and never decide what to do next. Maybe that's easiest.

"Freya?" a faraway voice calls. I turn, expecting to find small Olivia, wild-haired Garren or the well-intentioned blond boy.

I hadn't realized there were tears streaming down my face and as my eyes close in on Seth Hardy next to me I feel embarrassed, which is just as stupid as having to gather my books in the first place. Who cares about Seth or any of the people brushing by me in the hallway?

I need Garren. He has to help me. He's the only one. None of this means anything.

"Freya," Seth repeats. "Are you okay?"

I drag one of my sleeves across my face, smearing white makeup onto black cotton. Then I sniffle and try to clear my throat.

"Hey," he says, inching closer. "Is there anything I can do?"

I sense that he means that, despite the fact that I've treated him badly, and I thank him but tell him no, there's nothing he can do. On impulse, because he's being so nice, I apologize again for leaving the party without warning. "But I'm a mess," I add. "That's just the way things are right now."

I don't say why I'm a mess and he doesn't ask. His sympathetic eyes linger on my face until I break the silence again by saying, "I need to get to bio."

Seth nods and soon we're going our separate ways, him hightailing it down one end of the hallway and me the other, towards biology. I hate the days that I have double bio first thing. My morning concentration sucks and today I feel like I shouldn't be here at all.

As I slide into my seat, Derrick takes one look at me and then glances down at his hands, pretending that he hasn't noticed my bloodshot eyes.

"Hey," I say, dropping my biology textbook down on the counter in front of me.

"Hey," Derrick says back, his mouth inching open as though the thought of having to ask me what's wrong is making him tired.

Some people just aren't good at dealing with emotions and I save Derrick the trouble by saying, "Don't ask, okay? I don't want to talk about it."

Derrick bobs his head in relief. "You ready for the grasshopper dissection today? Payne's gone into the back room to get them."

Derrick and I actually had a debate about this on Tuesday, knowing that we'd be lab partners. Both of us wanted to be the one to cut the grasshopper open, like kids with a new toy. Dissection seems exciting compared to most of the other things we have to do in school.

"Do you still want to be acting surgeon?" I ask, because just trying not to dissolve or freeze the way I did at my locker a few minutes ago is draining my energy reserves; there's nothing left for pulling apart a dead grasshopper.

"Getting cold feet?" Derrick smiles. "Don't worry, I'm on it."

Sure enough when Mr. Payne hands us our grasshopper (a male) Derrick enthusiastically grips the scalpel. Mr. Payne makes us name all the specimen's external parts for him before getting started. The only ones I recognize by sight and name are the most obvious ones: simple eye, compound eye, head, antenna, wings and the ovipositor. I feel woozy as I listen to Derrick name the rest. When I close my eyes I see the interior of the Victorian school I walked through in my dreams last night. I never reached the classroom I was headed for before I spotted Garren but I can see it in my mind now—row upon row of wooden desks with cast-iron frames. The floor is wooden too and faded maps and diagrams hang on the walls like props in a Hollywood movie. The contrast between the historical setting and the students' perfect skin and features puzzles me. The oddly mechanical men escorting Olivia can only have been a product of my imagination but the thought of them makes me shiver.

"Are you doing all right there, Freya?" Mr. Payne asks.

It's time to pin our grasshopper into the dissecting pan and I mumble that I'm okay so Mr. Payne will leave us alone. He walks away, casting a final look over his shoulder.

With the pins in place Derrick drags the scalpel down the grasshopper's abdomen. Then he switches to the tweezers, digs into our specimen and pulls out a clump of mushy brown innards. "What the hell is this supposed to be?" Derrick asks, examining the gunk at the end of his tweezers. He turns to get my opinion but his face—the entire classroom—is fading to black with me in it. I fight the darkness, clawing my way back towards consciousness but not reaching it. As my body turns to jelly and begins to slide towards the floor, my lab partner's lightning-fast reflexes are the only thing that keep me from hitting cold linoleum.

EIGHT

The blond boy and I are weaving through a tangled mass of young people, some of them dancing with their arms stretched sensually up towards a hot summer night, others swaying—or even sleeping—as they lounge on blankets, towels and pieces of abandoned clothing. There are people upon people upon people as far as the eye can see—guys with long sideburns and flowing locks, girls with blissful smiles on their faces, some of them bare-breasted. The ground is squelchy underfoot and the air smells like mulch.

A curly-haired guy with grungy cheeks grabs my ankle as I step forward. I kick him loose and turn to shoot him an angry look. "Hey, man, what time is it?" the guy asks in a tone so mellow that he should be sitting atop a mountain, cross-legged, chanting for world peace.

"I don't know," I tell him.

"Don't sweat it," he says dreamily. "Stay beautiful."

I stare into the distance at the blond boy who's managed to get thirty feet ahead of me. "Latham!" I shout, not the least bit surprised that I know his name because it's second nature; I've known him forever.

Latham turns to wait for me. When I catch up to him in the dark he drawls "Far out" in a perfect drugged-up imitation of the hippies surrounding us.

"Out of sight," I declare, trying to match his dazed tone.

"Groovy, man," Latham adds.

We laugh together, thinking we're clever. Then Latham says, "I wish I could've been there for the real thing."

"I don't know—it was pretty unhygienic," I joke. But I know what he means. Life was rawer then but more innocent. People like these thought they could change things and that the changes would last.

We start pressing forward again, looking for safe places to put our feet as we near the stage. "You should come to the concert in Chicago with us," Latham says. "You know I can get more transit documents no problem."

"And you know that I can't go. Leila would explode. She's angry enough with me already."

Latham's opening his mouth to say something else when I begin to drift away from him and back towards my biology classroom. I hear it before I can see it—raised teenage voices and chairs scraping across linoleum. When I open my eyes Mr. Payne and Derrick are gazing down at me with matching looks of concern. They've laid me down on the floor after all but at least I didn't fall and crack my skull open. I can feel something soft under my head and notice that they've elevated my feet over a pile of textbooks.

"Don't try to sit up," Mr. Payne advises. "I've called for the nurse."

My mother comes to pick me up thirty minutes later. I'm lying in the school nurse's office under a scratchy gray blanket, staring at a cobweb on the ceiling and listening to the tinny radio that sits on the nurse's desk. The DJ's introducing a new Simple Minds song when my mom walks into the room along with the nurse, who's in the middle of telling her that I've perked up in the past few minutes but am running a low-grade fever.

"So she didn't faint because of the dissection in science class?" my mom asks as I sit up on the cot. My mother crosses over to me and spreads her right hand across my forehead.

"I'm feeling better," I say. "I just got light-headed watching my lab partner cut into the grasshopper."

"You do feel warm, though," my mother notes.

"I didn't sleep well last night. On top of that, there was the bio thing. I guess I couldn't handle it."

My mother faces the nurse. "She had a very rough case of flu a few weeks ago. We all did. But she's had some fairly bad headaches since then and I'd feel better if I could get her checked out by our doctor."

"Of course," the nurse says approvingly.

I continue to protest that I'm fine but my mother isn't interested in my assessment and asks the nurse if she can use the telephone. Then she calls Doctor Byrne, who tells her he can see me in an hour.

My mom propels me out of the office and towards her car as I repeatedly insist that I don't need to see a doctor and was the victim of a run-of-the-mill fainting spell. The truth is that my head feels like a balloon that's been overfilled and could pop at any second. If Garren hadn't told me about his father I might still suspect a brain tumor was the cause of all my strange thoughts and feelings over the past few weeks.

In the car, the sun feels like a jackhammer chipping into my skull and I close my eyes and sleep. We arrive in Toronto early and sit in Doctor Byrne's waiting room listening to his receptionist answer the telephone and book appointments. My mother leafs through a copy of *Life* magazine and I cross my legs and grip the armrests of my chair, determined that no matter what Doctor Byrne asks me, I won't crack and confess the sense of loss that runs deeper than my father, the holes in my memory, and feelings of distance from various family members. The only things I intend to reveal are physical symptoms.

"And where's he taking you this year?" the receptionist says into the phone during what sounds like a less formal conversation than the ones I've overheard so far. "Ah, very nice. Lucky you. I've only been there once and everything was delicious. But listen, as soon as he's finished with the patient he's in with, I'll have him call you back, all right?"

Not ten minutes later Doctor Byrne emerges from his office with a man in a ski jacket. The receptionist nabs the doctor before he can disappear back inside his office and informs him that his wife called. "Thanks, Marjorie," he says to the receptionist. Then he turns his attention to me and my mother and instructs, "Please come through."

"I have a wedding anniversary coming up on the weekend," he explains as my mom and I file into his office behind him. "So the pressure's on."

"Your anniversary?" my mother asks.

Doctor Byrne pinches at his eyeglasses. "That's right. Seven years."

Since Doctor Byrne looks about sixty, I would have guessed he'd been married for decades. Maybe it's a second wife and because I'm in no hurry to talk about myself I ask, "Where are you taking her for dinner?" I heard the receptionist ask his wife the same question over the phone.

"A place in Yorkville—the Bellair Café." Doctor Byrne smiles and launches into a series of questions about my fainting spell and how I've been feeling lately.

I admit that I have a headache (which I downplay the intensity of) and tell him it mostly happens when I don't sleep well, that school's been a big change from my old one in New Zealand and that I'm feeling a little stressed. The fainting I explain away by emphasizing that I was grossed out by the grasshopper even before my lab partner began slicing it open. I laugh and tell Doctor Byrne that I guess I won't be going to medical school.

"Well, let's have a look at you then," he says. Doctor Byrne listens to my heart, checks my glands, shines a light inside my ears and then whips out a tongue depressor and peers down my throat.

"I can feel the slight fever," he says, directing his comments at my mother. "It could be that she's fighting something off but since there are no other persistent symptoms for the moment I'm just going to suggest that she try to get more rest and drink plenty of fluids. You can give her acetaminophen for the fever if that's bothering her."

"It's not," I tell him.

"And of course if she develops other symptoms, I'd like to see her back here."

"What about the headaches?" my mother asks.

Doctor Byrne plants his palms on his thighs and looks me directly in the eye the way few people can sustain for long. It reminds me of how Nancy stared at me in the restaurant last Sunday. "Any confusion, Freya?" he asks. "Any dizziness—apart from today, that is?"

"What do you mean by confusion?" As soon as I've said it I wish I could take it back. I should've just told him no.

Doctor Byrne adjusts his glasses. "Disorientation. Memory problems. Word-finding difficulty. Hallucinations."

Hallucinations. Like thinking I'm someplace else. I see my mother scrunch up her shoulders at the word and I quickly shake my head. "Nothing like that. More like confusion over the difference between the metathorax and mesothorax." Two terms Derrick used in relation to the grasshopper earlier.

"I wouldn't worry about that unduly." Doctor Byrne's eyes twinkle briefly. "And I can hardly tell you to study harder when you're already under stress from changing schools and everything else, can I?"

The unnamed everything else is my father's death. People don't like to mention it unless there's no way around it, as though saying it will make it true all over again and send me into shock.

Doctor Byrne asks if I would mind waiting outside for a moment while he speaks to my mother. This must be the part of the visit when he and my mother confer over my stress and grief levels. I leave them alone, relieved to have made it through the examination without giving away too much but fixating on the other symptoms Doctor Byrne asked me about. The only one I'm not actively suffering from is word-finding difficulty.

I wish he'd explained what kind of condition all the other symptoms could indicate. On the other hand, even if he had I wouldn't have admitted to the symptoms. No matter what Doctor Byrne—or anyone—says I don't trust them the way I trust myself. It's how someone who is paranoid would feel but if I can't trust my gut I can't trust anything.

Back in the waiting room I skim through the same copy of *Life* magazine that my mom was looking at before we were called into Doctor Byrne's office. A girl named Brooke

Shields is in a skimpy swimsuit on the cover, striking an uncomfortable-looking pose that's probably supposed to be sexy. Minutes later my mother joins me and we walk out to the car together. "I want you to take it easy tonight, all right?" she says. "No homework. No going out. Lie down and relax.

"Humor me," she adds before I have a chance to reply.

"Okay, okay." I climb into the car and belt myself in while my mother, on the driver's side, does the same. "What did Doctor Byrne say after I left?"

My mother's face is weary. "Nothing new. He thinks you're a little worn out emotionally and that it's been taking a physical toll."

Exactly what I want him and everyone else to think, but I don't know how much longer I can keep up the pretense. At home I pop acetaminophen for my head and do as my mother suggests. Curled up on the couch with a glass of chocolate milk beside me on the coffee table and a mixture of music videos and soap operas playing out on the TV, my brain's on a rampage, alternately running over the details of the bizarre dreams I've had in recent weeks and racking my mind for a way to get through to Garren.

There must be a record of what happened to my father on file with the Canadian government. It could take a while to get my hands on it but it's possible my mother clipped one of the newspaper articles about the explosion from the *Herald*. If she did, they're likely somewhere in her bedroom, which I won't be able to ransack until she leaves for work tomorrow morning. The more I think about it, the clearer it becomes that I can't put off seeing Garren for long. I've covered for myself so far but that can't last. The dreams have begun to break through to my conscious mind.

Aside from the deaths of our fathers, all I have to offer Garren is visions and vague feelings. Without evidence he's not any more likely to listen to me than he was the last time but I have to try anyway. It's either that or end up locked in a rubber room.

The day feels endless and finally, around six o'clock, while my mother's cooking dinner and Olivia's parked safely in front of the TV watching a *Gilligan's Island* repeat, I scurry up to my mother's room and ease open each of her dresser drawers. The right-hand drawers are full of her things—underwear, hosiery, pajamas—and the left side contains a selection of my father's clothes that she couldn't bear to throw away—a Star Wars T-shirt, a navy cashmere sweater, jogging pants and an entire drawer of black socks.

I stare at the Star Wars T-shirt, an illustration of Luke Skywalker wielding a lightsaber emblazoned across its front. This was one of the T-shirts my dad liked to throw on for doing yard work or other household tasks. He was wearing it with his Adidas running shoes and faded blue jeans the day before he died, mowing the lawn while my mom planted lettuce, ginger and turnips in the garden. I glanced through the kitchen window at the two of them, Mom wrapped up in her seeds and Dad catching sight of me at the window. He paused to wave and I waved back, never dreaming that I'd only have him in my life for another day.

The memory of that moment feels as solid as yesterday, unlike many of my memories from before we arrived in Canada. I still can't believe he's gone and I lay my hand on the T-shirt and silently vow, *I'm going to find out what happened to you. I won't let the truth stay buried.* With my eyes smarting I continue scouring the bedroom. There's a squat filing cabinet stored within the walk-in closet and my heart quickens at the sight of it. I slide open the top drawer, sink my shaking fingers inside and discover copies of various financial statements, receipts and contracts, as well as my family's medical and education records. Disappointingly, the bottom drawer is completely empty. There are other parts of the closet left to search but I've taken too long already. Dinner will be ready any minute now and Mom will be sending Olivia up to look for me.

I've put my mother through enough today and don't want to have to scramble for a lie she might not believe. I grind my teeth together as I slip reluctantly out of the room, counting the hours until I can return to finish the job.

NINE

In the morning I don't remember my dreams but I feel profoundly unsettled, like I'm standing on a fault line while balancing on one foot. No one needs to come upstairs to urge me to get ready for school. I'm wide awake and moving long before my alarm goes off. Freshly showered and with my makeup done I watch Olivia crunch sleepily on her cereal and my mother brew coffee.

"How are you feeling, Freya?" my mother asks, tapping her nails on her coffee mug.

"Better," I tell her. "More rested." Truthfully, the headache's gone too.

"And the fever?" My mother coasts over to touch my forehead.

"You could just wait for me to answer, you know." I try to swat her away but she's already made contact. "I'm old enough to know whether I have a fever or not."

"You do feel cooler," she notes.

"I know," I chirp with only a dash of sarcasm.

My mother's front teeth peek out from under her top lip in an expression that's part smile and part grimace. "Try not to faint today."

I laugh, despite the tension whirring underneath my skin and once my mom and Olivia have gotten into the car and driven off I race back up to my mother's closet. Overnight I've grown more desperate and impatient and I make a mess, pulling things like spare blankets and shoe boxes from their shelves and leaving them abandoned on the carpet. I revisit the filing cabinet—and then the dresser and bedside tables—in case I missed the articles the first time around. But maybe she didn't keep them in the first place and there's nothing to find.

Just to be thorough, I search my own room in case I'm the one who kept the articles. With my memory full of holes that's a distinct possibility. However, there's no sign of them in my room either and as I'm slamming drawers shut it occurs to me that Olivia would have been just as likely to keep any record of the explosion as I would have. I rush into her bedroom, heading straight for her desk where I find the original December 18, 1984, clipping about my father's death in the top drawer.

GAS EXPLOSION CLAIMS LIFE OF CANADIAN DIPLOMAT AND LOCAL WOMAN

Daniel Morris

Staff Reporter

A Canadian diplomat and a local employee of the Canadian High Commission were killed in an afternoon gas explosion late yesterday afternoon. Firefighters were called to the house at 37 Coventry Terrace in Howick at approximately 5:30 p.m. after witnesses reported that property had been leveled by a blast and was engulfed in flames.

Marcy Cooper, who lives directly across the street from the destroyed home, said, "The sky lit up and the whole house collapsed in an instant, taking a car that had just pulled into the driveway with it. I couldn't believe my eyes. It was like something out of a nightmare."

The incident claimed the lives of Luca Kallas, a senior finance officer with the Canadian High Commission, and Brenda O'Callaghan, one of the owners of the Coventry Terrace home who had been locally employed by the High Commission as a property assistant. Two other residents of the Howick neighborhood were injured by flying glass and debris and were taken to Auckland Hospital for treatment.

Fire officials believe a natural gas leak caused the explosion. Investigators are continuing to probe the cause of the incident.

I slip the article into my biology binder to protect it from the elements and decide to leave two notes on the kitchen table in case I'm not home before Olivia or my mother arrives back at the house. The note to Olivia says I might be a few minutes late again. I apologize and tell her that something came up but that I'll be home as soon as I can. My mother's note is more difficult because I know she'll feel I'm letting her down. If I'm home in time I'll destroy both notes, but if I'm not my mother will be as angry with me as Garren was when I see her later. With that in mind I jot down:

Mom,
　　There's something very important that I had to do after school, which is why I'm not home with Olivia. I'm sorry I can't tell you more than that I'm helping a friend in trouble but I've made a promise. I know I'll probably be grounded and won't argue.
　　　　　　　　　　　　　　　　Freya

I fold the note into thirds and shove it into one of the envelopes my mother keeps to mail off bills, scrawling "Mom" across the front of it and then sealing it so that Olivia won't be able to cheat and read my words. Since most of what I've written is a lie it wouldn't really matter whether she reads my mother's note but if I *were* telling the truth I'm sure I'd be secretive.

With the notes finished I dart into the family room and

pull a 4 x 6 snap of my family (my mother in the center of the frame with her left arm sloped around my father and her right around my grandfather, Olivia and me standing in front of the trio, me hunching down so I don't block my dad's face) out of its mantelpiece frame. I hide the empty metallic frame underneath the TV stand and hope that no one will have a chance to notice it missing.

There's no photograph of my father in the *Herald* article so technically the family photo doesn't prove anything but it can't hurt for Garren to see me with my parents and little sister when he's been thinking of me as someone who's toying with him. The blond version of myself in the photograph doesn't look evil or conniving; she looks happy and loved.

I drop the photo into my binder along with the news clipping and troop out to the nearest bus stop to begin the journey to Toronto. My head's surprisingly clear but I'm nauseous with nerves that worsen when I reach Garren's house on Walmer Road and he fails to answer the door. I knew he might not be here—that he likely has school, work or something else to keep him busy—but I also know that I can't leave without speaking to him a second time.

At first I circle his neighborhood, intermittently ringing the doorbell in case he arrived home while the house was out of my view. After an hour it's too cold to continue loitering on his street—even for me—and I give in to the bitter arctic wind and walk down to Bloor Street where I dip into a coffee shop and order hot chocolate and a honey-glazed donut.

The radio's playing and the same Simple Minds song I heard yesterday comes on as I'm finishing my donut. The DJ says it's from a new movie called *The Breakfast Club*. He sounds excited about it and I wonder if I'll ever in my life be able to enjoy anything as ordinary as a movie.

It's only 1:10 in the afternoon but I'm already picturing my mother reading my note. I'd rather she be angry than anxious but I want to beat her home so she won't be either. If I left now I'd only be a little later than usual. Olivia wouldn't rat me out and my mother wouldn't need to know a thing.

But nothing will make me leave the area without speaking to Garren; I'm not going anywhere . . . except back to Walmer Road. I tuck my binder tightly under my arm as I venture out onto Bloor again. The wind whips at my cheeks, bringing tears to my eyes. I move decisively in the direction of Garren's house, pretending to myself that I can't feel anything, like a machine.

From down Garren's street, I spy a car in his driveway and my legs turn to mushy broccoli stalks underneath me. *Someone's home.*

I hurry up the road, telling myself everything will be okay—that I'll make him listen. My gloved finger is freezing as it taps the doorbell. I already know that when I open my mouth, my voice will crack. Too much depends on this.

The door inches open to reveal a stunning brunette roughly the same age as my mother. She's rubbing her hands together to combat the blast of cold air she's allowed inside.

"Yes?" she prompts, staring particularly hard at my eyes, which must be a sloppy mess of smudges that I should've thought to clean up before ringing the bell.

"I . . . Is Garren home?" I stammer.

"He is," she confirms. "And you are?"

"Freya. Freya Kallas." My stomach flips over as I stare at the woman standing in the doorway. She's not as familiar as Garren but she doesn't look like a stranger either.

The woman motions for me to step inside. Then she retreats to the kitchen. I hear running water in the distance. It stops as Garren's raised voice peals through the house. I can't make out many of the words but then I hear his mother advise, in a steely stone, *"Be nice about it."*

Garren advances through the hallway towards me wearing the face of someone who has been lied to one too many times. *"You,"* he says accusingly.

I reach into my binder and shove the article at him. "Just read it. Please."

He must not want his mother to overhear us because he hasn't started shouting yet. "This doesn't mean anything," he says as he takes the scrap of newspaper from me and begins scanning from the top.

I slide my New Zealand driver's license out of my wallet and show him that too. "Here, look at the last name—Kallas. The man in the article—the diplomat they talk about—he's my father."

Garren refuses to take the ID but he looks it over as he commands, "Outside." He jams his feet into a pair of running shoes on the mat beside me, jerks open the door and steps onto the doorstep.

I follow cautiously, afraid it's a trick and he'll abandon me outside. But if he thinks that will make me disappear, he's wrong.

While Garren's scrutinizing the article a gust of wind catches the photo tucked within my binder, steals it from between the covers and dashes it to the ground. As I bend to snatch it up, Garren's attention shifts to the image between my fingers.

"What's that?" he asks, his cheeks already blushing from the cold.

"My dad—and the rest of my family. I thought . . ." Garren's holding out his hand for the photo and I don't bother to finish my sentence.

He takes the photograph from me, suddenly very still and quiet despite the second gust of wind cutting through us on his porch. I squeeze the binder to my chest and say, "Did you tell your mom why I was here?" He must've told her something since I heard her warn him to be nice.

Garren glances up from the photo, his green eyes unreadable. "She's been through enough—and I still don't know why you're really here." He moves closer to me, his thumb tapping my grandfather's image. "Who's this?"

"That's my grandfather on my mother's side." I point at my father's face. "And this is my dad."

"What's your grandfather's name?" Garren asks.

"Henry Newland. Why?"

Garren's mouth jerks open. "You're the one who came to me with a story that makes you sound like a paranoid schizophrenic. Don't you think I should be able to ask you whatever I want?"

"You can. I'm not hiding anything—I was just curious."

Garren's head drops. He hands the photograph and newspaper article back to me. "Wait here while I get my coat. It's fucking freezing."

He turns to grab the doorknob and I snap, "You can't ditch me that easily."

Garren shoots me a look over his shoulder. Something in his face has changed. "I'm coming back. Just give me a second."

I don't really have a choice except to trust him. So I wait, and in a moment Garren reappears, wearing the same black coat he was sporting that day outside the museum. "Walk with me," he says, like it's not a question but a demand.

We fall into step together as we head away from his house. "Tell me again what makes you think you know me," Garren says, his eyes on the sidewalk ahead.

I'm glad that he hasn't turned me away but so far speaking with him hasn't provided me with a single answer. If I have to go home feeling the same lost, crazy way I've been feeling for weeks now, I don't know what I'll do. I need Garren to start opening up and tell me what he knows.

"I can't explain it," I tell him, my teeth as cold as metal as we walk. "I wish I could. It's only a feeling but not like a hunch, much stronger than that. Something a part of me knows but that my conscious mind can't access." I'm still clutching my binder in front of me, like a shield, and there are tears in my eyes because of the wind but I don't want Garren to think I'm crying. Just because I need his help doesn't mean I've given up my pride. "I dreamt about you a couple of nights ago," I confess, blinking back the tears. "We were in a strange, old-fashioned kind of school. We were both a little younger and I already knew who you were."

Garren shakes his head resolutely as I speak. Once I'm finished he looks at me sideways and says, "I don't remember you. We've never met. I've lived in other places most of my life too—Denmark, Japan, Switzerland—but none of the countries you mentioned. We never went to school together, Freya, but"—Garren straightens his back, ripping his gaze from me again—"the man in the photo that you say is your grandfather, he's my grandfather too."

I freeze on the sidewalk for a second but Garren hasn't stopped and I have to rush to catch up to him. "On my mother's side," he specifies. "My grandmother died a long time ago, from cancer."

"Mine too," I whisper. "I can hardly remember her." This is not what I expected—that apparently Garren and I are related—and I don't understand how or why our families would've hidden it from us all these years and what the relationship has to do with our father's deaths. The shock makes me stumble on the sidewalk and Garren automatically reaches out to steady me. "What about your other grandparents?" I ask breathlessly.

"Dead too. In a car accident just a couple months after my parents got married."

My ears are ringing. The sidewalk rises and falls in front of me, like a series of cement waves. I stop short and sit in a snowbank next to someone's blue spruce. Then I fold my hands behind my neck and lower my head to my knees so I won't pass out like I did yesterday.

Garren stops and hunches down next to me, balancing his weight on the balls of his feet. "No," he says quietly. "*Don't say it.* You have to be lying. There's no way any of this can be true."

"I don't know what's true," I mumble to the ground. "I only know what I've been told." And I was told exactly what Garren relayed—that my father's parents died in a car accident before I was born.

My binder's cradled in my lap and Garren eases it away from me. He gets to his feet again and stares at the article and photograph as he says, "My dad was killed in a train accident in Switzerland on December seventeenth. Two cars derailed and four people died. Thirteen more were injured."

The same day even. It must not have been an accident— our fathers were murdered. But what about our grandparents? Who has the power to control that many events and why have they done this?

I've begun to feel the cold in the back of my legs. It keeps me conscious and, as much as possible, restores a semblance of calm. "Do you remember your life in the other places you lived?" I ask. "I mean, do you remember them in the same vivid way that the present's happening?"

"Of course I remember." Garren furrows his eyebrows. "Are you saying you don't?"

I begin to describe the bizarre feelings and thoughts I've had since returning to Canada with my family. I tell him about not being able to remember details from the past that I should know, like my best friend's favorite band, and about feeling as though my sister and grandfather aren't my real family.

"Like they've been replaced?" Garren asks incredulously.

"I don't know." I unlock my hands from around my neck and straighten my back.

Garren slams the binder shut. "How do I know that any of the things you're saying about your grandparents are true? It would be so easy for you to just say your grandparents died the same way as mine. Can you prove it?"

"Can you?" I fire back, suddenly angry that after everything I've said I'm still the one being cast as the potential villain. "*I'm* the one in the photo with my grandfather. That's proof of something. How do I know *you* even know him? And I brought evidence of the accident that they say killed my father. Where's your evidence about the train accident?" I believe Garren one hundred percent but I'm tired of him doubting me. "And for the record—I was told that a kid without a license was the one who crashed into my grandparents' car. Some boarding school rich boy who took his father's car out when he was home one weekend and lost control of it on a patch of black ice. My father said that my grandfather was dead at the scene but my grandmother lived another three hours."

Garren turns in the street, peering steadily back at his house in the distance as though he'd like to rewind history to a point when his life felt solid, a time before I knocked on his door and made him question everything. The cold has turned his skin a blue-gray that strengthens his resemblance to a statue. I can imagine him frozen that way forever, trapped in a moment of perpetual confusion and denial.

"I don't understand any of this," he says. "Who are you?" His expression and tone are stark enough to make me wish I didn't have to do this to him.

I stand up, brushing the snow from the underside of my legs. "I only know what I told you; I don't know what it means. That's why I had to come to you. You're the only one I've had this feeling about. I thought . . . I thought you'd know me." I can't keep the disappointment out of my voice.

"I don't," Garren says. "I still don't. But that's what I was told about my grandparents too, that some kid not old enough for a license smashed into them. Even the part about my grandmother dying in the hospital later that same night—the details match."

I ask him their names, which are different from my father's parents. It turns out Henry Newland is the only name we have in common—Garren says his grandmother's (Henry's wife's) name was Irene while my grandmother's name was Evelyn. I continue to question him about the people closest to him—especially those in Canada who he sees regularly. Garren tells me he has an aunt (on his father's side) who never married but that aside from her and his grandfather, he and his mother don't know many people in the area.

"That's like us," I say. "My mom has one close friend but really there's no one else except my grandfather." I explain how the three of us were really sick with the flu right after we arrived from New Zealand and about the doctor my grandfather set us up with.

Any remaining color drains rapidly from Garren's face. "We were sick when we got here too. For almost two weeks. My grandfather called his doctor, Doctor Byrne. He came to see us a couple times."

"Yes, Doctor Byrne!" I cry. "His office is on Yonge Street, near St. Clair. I had to go in and see him again yesterday."

Garren nods slowly, his mouth a pale slash. Without further warning he crumples into the snowy lawn next to us, like his mind and body can no longer stand the shock.

My binder lands next to him, flipping open and releasing the article and family photo into the wild while my useless biology notes remain safe (thanks to the three metal rings fastened inside). The newspaper clipping and snapshot jolt along the sidewalk, powered by frigid northern air, and for a split second I hesitate, not sure whether to sprint after them or check Garren's condition.

"Fuck," I mutter as I dive down next to him. "Fuck, fuck,

fuck." Garren's eyes are shut and I hover over him, feeling for his breath. It's warm against my palm and I pull back, trying to remember what Mr. Payne did for me when I fainted yesterday.

The first thing that comes to me is that he'd raised my legs. I rush to Garren's feet, sit on my knees on the sidewalk and prop up his feet on top of them. Then I give him a minute to wake up.

Before long his eyelashes are fluttering. I watch him stare blankly up at the sky like an upended turtle that doesn't know what happened to it.

"Don't try to move yet," I advise. "Just lie there a minute."

Garren props himself up on his elbows to look at me.

"Lie back," I repeat. "Do you want to pass out again?"

Garren groans but obeys. "What happened?" he asks from his place in the snow. If he'd stretch out his arms and legs he could make a taller snow angel than I've ever seen.

I glance down at Garren's Nike running shoes in my lap. Could he really be my cousin or some other kind of relative? We don't look alike but Garren and his mother have the kind of photogenic good looks that make people turn their heads. My grandfather, Henry, on the other hand, looks like an ordinary person, a retired school principal or former department store employee.

"I'm getting up," Garren announces, slowly shifting his weight to his elbows and lifting his feet from my knees. As he sits forward in the snow my mind turns to the lost photo and news clipping and I shoot up, scurrying off in the direction I last spotted them.

I scan the unevenly shoveled sidewalk, slushy street and nearby lawns, picking up speed as I stagger forward. There—ahead, caught in the naked, low-hanging branch of a maple tree, sits my family photo. I run towards the tree and rescue the photograph but the clipping is nowhere to be found and as I'm searching for it, Garren gaining on me, a car honks.

I turn to see its lone female occupant wave. *"Shiiiit,"* Garren rasps from behind me. Only then do I realize the woman was his mother, disappearing down the road. "Now I'll have to wait until she's back to talk to her." Garren's front teeth scrape together and tension lines etch into his forehead.

I tell him she might not know anything—that I tried fishing for information from my mother without any luck. Then I ask if he's okay now.

Garren's hands dive into his pockets. He nods, his breath streaming out a frosty white. "As okay as I can be, considering." He jogs back to the place he fell to retrieve my binder from the snow and then sets it in my hands. "I don't know how that happened. I've never passed out in my life."

"Not that you remember," I correct, my eyes still scanning the surrounding area for the newspaper article. It's just a scrap of paper and shouldn't matter now that Garren believes me, but it feels like losing a small part of my father a second time.

"I remember *everything*. Not like you. I was just"—Garren yanks his hands halfway out of his pockets and inhales sharply—"lied to."

I don't argue about his memories; it's enough that he's no longer fighting me.

"Come with me to see my grandfather," Garren urges. "We'll catch him off guard. He won't have time to come up with a cover story." He sounds decisive, like when he asked me to leave yesterday, and it's a good idea. My grandfather will be shocked to see me and Garren together. What choice will he have but to tell us the whole truth when we've figured out so much of it already?

"We should go right now," I agree. "But the article . . ."

Garren frowns, his eyes turning over the neighborhood like mine have. "The wind is blowing westerly." He points at the estimated trajectory, which we follow for approximately twenty-five feet without success.

I could look until nightfall and never find the clipping. It feels as if it could be halfway to New Zealand by now, like the world's working against me, stealing the truth at every opportunity. "Forget it," I tell him. "It's gone."

"I'm sorry." Garren shakes his head in regret.

"It's not your fault." I think of the Garren from my dream and how I felt about him. Definitely not the way you feel about a relative. There was enough longing inside me to fill an entire museum. But neither of us are those people now and I'm not sure we ever were entirely. A dream isn't the same thing as a memory. It has a life of its own.

"We should just go," I add. "Catch the subway over to Henry's place." I don't want to call him my grandfather anymore. He'll have to prove he deserves the title.

Garren and I push on against the wind, neither of us wasting another second looking for something that doesn't want to be found.

TEN

walk to the Spadina subway station with Garren and follow him down to the platform where we hop into a waiting
subway car. Since Garren lives in Toronto and is undoubtedly
more familiar with the transit system than I am, I don't pay
much attention to our surroundings until I happen to notice
that we're pulling into Christie Station. There, I check the
subway map hanging above our seats and find we've been
moving farther away from my grandfather's house in Davisville ever since we stepped onto the train.

"We're going in the wrong direction," I tell Garren. "We
should be heading east and then transferring to the Yonge
line."

"It's west all the way to Islington," Garren argues. "And
from there we have to catch a bus."

"But he lives near Davisville Station." I've only been to
Henry's house on Hadley Road once since we've been back

in Canada (mostly he comes to us) and we didn't go by subway, but Henry's mentioned the station several times.

Garren's left leg jerks. He stretches it out into the aisle and folds his arms in front of him, his fingers digging into the fabric of his coat. "The address we have for him is in Alderwood, Etobicoke."

Two addresses. Two wives. What other bombs will Henry drop on us when we see him?

Garren says we should go to the Davisville address, since it's closer, and that if he's not there we'll jump on the subway again and head for Alderwood. We decide against making phone calls to either address to check Henry's whereabouts since that could backfire on us and ruin the element of surprise.

Once we're headed in the right direction, squished together on an eastbound subway car that grows more crowded with every stop, Garren and I exchange basic information about ourselves. I learn his last name's Lowe and that he's eighteen and all but finished high school, requiring only two more credits to graduate. He's been going to school part-time since he and his mom arrived back in Canada and, for the last couple of weeks, has been working as a dishwasher at a restaurant several times a week.

"I'm due in there at four-thirty," Garren says, checking his watch, which has a slew of buttons on it and must be one of those calculator ones that I've seen around the wrists of some of the kids at school. "I'm not sure I'll make it."

I tell him I'm supposed to be home after school to watch my ten-year-old sister and that I won't be there for that either.

"Your impostor sister," Garren says. "You really think she's not who she says she is? Even if that were possible, a ten-year-old would slip up—there's no way she'd be able to hold the act together."

"I know. But I feel what I feel. And look, I was right about you."

A shadow-smile appears on Garren's lips for the briefest moment before fading into unhappiness. He makes me describe my Victorian school dream again. I leave out how I felt about him in the dream (it's not necessarily relevant anyway) but even on the subway, where the majority of people are cloaking themselves in urban anonymity and avoiding looking in people's faces, I notice women notice Garren.

He must notice them noticing too and I wish I could ask him if it was the same in Switzerland or whether it only started in Canada, like it did for me with the boys in my school.

When we segue into discussing our fathers Garren says his was rarely home and that when he was, he was like an absentminded professor, permanently in his own world. He tells me that his mother almost left his father about a year ago but that she wouldn't know he was aware of that. "I heard things, though," Garren says. "It's funny how they think you don't."

Garren, slumped in his seat, looks over at me. "So you

see, I do remember everything. I don't know exactly what you think has been going on with you, but it's different than what's happened in my life."

We get off the subway at Davisville Station where Garren and I study a map posted on the wall near the ticket booth. Having pinpointed Hadley Road, Garren estimates it's a fifteen-minute walk and I begin to get nervous again, unsure what to expect from Henry when we arrive.

"I feel like I'm dreaming," Garren says as we step onto the sidewalk. "You asked me if the past seemed as vivid as the present but it's this that doesn't seem real."

His ears turn beet red as we walk and maybe I'm turning red from the cold too but there's a second where I have to fight the impulse to cover his ears with my gloved hands to warm them. I catch myself in midair, my arms poised to swing around either side of his head.

The movement doesn't register with Garren; he's thinking of other things. "We can't let him try to sweep any of this under the rug," he says. "And I'm not going to keep any bigamy secret for him either."

A current of confusion and anticipation's swimming through my veins. I slow my pace, trying to get a grip before we reach Henry's house. The feeling's not as overwhelming as when I was approaching Garren's door earlier and I funnel it into anger. We deserve the truth about our families. No one has the right to hide it from us.

"It's there." I motion to the redbrick house across the street. "Supposedly he's lived here for over thirty years."

Henry's blue Buick is parked in the driveway and Garren says, "That's his car all right."

We march past it, up the steeply narrow steps to his porch. The steps are caked with ice and if Henry was really my grandfather I'd be worried he could trip down them and break his neck.

Garren raps loudly on the screen door. We stand like police officers or soldiers waiting for Henry to answer. Garren's raising his hand to knock a second time when Henry pulls the wooden front door open. Expressionless, he pauses in the doorway before reaching for the screen door too.

"Surprise," Garren says, his unsmiling face as hard as granite.

Henry pushes the screen door open and motions for us to come in.

"We found each other," I announce as I step through first. "I guess you didn't think that would happen."

Garren trails me inside and the two of us, jammed into the close quarters of the entranceway with the man who calls himself my grandfather, hover on the edge of a moment that could change everything.

"Say something," I demand. "Tell us why our fathers died on the same day in different continents. Did you have something to do with that?"

My so-called grandfather's silence speaks volumes. His piercing gaze shifts continually between Garren and me.

"Answer the question," Garren growls. His arms are stiff at his sides and his legs are solidly rooted to the floor. "We're not leaving until you tell us everything. Why does so much of my family tree match Freya's? Everything but people's names are identical and you must know why."

"Calm down, son." Henry raises a cautionary hand, like he's afraid Garren might take a swing at him.

"We don't want to calm down," I spit out. "We've been lied to and our fathers have been *killed*."

"They weren't killed," Henry replies. "I don't know who told you that, but it's not true."

"And our grandmothers, Evelyn and Irene? How is it that they both died of cancer? How do you explain your two addresses and two wives?" I've begun to shout.

"Come inside," Henry beckons. "Sit down. Please. I'll tell you everything you want to know but there's something I have to take care of first."

Garren and I twist to look at each other, our gazes steeped with skepticism. We watch Henry shamble towards the living room, following him in from a distance of roughly ten feet behind. There's a wedding picture of him and Evelyn on the wall and I nudge Garren to point it out to him. Various photographs of my family are planted around the room too. On an end table beside the couch sits an old snapshot of Olivia and me. She's about five years old and wearing a gauzy fairy costume. I have both my arms around her and am hugging her to me while baring a vampire grin. I remember that Halloween the way I remember most other parts of my life—as though they were something that happened to someone else.

"Please sit," Henry says worriedly, his outstretched hand indicating the couch. "I have something to show you that will explain everything."

Garren scoffs as he glances at Henry's mottled hand. "Something you should've shown us long before now."

"I have my reasons," Henry insists as his hand drops to his side. "When you see what I'm talking about you'll understand."

Reluctantly, Garren and I move towards the couch.

"I am sorry for what this must be putting you kids through," Henry says as we sit down. He sounds as harmless as an old wool sweater, the same as always, and regards us with a sympathetic gaze. If I felt even a slight attachment to him the kindly tone and matching stare would probably make me feel better. They don't. The couch is equally uncomfortable. Any support it had in it feels like it expired a decade ago. I take off my gloves and lay them on the arm of the couch along with my biology binder.

"Just give me a moment to access it," Henry continues, lingering in the living room doorway. "It's upstairs, in a safe place." He backs out of the room and soon we hear him on the steps.

I'm relieved that Garren and I are in this together but as Garren shifts his weight on the couch, it emits a creaking sound that makes me shiver. *Something's not right.* Even beyond the lies my grandfather has promised to come clean about. An image of armed men jumps into my head and I can't explain how I know that they're coming for us but the truth of it is there in the pit of my stomach because I want to run.

I grab Garren's arm, my fingers closing viselike around it. "We have to get out of here. Someone's coming."

"What do you mean?" Garren's eyes bore into mine, expecting an explanation.

"I think we're in danger." I don't know what I expected coming here but it wasn't that. Already there's a flame of doubt inside me but in my mind the men are hurrying—they don't want us to elude them. "You have to trust me on this." I can't afford to second-guess myself.

Garren gets soundlessly to his feet and creeps towards the staircase. I trail behind him, listening for any sounds from Henry upstairs. There's dead silence from the second floor.

"Someone killed our fathers," I whisper, tugging at his jacket. "You don't know what they could do to us."

"But . . ." Garren's eyes drift into the empty space on the stairs. He must still be thinking of Henry as his grandfather, at least in part; he can't conceive that we might have something to fear from him. "The evidence . . . just give him another minute to come down with it and after we've seen it, we'll go."

I shouldn't listen to Garren. So far my instincts have proven better than his. They've brought us this far, after all. But I want to see Henry's proof as badly as he does and we edge quietly back to the couch together where I say, "Two minutes and then we go up after him."

Garren cups his hands around his kneecaps. "Deal."

Three and a half minutes later Henry has yet to reappear and Garren storms over to the staircase and yells, "What're you doing up there?"

A set of footsteps thumps along the ceiling and then tackles the stairs. From my spot on the couch I listen to Henry apologize to Garren. "But you see," Henry continues, "it turns out that what I was speaking about isn't in my possession at the moment after all. I was sure it was, but . . . well, I'm not the only person involved in this."

Henry reemerges in the living room to face me, Garren three steps behind him. "I've had to contact a friend who is bringing the documents, so if you'll just sit tight awhile longer," Henry adds hastily.

"What kind of friend?" I ask, a knot of fear tightening in my stomach. The armed men are closer. I see them in a black sedan. I can't exactly read their minds but their intent clings to them in a way that makes my toes go cold—they're not just after us. They don't plan to arrest us or bring us home to our mothers. This is deeper and darker than that. They'll do whatever they believe they have to in order to clean this situation up. There's an inexplicably familiar urgency to my fear that lifts it beyond any remaining doubts.

"It'll be clear soon enough," Henry replies. "I understand your impatience and why you're upset but I need to do this correctly so you'll see why it was all necessary."

Garren's still standing. His jaw's clenched and he says, "Start without your friend. The blanks can be filled in later."

Henry presses his palms together and fits them under his chin. "It's not that simple, I'm afraid." There's a dispassionate glint in Henry's eyes that makes him look like someone else.

I stand and move away from the couch. "Are you really my grandfather?" I point to Garren. "Are you his? You must know that much." As I'm asking the question the black sedan turns up Hadley Road. I see its presence in my mind and run to the window where I yank back the thick maroon drapes just in time to spy the car pull into Henry's driveway.

"They're here," I tell Garren. "We have to go!"

We're about to lose everything. We should never have come.

"There's nothing to worry about," Henry says calmly. "That would be my friend. Let me get the door and see him in."

I jump in front of Henry to stop him from reaching the door. "You can't let them take us!"

Henry's veneer of calm drops with a thud. "How much do you know?" His pupils are pinpricks and his intent stare gives me a better glimpse at the real Henry behind the grandfather façade.

Henry must have left the door unlocked because two men in dark suits are bolting into the living room. The first is about thirty years old and has a buzz cut and sunglasses, like a Special Forces officer in an action movie, and the second I don't have time to look at. "Be careful with them," Henry urges the men. "They won't resist."

Wrong. Garren's already reaching for the coffee table, swinging it into his arms and launching it at the dark suits.

Everything seems to happen in the same instant. Henry reaches for Garren, who shakes him off as though he's nothing more than a spider. My legs are hauling me away like they've already formed an escape plan and then I'm twisting to check that Garren's behind me. "Follow me!" I shout, remembering the back door through the kitchen. One of the men is reaching for his gun and Henry's shouting something in a horrible, high-pitched voice.

In my panic, I can't tell what it is but he sounds scared and I don't understand that. Why should he be afraid? Garren and I are the ones in danger.

Then I'm flying past Henry's fridge, into the back hallway and outside into daylight. I don't even feel the cold. I don't feel anything except my heart pumping.

"Over the fence," Garren calls from behind me. I veer left, flinging myself onto the chain-link fence. Garren's neck and neck with me now, effortlessly clearing the fence. He pulls me over the other side. We fall in a heap together. Then we're up and springing forward, Garren tugging me towards the back of the neighbor's yard, another chain-link fence.

I chance a look back and see one of the men hot on our tail. I don't know where the other one's gone. Garren heaves me up onto the next fence like a doll. He's saying, "Go, go, go, go!" and then he's next to me again, running with me like this is the end of the world. A Dalmatian bares his teeth and barks at us as Garren and I tear through the dog's territory but we're already onto the next fence, which is tall and wooden with nowhere to get a foothold. Garren locks his fingers together to give me a step up. As my right sole lands on his palms, he hoists his hands into the air, sending me flying towards the top of the fence. I grab hold of it, pulling my torso over the edge. In what feels like a single sweeping motion I'm up, over and dropping clumsily to my feet.

I survey the backyard, Garren landing next to me. The snowy landscape is littered with paw prints and fresh dog shit. Someone's left the back door to the house ajar and no matter who we'll find inside they'll be easier to deal with than armed men. I point as I run headlong towards the door, not wanting our position to be overheard by the men with guns.

There's an empty metal dog dish on the floor that I don't notice until it's too late. I kick it as I burst through the doorway. The clang echoes through the house as Garren follows me inside, locking the door behind him.

"Who's there?" a woman calls.

Garren and I freeze in our tracks. I hold my breath, as though even that could be too loud.

"Jerry?" the woman calls. "Was that you?"

The woman, in brown cords and with her hair tied back in a neat ponytail, wanders into view, feeling her way along the hallway towards us. There's a series of clicking sounds from behind her, which turns out to be a Labrador retriever.

She spins to face the dog, bending to loop her fingers around his collar. "Do we have company, Jerry?" Jerry's wagging his tail, evidently not as talented a guard dog as the Dalmatian next door.

"I know you're here," the woman says, visibly shaken. "Just take what you need and go. My purse is in the kitchen, hanging over a chair."

My lips part. I stare searchingly at Garren and decide to take a chance. "We don't want anything," I tell her. "I'm sorry we charged in like that—we're being chased."

"You and who else?" the woman asks. There are faint laugh lines around her mouth and the corners of her eyes but aside from those she looks youthful.

"Me," Garren answers. His voice is deep and therefore more alarming than mine but Jerry the dog is still wagging his tail.

"Who's chasing you?"

I twist my hands in front of me. "We don't know who they are. There were two of them and they had guns, like police, but I don't think they are."

The woman blinks slowly, like she doesn't believe me.

"We don't want to take anything," I say again. "Can we just hide here for a minute or two until they're—"

An aggressive knock at her front door cuts my sentence short. The woman flinches, hesitating in the hallway. Then she says, "Go upstairs and don't come down until I tell you it's all right."

We do as we're told, Garren whispering to me on the steps, "Would they hurt her?"

"I don't know." We shut ourselves up in what appears to

be the master bedroom and sit on the hardwood floor. I can't believe that someone who doesn't know either of us would do a stranger such a favor. But maybe the woman believes we're dangerous and sees this as the safest way of turning us in.

The knocking hasn't stopped yet. Then we hear the woman's voice, muffled by the floor that separates us, and brace ourselves for a barrage of noise that doesn't come. Two minutes later she gingerly opens the bedroom door. "I think they've gone," she tells us. "But don't look yet. They could be watching the house."

"What did they say to you?" Garren asks.

"I wouldn't open the door for them. They told me, from the other side, that they were CSIS—Canadian Security Intelligence Service—and that there'd been reports of suspicious activity around the neighborhood that related to national security threats."

Jerry pads up behind the woman, skirting by her to sit in front of the bed with us. I automatically reach out to run my fingers through his fur. The repetitive motion, along with the rise and fall of his breath under my hand, keeps me anchored.

"But I don't believe they were who they said they were," she continues. "People sound different when they're lying."

"They were lying," Garren confirms, although we can't really say that with any certainty because we don't know who they are, just that they seemed prepared to shoot.

I can't help but ask, "Why didn't you hand us over to them?"

The woman's eyes move like she's focusing on me, although I know she can't see. "You sounded afraid." She brushes invisible hair from her face. "I had problems with the police in another life."

Garren thanks her and says that we'll leave as soon as we can. The woman asks whether we have a place to go and Garren's eyes zoom over to mine. Where is safe? We can't go home again—Henry knows where we live. What will they do to our families, who know nothing of any of this?

"We'll think of someplace," Garren replies, his voice soft so that although he's answering her question I know he's really saying it to me.

The woman fits her fingers around her ponytail and tilts her head. "I can give you a little money. Not much. Just some of what I have in my wallet. And a bunch of subway tokens, if that would help."

Money. I hadn't thought about that but I know I don't have a lot on me and I doubt Garren came prepared either. "Anything would help," I say gratefully. "Thank you."

The woman nods sort of sadly, and I hope there was someone to help her when she had problems with the police. There's a spark of panic inside me that I concentrate on squeezing down under my ribs so it won't grow. If it gets any bigger I won't be able to move.

It never occurred to me that I wouldn't be able to return

home tonight. If anything happens to my mom or Olivia because of this I'll never forgive myself.

Jerry follows his master out of the room and, left alone, Garren and I turn inward, like the other doesn't exist. The spell's broken when he gets up to pace the room. As he nears the window I warn, "Don't look out there." I'm not ready to be chased again.

"I know," Garren says impatiently. Then he stops and rocks on his heels. "How did you know they were coming for us?"

There's no way for me to explain it. "I just knew. I could see it happening." Not a brain hiccup like I'd convinced myself when I guessed about Christine's mom, a phenomenon.

"In your head?" Garren asks, running one of his fingers over his bottom lip.

"Yeah." I shiver in my coat.

"So what do you see now?"

I turn inward again and attempt to listen to a deeper silence. I picture the man with the buzz cut and glasses. Think of him, think of him, think of him. Where is he right now? What will become of Garren and me when we walk out the door?

But there's nothing there to see. There's just this. Us in a strange woman's bedroom, scared and confused. I throw up my hands in futility. "Nothing. It's blank."

Garren pulls the collar of his coat up, retreating into

it. "We have to go to the real cops. Tell them what's happened."

They'd never believe our story. There are too many gaps and besides, the men outside have had a head start to set their plan in motion.

"We need to warn our families," Garren continues, zeroing in on the phone atop the bedside table. "My mother had an appointment at the bank. I have to call her there and tell her not to go home." Garren picks up the receiver and calls directory assistance to ask for the bank's telephone number. By the time he's gotten through to the correct branch and uncovered the name of the person who his mother was meeting with he's informed that his mother has already left the premises.

Olivia would've already left school too. Whether she's my sister or not, I'm afraid for her, and then it occurs to me that Garren and I only seemed to be at risk when Henry (if that's even his name) found out that we knew things we shouldn't. Maybe our family's ignorance will keep them safe.

I tell Garren my theory. His eyes shrink as he says, "But you can't see what's going to happen to them, can you? So you don't know."

I don't *know it* the way I knew about the men coming for us but it feels true. Maybe only because I want it to be.

"I'd never get to my family in time." My voice splinters. The words are jagged and rusty in my mouth. "Henry would've told them everything—where my mom works, where my sister goes to school, where we live."

Garren digs his fingers into his scalp. "I wouldn't make it either. Not if they're trying to get to my mom." He sits on the bed and stares at the floor. "Who are these people? What do they want from us?"

Jerry patters through the open door, his owner behind him clasping several ten-dollar bills and a fistful of transit tokens. "Here," she says, holding them out to us. I stand and take the offered things from her hand.

"Thank you," Garren and I say in unison. As much help as Jerry's owner has been to us, I have the distinct feeling that we've begun to outstay our welcome and Garren must feel the same way because he motions to the window and says, "I'll have a look outside and if it's safe, we'll be on our way."

He crosses to the other side of the room, peels back the blinds two inches and studies the neighborhood sideways through the gap. "I don't see anything—what did their car look like?"

I take Garren's place at the window, scouring the road for a black sedan. It could still be parked back on Henry's street (the nearest parallel road to this one) as the armed men lie in wait in the shadows, crouched down beside someone's porch or harmless-looking station wagon.

But I don't see anything either and we can't stay here forever. I hand roughly half the tokens and bills to Garren and watch him deposit them in his front pockets. Two of his fingers brush against my wrist. "Ready?"

I nod and thank the woman a third time. We exit through

the front door, our eyes flitting from house to house and all the spots in between where gunmen could easily conceal themselves. "Quick," Garren urges. "We need to get off this street and onto a busier one so there are people to blend with."

We walk rapidly in the direction of Mount Pleasant Road, constantly looking over our shoulders like we have targets painted on our backs. Surrounded by stores and cafés, I begin to relax my shoulders but not my mind. Garren hurries us along to Yonge Street (which is bustling with people of every description—teenagers, office clerks, construction workers) where he pulls me into a phone booth with him and calls home.

I can tell his mother has answered the phone by the way Garren exhales—she's answered and she's all right (just as I'd hoped) because she's oblivious to the things we've discovered. I lean back against the cold, dirty glass of a phone booth that isn't really large enough for two people, and allow myself a moment of happiness before I'll have to face the fact that although our families are safe, Garren and I have no place to go.

ELEVEN

Garren doesn't stay on the phone long. When he hangs up he tells me we should move on in case they're somehow tracing calls to and from his house. As we're trekking along the sidewalk, Garren explains that Henry got through to his mother first and told her that Garren had dropped in to see him, asking for money and acting aggressive and strange. "Paranoid," Garren specifies. "He told my mother that he thought I must be on drugs and that he was very worried about me. He was trying to fish for information and find out what she knows. He asked if I'd been saying any weird things lately or hanging out with a bad crowd."

Since I heard Garren's half of the conversation I know he didn't tell his mother what really happened at Henry's, just that she shouldn't worry because he's all right. I tell Garren I want to phone my family too and we pick a different telephone booth, one that makes my stomach rumble because it smells like French fries. My mother's extension is busy so I call Olivia who has read the note I left her and wants to know where I am. "With a friend," I reply. "When Mom gets home just tell her I'm fine, okay?"

"Won't you be home by then?" Olivia asks.

"Probably," I lie.

When I hang up Garren starts talking about going to the police again. He says there's bound to be a station nearby and that all we need to do is stop someone in the street and get directions. I shut my eyes and when I open them again he says, "What? You don't think we should go to the cops? This isn't something we can handle ourselves. We're being hunted. And we still don't know what they could do to our families. Okay, they haven't made a move yet but that doesn't mean they won't."

I push the phone booth door open and step outside, Garren following me. My lips feel chapped from spending so much time out in the brutal wind and nerves are bouncing around my throat, making me wonder if I really have to puke or whether I can talk myself out of it. *Mind over matter*, I lecture, but the trouble is, my mind is terrified. I don't know what we're supposed to do next but I know what Garren's suggesting could get us killed or at the very least taken.

"The first thing the police would do is call our mothers," I tell him. "They'd think we were making it all up—that we're either nuts or high, like Henry told your mother."

Garren's dumbfounded. "But our dads—their deaths must be a matter of public record. The stuff about our grandparents too, if it's the truth. Henry's two addresses and Evelyn and Irene."

"You really think the cops are going to look all that up?"

Garren's head snaps back like he's only now beginning to understand the ramifications of our situation. We can't go to any of the usual people for help. We're on our own.

"We need someplace to go," I continue. "Someplace we can just take a minute to figure out what to do next." My mind speeds to Christine and Derrick. But their parents might ask questions and they certainly wouldn't allow Garren to stay over with me, even for one night. Besides, my grandfather will probably have my mother looking for me, calling everyone she can think of.

Nancy. Is she in on this with Henry? And what about Doctor Byrne? Aside from Henry he's the only known living common denominator between me and Garren.

The abrupt realization makes me cry, "We have to talk to Doctor Byrne!" The traffic lights ahead change and Garren and I are forced, by an onslaught of cars, to pause on the corner. "Henry said he and Doctor Byrne have been friends for years and he examined your family too. He could know something."

"He could," Garren agrees. "But if he did, wouldn't they warn him about us?"

Now Garren's the one seeing a clear picture and I nod. "You're right." The armed men could be waiting for us at Doctor Byrne's office as we speak but . . .

"I know where he's going to be this weekend." My words spill out with such velocity that I'm not sure whether I'm putting them in the right order. "It's his anniversary and he told me and my mom he was taking his wife to dinner at a place called the Bellair Café."

"When?"

"I'm not sure. We could call the restaurant. Pretend we forgot the time of the reservation or something."

It's the only thing we have to cling to right now—the idea that Doctor Byrne might be able to deliver the truth—and I watch a sliver of hope steal into Garren's face. The sight of it instantly doubles my own hopefulness.

The walk symbol flashes and the crowd gathered at the lights with us pushes on, Garren and I straggling behind as he says, "I have an idea about where we could go. Somewhere no one would think to look for us."

"Sounds perfect." I feel jumpy wandering the street—anyone who gives us a second look could be working with Henry. We need to duck out of sight as soon as possible.

Garren arches his eyebrows. "Not exactly. It would mean breaking in." He tells me that the girl I saw at his house the other day, Janette, has a thirteen-year-old brother who shovels snow for some of their neighbors. "One of the families he shovels for has driven down to Florida on vacation for two weeks. He's supposed to drop by and clear the snow and pick up mail and stuff every few days so it's not obvious that the house is empty."

Garren adds that he knows which house it is.

I can't think of a better idea but it still sounds risky. "Your girlfriend—she lives in the same neighborhood, though, right? What if she sees us or what if Henry has someone watching her street?"

Garren shakes his head. "He couldn't have anyone watching the street. My mom doesn't know about her. Neither does Henry. And Janette's house is close to Lawrence Station—at the closer end of the street than the empty house I'm talking about. We could take the long way around, across Lawrence and up Duplex Avenue. Janette wouldn't have any reason to be that far down her street. We'd just have to look out for her brother."

I'm cold and scared. I've only been in danger for an hour and I've already forgotten what it's like to feel safe. "Okay," I tell Garren. "Let's go."

We head for Eglinton Station where we huddle in front of a pay phone (our third in half an hour) and I call directory assistance and then the Bellair Café. "Yes, hello," I declare in what I hope is a mature (and somewhat annoyed) voice. "I'm hoping you can help me. My husband placed a dinner reservation with you for this coming weekend and has *inconveniently* forgotten the date and time of the reservation."

The man on the other side of the phone laughs goodnaturedly and asks what surname the reservation is under.

"Byrne for two," I tell him. "B. Y. R. N. E."

"Bingo," the guy sings. "That would be seven o'clock tomorrow evening, Mrs. Byrne."

"Ah, thank you. We'll see you tomorrow then."

Garren's staring at me as I hang up the phone. "You were good," he says.

"Not good enough to convince you two days ago." Behind us a middle-aged couple is kissing passionately goodbye like they'll never see each other again. I've never seen anyone older than thirty kiss in public that naked and unashamedly and for a moment the act distracts me.

When my attention shifts back to Garren, his gaze has dropped to my Doc Martens. "Two days ago everything was different," he says.

We go down to the platform together and ride the subway one stop north to Lawrence because Garren says it's farther than it looks on the map, especially on a day like today, and that anyway, it'd probably be harder to spot us on the subway than on the street.

Along the journey he admits that when I came to his door earlier this afternoon he told his mother I was just some girl who was chasing him but that he wasn't interested in. "I didn't want her to know you being there had anything to do with my dad," he continues. "She hasn't been the same since his accident and I thought the things you were saying were . . . I don't know . . . some kind of fucked-up joke."

I guess I might've thought that, too, if our situations were reversed. As it is, I've slipped into a frame of mind that won't allow me to think beyond the next twenty-four hours. We'll go to this place Garren knows and spend the night there. Tomorrow we'll ambush Doctor Byrne and make him tell us what Henry wouldn't.

The moment after that is a complete mystery. If I try to think beyond it panic will swallow me whole.

I get off the subway with Garren at Lawrence Station and then we walk the long way around to Cranbrooke Avenue. I was envisioning a neighborhood where the houses were much farther apart (and hopefully backing onto a park or otherwise unpopulated area) so that it would be possible to break in without anyone noticing. I was also imagining it would magically be dark out by the time we arrived. Neither of those things is true and the only thing that keeps me from turning back is lack of options.

"We could try the windows and see if one's unlocked," Garren says as we near the house. "But that could take a while and since they're out of town they probably locked everything up tight. I figure the best thing to do is jump the fence and then kick the back door in."

I've seen that done on television where the doors give way easily but it can't be that simple in real life, can it?

The only saving grace is that the house—which looks similar to Henry's—is detached. If we can get inside without being spotted no one should be able to hear us. There's no one out on the street as we walk hurriedly towards the house and Garren points at the empty driveway and says, "Follow me fast. I'll try to unlatch the back gate—unless there's some kind of lock on it—so you won't have to climb over."

I'm right behind him as he whisks up the driveway and scales the high wooden gate, disappearing into the yard. I'm instantly more nervous at being left alone and exposed on the other side but then Garren's swinging the gate open for me and we're both in the yard, edging around the house and searching out a back door, which sits right where you'd expect it to, at the top of a compact porch.

"Do you know how to do this?" I ask under my breath.

"I've never tried." Garren zips up the steps and examines the door while I anxiously scan the area. If anyone in the vicinity happens to be peering out their back window right now, we're doomed.

A lone goose that should've flown south long ago honks accusingly as he flies overhead. The sound makes me jump in my skin and Garren's ashen as he says, "Okay, I'm going to aim right below the doorknob and kick the shit out of it. That's my plan." He says that like he knows it's not much.

I move away to give him room and Garren stands sideways, several feet from the door. His left leg's firmly on the ground as he launches his right heel fiercely into the door. The noise of the assault rockets out into an otherwise noiseless neighborhood and suddenly I'm positive we'll be caught, not in a sixth-sense way but because there surely must be a spooked neighbor within hearing distance.

The door shudders visibly under the force of his effort but doesn't break. Garren's already repeating the process like the door is his mortal enemy. The second time the door frame begins to splinter and on the third I hear it crack and part of the jamb splits off and shoots into the house. Garren staggers through the doorway. I race in after him, glancing at the door frame as I go and hoping the damage isn't visible from the house directly behind us.

Inside, I press some of the larger bits of jagged wood back into the frame so I can close the door behind us. With the lock destroyed, the door begins to swing open again. Garren's the first one to spot the door stopper on top of the shoe rack next to us. He snaps up the stopper and wedges the door shut.

I'm shaking and I can hear Garren breathing. We stand motionless in the back room (which has been decorated as a children's playroom with shelves full of toys, a dark green carpet and forest wallpaper) for a full minute, waiting to hear some sign that we were spotted. When nothing happens I suggest we go upstairs and watch the street from one of the bedrooms. If we hear a siren or see a police car it will probably be too late to make a getaway but it's not as though we can sit back and relax.

The first room we come to upstairs is a children's bedroom with two single beds. Someone's painted a Smurfs mural on one of the walls and there's a Wonder Woman alarm clock on the dresser next to a stout pink night-light. Children's books line the top two shelves of a red plastic bookcase. The bottom shelves are filled with things I've seen advertised on after-school television—My Little Pony figures, a giant Barbie head to style, plush Care Bear toys and two identical Strawberry Shortcake dolls.

Garren and I dart over to opposite sides of the window

and cautiously pull back the minimal amount of curtain that will allow us each a view outside. Every so often a car jogs along the roadway and after several minutes we see a woman dawdle by with a little girl in her arms, the two of them bundled up against the cold. Garren releases his hold on the curtain and moves to the nearest bed, lowering himself onto the purple bedspread.

"Is your foot bothering you?" I ask from the window.

Garren curves his fingers around the edge of the bed. "Not really."

That's not the same as no and I say, "Maybe you should ice it. I mean, if no one comes for us."

"It'll be fine." Garren folds his hands around the back of his head and lies back. "I'm just having a hard time processing all this. *It's unbelievable.* Those guys with guns coming for us and Henry being in on whatever the hell's going on. It must go back to our fathers and something top secret they knew but I don't get how it can stretch back to our grandparents too." He rubs his eyes. "I don't understand any of it. With the scope of this you'd think our mothers would have to know something but mine seems clueless. I don't just mean today. I feel like I'd know if she'd been hiding something this big."

I don't have any more facts than Garren does but the uneasy feelings I had before this served as a warning and our current situation doesn't come as quite as much of a shock to me as it does to him. I think about describing my dreams about the blond boy for him but I don't want to risk upsetting Garren by telling him about the boy snarling like a wild animal and wanting to hurt me.

Instead I talk about Doctor Byrne and the flu my family had after flying home. It turns out that Garren and I both traveled through Australia to reach Canada. My family never left the airport in Sydney but Garren's father lived in Melbourne for two years in his youth and Garren's mom wanted to sprinkle some of his ashes there. He says they were fine while they were in Australia but that the flu hit after they'd been back in Canada for only a couple of days.

Neither of us has an inkling of how the flu ties in to everything else but it must. All the similarities between our lives must add up to the same thing. We go over it and over it, talking in circles as I, at first, continue to glance out the window and then gradually drift towards the other bed. Darkness has begun to fall and it's chilly in the house (the owners must have turned the heat down before they left) but still warm compared to outside.

I lie down in my coat and shut my eyes, intending to open them again in a minute because it's important to stay alert. When I do force my lashes open the room's dark and I have no idea how long I've been asleep for. The tension must've drained me more than I'd realized.

I get up and feel for the light switch, realizing just in time that I shouldn't flick it on because I'm not supposed to be here. The house needs to appear vacant. I stumble over to Garren in the blackness and reach for his leg. "Garren, I'm going downstairs to look for flashlights or candles."

He turns over in his sleep and I try again, saying his name until he stirs more wakefully. "What time is it?" he asks.

I tell him I don't know and repeat what I said about looking for sources of light that won't announce our presence in the house.

"Good point," Garren says, sitting up on the bed. "Something to eat would be a bonus."

Food, yes, I'm starving.

We shuffle downstairs in the dark. I feel like a ghost haunting a stranger's house, only a ghost wouldn't need to hold the banister and wouldn't feel hungry. On the ground floor, I head directly for the kitchen, which is solidly in the middle of the house, between the play room and combination living/dining room, and swing the fridge open so that we'll have something to see by.

"I'll make sure all the curtains down here are shut," Garren says before wandering off into the adjacent rooms.

I shove one of the chairs from around the kitchen table against the fridge door to keep it open. The refrigerator is depressingly empty except for a selection of condiments—ketchup, mayonnaise, mustard, pickles, relish, Cheez Whiz—and a jar of applesauce and half a carton of orange juice. Inside the freezer there's a package of waffles, a carton of Neapolitan ice cream and a box of frozen hamburgers. I check inside the box to see how many hamburgers are left and am relieved to find five remaining.

Garren returns while I'm rifling through the cupboards

and says, "I turned up the thermostat. It should start to warm up in here soon."

I can't believe we're camping out in someone else's house. Bizarrely, on some level that feels weirder to me than having Henry turn against us and being chased by men with guns. We're an intrusion here; we've invaded other people's lives.

Garren adds that there are drapes in each room and that the ones in the living room might even have a thick enough lining to block out the light from the TV if we wanted to turn it on but that he's not sure.

"I guess we should leave it off then," I say as he begins to explore the contents of the cupboards with me. We find a jar of peanut butter, instant coffee, olive oil, Worcestershire sauce, a box of crackers, two cans of tuna, two jars of Ragu sauce, one can of sliced mushrooms, one can of peas, an unopened box of Count Chocula cereal, a large can of Beef-aroni, four Cup O' Noodles packages, three cans of Campbell's soup, three lunch-size fruit cups, a package of dried spaghetti and multiple sachets of Kool-Aid.

We could stay here for a week without going hungry. *Not that we'll have to,* I tell myself. Tomorrow everything could change again. Tomorrow Doctor Byrne could supply us with all the answers we need to free ourselves from this.

As we continue searching the kitchen, Garren discovers an emergency fund of thirty dollars stuffed into the smallest of three red canisters and I locate a working flashlight behind a box of garbage bags. Garren says he bets there's another in the garage but since there's no entrance to it from the house we can't check. In the dining room we find matches and a box of long taper candles. I stick two of them in pewter candleholders (which were in the same drawer as the candles) and light a candle for each of us so we can explore the rest of the house.

"There has to be more money somewhere," Garren says.

If we weren't in so much trouble I'd feel bad about taking from these people. There's a formal family portrait of them hanging in the living room and their grinning faces make them look like understanding folks—father, mother, and two daughters who both appear to be about seven years old but who must be fraternal twins because one's a blond and the other a brunette.

Garren looks at the picture too and I assume he's feeling guilty, but then he says, "Your binder with the photo of your family in it—did you leave it at Henry's?"

That's the first time I've heard Garren refer to our supposed grandfather as Henry the way I've been since this afternoon. "Do you really think he's our grandfather?" I ask. I'd forgotten about the photo until Garren brought it up. The last time I had it was when we sat on Henry's couch.

The article's gone. The photo's gone. I don't know which parts of my life are real. There's nothing concrete for me to hold on to.

"I don't know." Garren looks tired in the candlelight. "Maybe he's the impostor—not your sister."

"Or maybe they both are. But anyway, the photo and binder must be back at his house." I try to make a joke out of it. "He can spend the night trying to crack the code of my biology notes and figure out where we've gone."

Garren smiles but it doesn't make him look any happier. We go back upstairs and, after making sure the drapes are shut, root around in the master bedroom, which feels like the worst invasion of privacy yet because I uncover copies of the *Kama Sutra, The Joy of Sex* and *More Joy of Sex* beneath several issues of *National Geographic* in one of the bedside tables.

In the walk-in closet Garren finds a forgotten ten-dollar bill in the back pocket of a pair of the father's jeans and I come across a glittery silver clutch purse that has a tube of lipstick in it along with a crumpled five-dollar bill and a compact of blue eye shadow.

That brings us to a total of eighty-five dollars plus whatever cash we each happened to have on us earlier and Garren and I empty our pockets to count it up properly. Between us we began the afternoon with thirty-six dollars and fifty-seven cents, which means we now have just over a hundred and twenty dollars. It sounds like a fair amount but Garren says, "We need to spend as little as possible. Who knows how long this might have to last us?"

I don't want to think about that. Doctor Byrne has to be the answer. "Let's go eat," I suggest. "We can try the burgers."

We fry them up along with the mushrooms while listening to top-forty radio on low. Neither of us has much to say as we eat by candlelight but a few minutes into the meal we hear a thud from the second floor. We race upstairs with the flashlight to discover that some of the clothes we'd disturbed in the master bedroom closet had caused a previously unseen briefcase to fall to the floor.

The leather briefcase is lying open on the carpet and I bend to start picking up the papers that have spilled out (Garren shining the flashlight on the mess), automatically skimming through the typed pages, as though any information I run into now will inevitably be about us. It's not. The only things in the file are a lengthy marketing statement for the company the father or mother probably works for and a bunch of corporate invoices.

I feel Garren's eyes on me as I shove the papers anxiously back into the briefcase. "I don't know why I had to look at them," I mumble. "You don't even know these people so they can't have anything to do with us."

Garren aims the flashlight away from me. "You don't trust anything anymore," he says simply. "Of course you'd look."

He's wrong, though—there's still something left I trust and that's him.

TWELVE

Later we listen to the news station in case there's any-thing about us on it and devour mountains of ice cream. We spend most of Friday night planning out how we'll approach Doctor Byrne outside the restaurant tomorrow. It's not far from Garren's neighborhood so he knows precisely where it is and what's around it. We decide that we'll have to make the doctor think we have a weapon; otherwise it will be too easy for him to pull away from us. We need to seem like a threat. If his wife isn't involved her presence might work in our favor because he won't want her to get hurt. We'll need to stay on the move while we talk to him too. A moving target is much harder to locate.

Garren and I agree that if either of us is taken the other should run rather than surrender, but not return here because the house might no longer be safe. By that we both mean, although neither of us says it, that the captured per-son could be forced to talk. I don't want to believe that I'd turn Garren in and I don't want to imagine what they could do to me to make me change my mind.

Just before we go to bed, when hopefully most of the neighborhood is asleep, we do a quick evaluation of the back door. Luckily all of the visible damage is on the inside and won't advertise the break-in.

Garren retreats to the spare bedroom and I take the twins' room (because it feels safer than the master bedroom—like the parents have cast a protective spell over it) where I lie awake for hours worrying about Garren or me being taken. I wonder repeatedly whether Doctor Byrne remembers mentioning the Bellair Café while I was in his office yesterday and whether he'll be expecting us, laying a trap. No amount of worrying I do will make a difference and being tired tomorrow will only slow my reaction time and increase the likelihood that I'll be caught. But naturally, pressuring myself to sleep in that way only helps drive sleep farther away and the sun is starting to rise by the time I finally drift off.

I dream that my younger self is sitting in an airy room with my mother and she's just told me something that has me frantic and furious. Nothing will be the same afterwards. I will never love her like I used to, never trust her. There's a fire inside me when I go to school in the morning and when a guy, no more than a child really, bumps into me hard and fails to apologize, I turn on him in the school's neatly manicured front lawn, pummeling him with my little fists.

I'm vicious in a way that is not me. I've been betrayed. Somebody has to pay for it.

The men who are not men apprehend me quickly. Hold on to me with an iron grip. I can't blame them either because the boy's nose is bleeding and I'm already sorry.

The dream Garren—the younger Garren, just as I am a younger me—appears beside the men and tells them, "You better be careful there—you know that's the boss's daughter."

One of the men replies, "Thank you for your concern. The situation is under control."

When the men release me after filing a discipline report I know it's not because of anything Garren said—that's not how they work. A tear snakes down my face. It doesn't seem right that I can feel so lost and hopeless and yet the world carries on as usual.

"I did punch him," I say to Garren. "I made him bleed."

Garren folds his arms in front of him. "I saw. But I also heard what happened at your house a few days ago." He doesn't elaborate and I don't know where he could have heard such a secret but he adds, "It's inhumane, what they do."

In my dream we both know the "what" and "they" he's referring to but when I wake up at twenty after two in the afternoon with a dry mouth and grit in the corners of my eyes the knowledge instantly evaporates. I lurch into the bathroom and brush my teeth with one of the twins' toothbrushes, my brain fuzzy. Then I dip into the master bedroom closet again and pick out some of the woman's clothes to change into after I've showered. The things I select (a big-shouldered, belted beige sweater and tailored dress pants that are several inches too short) look nothing like what I'd normally wear, and once I've cleaned up and have them on I feel like a bank teller or class valedictorian waiting for a flood.

My hair, I scrunch up into a ponytail and intend to hide under one of the woman's many winter hats. I even decide to apply her horrible blue eye shadow and perky pink lipstick. If there's anything I can do to avoid being spotted by the men who were after us yesterday, I'm ready to do it.

When Garren sees me he jokes that he was beginning to wonder if I'd slipped into a coma. Before I can joke back that I was saving the coma for tomorrow he adds, "You look like a completely different person."

"That's the idea," I tell him. I don't say anything about my dream or the strange men who keep showing up in them; talking about that won't help with tonight.

The next few hours go by in a blur. I toast a waffle and eat it with a fruit cup. Garren shows me the two additional flashlights and a slew of batteries he found while I was sleeping. We pore over the few bits of information we already have, comparing our life stories further. Henry has spoken about Cooke and his wife to both of us, likely as a ready explanation for his many absences while he was spending time at his other address or with his other "family." We don't discover any other overlaps between our lives but there are already enough to deal with and I keep coming back to Henry and the question of whether he's our true grandfather or not.

Surely if he were he wouldn't have called those men to take us.

I'm glad it's dark by the time we have to leave the house. Because the only thing keeping the broken back door closed is the stopper Garren shoved underneath it last night, popping out the front entrance seems like our best bet. If we're spotted by someone who knows the owners are away it will look extremely suspicious but the sound of the back door banging open and shut with the wind for hours would be a problem too. There's a chance we might have to return to the house later and if that's the case the fastest way to slip back inside will be through the unlocked front door.

Garren and I are both in disguise, my feet squished into the woman's tall boots and each of us wearing a borrowed coat and hat, but if I saw Garren on the street I'm sure I'd still know it was him. I'd *feel* it and as we're sneaking out of the house (after we've scanned the street twice to make sure no one's around to see us go—once from an upstairs bedroom and once from the living room) my nerves flare one second and then die down the next. The secret sliver of my mind that knows things doesn't believe we're at risk yet.

I shouldn't rely on that feeling too much. Anything can happen. The future hasn't been written. In this instance the feeling's correct, though. We make it safely out of the neighborhood and take the long way down to Lawrence Station.

From 6:40 onward we stroll Cumberland Street awaiting Doctor Byrne's arrival while keeping a cautious lookout for whoever might be watching us. At about ten minutes to seven Garren says, "Do you see anything? Any visions?"

I don't but maybe it's just that the sense doesn't work on command. We round the corner onto Bellair for the umpteenth time, then cross the street and circle swiftly back to the restaurant where a fifty-something-year-old woman in a long green coat and high heels is emerging from a silver car. I stare at the driver through the front window as the car pulls away. Without enough time to look him over I can't be positive it was Doctor Byrne but there was a general resemblance and I grab Garren's arm. "Did you get a look at the driver? Was it him?"

"I think it was," Garren concurs, and my heart starts galloping.

He must've gone to park the car and in that case he'll be back soon. We pace the sidewalk directly in front of the restaurant, intermittently checking our watches like we're expecting someone long overdue. Then I spot Doctor Byrne trundling down the sidewalk, the gap between us fast closing. "There he is," I gasp.

We stride forward and stop directly in front of him, Garren and I binding together like a human wall so he can't get by. At first he doesn't recognize us because he's doing the typical big-city thing of not looking anyone in the face, but as Doctor Byrne glances up to step around us, he wrinkles his nose and then frowns deeply in recognition, his shoulders sagging.

"Come with us," Garren commands, sinking his right hand into his pocket to suggest that he's armed and that Doctor Byrne doesn't have much of a choice.

Doctor Byrne glances from Garren to me, a mild amount of surprise in his eyes but no fear. "What do you intend to do to me?"

"We don't want to hurt you," Garren tells him. "We just need information."

"Walk with us," I bark, indicating that he should turn and continue onward. Doctor Byrne obliges, swiveling on the sidewalk, and Garren and I sandwich him between us. We storm off in the opposite direction from the restaurant.

Doctor Byrne's shorter than I am and I can see the bald spot on the crown of his head as we head west along Cumberland. The two things make him look vulnerable, despite the fact that he doesn't appear to be afraid. He pinches his coat lapels together as he says, "Where are we going?"

Since we've been able to stake out the restaurant and make it this far down the road with the doctor unimpeded, Henry and his people must not have suspected we'd be here, but I'm afraid our luck will run out at any second and I say, "Why do they want us? Who is Henry Newland really? You need to tell us everything."

Doctor Byrne touches his glasses. "I can't, Freya. That's physically impossible."

"Physically impossible," Garren repeats darkly.

"You mean you *won't* tell us," I clarify, because Doctor

Byrne can't literally mean what he said about it being impossible. We veer down a lane, the doctor still in lockstep with us.

"Believe me, the matter of telling you has nothing to do with whether I'd like to or not. I can't. It's *not possible*. The second I attempt it . . ." His voice trails off. "In effect, you could do whatever you want to me and it wouldn't make a difference. What you're looking for is an impossibility, or at least seeking it through me is."

"We don't have time for this," Garren says, his hand in his pocket again.

Doctor Byrne is quiet. We've reached a parallel road and Garren closes his right hand around Doctor Byrne's arm and guides him across the street. People watching us might think we were out for a stroll with our aged father or grandfather.

"I don't believe either of you would hurt me," Doctor Byrne says. "And I would help you if I could. I've tried, in my own way. You have to understand none of this was meant to hurt you."

"If that's true, why do they want to hurt us now?" Garren asks as we veer onto Hazelton Avenue.

"Things aren't as they seem," Doctor Byrne replies cryptically. He turns to me and adds, "If you're smart, you'll take the advice I'm about to give you and follow it to a tee." Garren and I lean in closer and listen to him say, "Don't say anything about any of this to anyone else you meet. Get as far away from here as you can and don't leave a trail. Don't contact your families. Get yourselves new names and new identification. That's the only way you'll remain safe." Doctor Byrne reaches inside his coat and Garren's head jerks like he's expecting the worst but the doctor opens his wallet and hands me two stiff fifty-dollar bills.

I hesitate and Garren reaches between us to take the money.

"Will they leave our families alone?" I ask. "They don't know anything."

"Both your families are fine. I'm sure they're very worried about you but they'll be safer now if you stay away from them. Do it for their sake if you can't do it for your own." Doctor Byrne relaxes his hold on his lapels and adds, "I don't want to be your enemy. But sometimes there's a greater good to consider. I know you can't understand that from where you're standing." He quivers in his coat. "If I don't get to my wife soon she'll raise some kind of alarm. I don't think you want that to happen."

The doctor stops walking and I can read in his face that he's made up his mind not to take another step with us, no matter what we say.

I stop too. Desperation surges through me. I can't walk away from this meeting with nothing. "Please, you have to tell us *something*. None of this makes sense to us. Our fathers, our grandparents. And I can't . . . I can't remember certain things and then there are dreams that feel like they must be memories but can't be because they're so—"

"Freya." Doctor Byrne's hand grazes my shoulder in

sympathy. "I can't help you. If you think memory is a problem maybe there are other places you can look for help eventually, but the best thing you can do now is leave here as quickly as possible. If they find you . . ." Doctor Byrne shakes his head like he doesn't even want to consider the matter.

Garren's hands hang limply from his arms. "What happens if they find us?"

The doctor's stare is frank, his pupils heavy with apprehension. "Something you wouldn't want." With that, he turns on the sidewalk and begins walking steadily away from us. Neither Garren nor I make a move to follow him. Doctor Byrne was right that we wouldn't hurt him. I guess he knew each of us just well enough to make that call.

I stare at Doctor Byrne's back and watch him disappear into the distance. Now we have nothing. No information and no further plan of action to get it. I feel empty the way I did in my dream last night. There's nothing left to hope for. Just the gnawing sense that Doctor Byrne's words are no exaggeration.

I felt it when the men were coming for us. I didn't know where they'd take us or what they'd do. Only that whatever it is makes me want to recoil and revolt.

"We have to go," Garren says. "He might call them."

Doctor Byrne said he wasn't our enemy but obviously he's not on our side either. How does he expect us to leave town? Are we supposed to live out the rest of our lives hiding under a rock somewhere while still wondering what the truth is?

"We have to go," Garren repeats, and he sounds hollow but with a streak of urgency, as though he's trying to put on a brave front for me. It's because I can hear all that in his voice that I start moving and don't make him say it a third time.

At first I follow him without an awareness of where we're going, through busy city streets and then back underground into the subway system where I hear Winston Churchill in my head, as clear as day. The way his voice keeps returning to me is a minor enigma enfolded in a larger one, like a trove of Russian nesting dolls. He says, "Courage is rightly esteemed the first of human qualities, because it is the quality which guarantees all others."

I don't feel courageous but I can't stand for both of us to feel defeated either—it's much worse than just feeling it for myself—and my mind starts whirring again. Doctor Byrne said if I thought there was a problem with my memory maybe there were other places I could look for help. It didn't mean much to me when he said it but maybe there was something to those words. I repeat them to Garren and ask if he thinks they were a hint.

He shrugs wearily. "I don't know that there's any connection between your memory issues and the rest of this. Even if there is, you can't go see another doctor here. You heard Byrne—we have to get out of here as fast as possible."

And go where? I'm barely sixteen, not ready to take ultimate responsibility for my life.

"The greater good," Garren says bitterly. "What the fuck

is that supposed to mean? How can we be any threat to the greater good?"

"We don't have to be. They only have to think we are. Anyway, how can you not believe my memory—and maybe yours—isn't related to this? *I knew you.* I knew you before we met two days ago."

Garren leans down over his knees, his long arms stretched across them like a blanket. "You have some ESP thing, that's for sure. But I'm telling you, we've never, ever met. There's nothing wrong with my memory and I'm not having any weird dreams the way you are. All those things have to somehow be linked to this ESP thing you have." He sighs through his teeth. "And thank fuck you have it because otherwise those guys would've had us yesterday. Maybe it'll help us get out of here and figure out what to do."

I'm not ready to leave without answers. I won't go anywhere near my family since that will put them at risk but there has to be something else I can do. *Other places I can look for help.* Who helps people remember things when they can't? A hypnotherapist.

The subway train screeches as we pull into the next station. I watch Garren grit his teeth and I know he won't like what I'm about to say either but on a certain level it doesn't matter; I have to do this. "There's one last thing I have to try before I think about going away. Not a doctor, but a hypnotherapist."

Garren doesn't even blink. "We have to leave, Freya. We don't have time to worry about your memory."

"But it could help. We don't know what we're really running from. We need all the information we can get if we want to outrun them." And I can't stand not to know. I'm like a shell of a person.

"Just give me one more day," I continue. "It'll take us that long to figure out what we're going to do anyway, won't it? We'll have to go back to the house and get supplies and—"

"We're lucky they haven't caught us already. You can't take that kind of risk on a whim when there's every chance that it might not help at all." The vein in Garren's neck is throbbing. "And do you know how much something like that would cost? We can't afford to waste a cent."

"I'll get the money." There has to be more back at the house—or things we could pawn for it. Whatever I thought was the matter with my life, I didn't think it would come to this. We're about as far from safe and sound as two people can be. We have nothing and no one, except each other. We've stolen from people and will probably have to do it again. The grim facts make me more determined to uncover the truth.

"How the hell do you think you're going to manage that? You don't have a clue what you're doing." Garren slaps his pocket, the one with Doctor Byrne's cash in it. "This is for getting us out of here and believe me, it won't last long or take us far. The last thing we need right now is to make a stupid mistake."

I don't need a lecture in priorities—my life is on the line same as his—and two seconds later we're hardcore arguing in the middle of the subway car, the two teenage guys sitting closest to us grinning toothily like they think it's funny.

It's not remotely smart calling attention to ourselves this way and the second that hits me I shut up and refuse to say another word. When Garren realizes I've taken an unofficial vow of silence he joins me inside it, the two of us glowering quietly. We pass station after station, descending Yonge Street. With every second we're putting distance between us and the house near Lawrence Station until I finally say, "Where are we going?"

Garren's fingers creep up the back of his neck. For a couple of seconds I wonder whether he's stopped speaking to me entirely. Then he says, "You mean now? I don't know. It seems like you want to be the one to call the shots so why don't you tell me?"

He's still angry. It makes me want to fight him again because it's not like I'm doing any of this for fun. I control myself and stare out the window into the pitch-black tunnels we're hurtling through. Garren's the only person I can depend on; I shouldn't argue with him.

"I don't think we should go back to the house yet," he adds before a full-fledged silence can take hold between us a second time. "It's Saturday night—there'll be more people coming and going, a bigger chance neighbors could spot us heading into the house and if that happens we're screwed. We're better off killing a couple of hours somewhere that we can keep a low profile or blend into a crowd." He drops one of his hands to his thigh and trains his eyes on mine. "So where do you want to go?"

He says that like he really wants to know, almost like the dream Garren, and the feelings I had for him in my sleep bleed through to my consciousness in a way that I've been resisting for the past two days. There's no time to feel like that about *anyone*. I push the feelings down under my ribs along with the panic and irritation.

"If you know of a theater, the movies could be a good place to hide out for a few hours," I reply. Once we make it inside no one will be able to recognize us in the dark.

Garren nods and says he knows a couple of places close by. We end up in a line for the Market Square Theatre on Front Street. Being stationary in such a public place makes me edgy. The subway itself seemed womblike in comparison; maybe we should've just ridden it until closing time.

As we near the ticket booth I scan for a pay phone and notice one about thirty feet away, by a city trash can. Garren sees my eyes land on the phone booth and reads my mind. "Go do it if you want to that much," he says resignedly. "I'll get the tickets."

I rush towards the phone booth where my fingers fly through the yellow pages. Someone's torn the pages S through Z out of the book. Fortunately, I don't need them and I sink a quarter into the phone and call the first hypnotherapy number listed. It rings eight times before I hang up and try the next three numbers with the same result. Being a Saturday night, naturally most of the offices would be closed and I begin searching for listings that don't have the name "clinic," "center" or "doctor" attached to them. Someone who's in business for themselves would be more likely to pick up the phone on a Saturday night.

On my fifth try, to a woman named Barbara Trower, I finally hear the sound of a human voice. When I explain that I need help remembering parts of my life Barbara Trower declares that it sounds like a case for a therapist and that she doesn't deal in trauma. My spirits plummet. I tell her I don't have any reason to believe there's been any abuse but she apologetically declines and advises that I seek a professional recommendation from my doctor.

The next three numbers go unanswered and I'm on my ninth attempt, to someone named Lou Bianchi, when Garren raps against the phone booth with his knuckles and flashes me the movie tickets. I notice they're for *The Breakfast Club,* that movie I heard about on the radio.

"Lou Bianchi," the man on the other end of the line chimes.

I hold up a finger to Garren, then turn my back to him to concentrate on Lou Bianchi. If he's as principled as Barbara Trower, telling him the truth won't help me, so I say, in a calm but melancholy voice, that my twin sister died when I was almost five and that my memories of her have faded with age. The loss could be regarded as a kind of trauma too but at least Lou Bianchi won't suspect I've been abused.

"I want to remember our time together," I plead. "I've

tried to do it on my own but I can't. There's nothing left of her in my conscious mind. Can you help me? I don't care how much it costs."

"I charge everyone the same amount," Lou says evenly. "It's forty-five dollars a session."

"And do you think you could help me? I want to do this as soon as possible—tomorrow if you could." I feel Garren's stare on my spine and will Lou Bianchi to say yes.

"Oh, no, not tomorrow. I don't see clients on the weekends. Family time, you understand. But I can squeeze you in on Monday afternoon. One o'clock?"

"One o'clock," I agree, pretending to write down his address as he offers directions.

The last thing I do before I leave the phone booth is tear the entire hypnotherapy page out of the yellow pages. Then I open the door to meet Garren, hoping to God that he'll understand about the extra day and that making that judgment call for myself won't cost our lives.

THIRTEEN

On-screen a teenage redhead is applying lipstick by sticking the tube in her cleavage and then lowering her head to her blouse. The girl reminds me of one of Nicolette's friends and the second I find myself thinking that, I miss Sir John A. MacDonald High School with a passion, even the stupid parts of it like how everybody hung out in tribes and there was a permanent draft in our English classroom. I miss the morning Derrick and I hung out at the museum together and the day Christine dyed my hair. I miss kidding around with Kyle about Greek myths and how he told me he liked my hair, even though I'd turned him down just the week before.

I wish I'd paid more attention to all of them and I wonder, if I hadn't seen Garren outside the museum ten days ago, could I eventually have been happy in my new life? It's a traitorous thing to consider—being happy with a falsity when my father's been murdered—and I only think it for a moment.

Next to me Garren is quiet, facing the movie screen but not really absorbing the images. I know what he's thinking without having to ask because I'm thinking most of the same things. That the life we thought we had is in the past. We'll never see our mothers again. We won't be able to graduate or get degrees. I'm not sure how we'll even feed ourselves.

On top of that he's unhappy about the extra day's wait to leave town. He didn't protest when I told him about the Monday afternoon appointment I'd made with Lou Bianchi and that almost made me feel worse than if he had, like he's either given up on some level or is planning to run off without me during the middle of the night.

By the time the credits have rolled and we're stepping into the darkness again I'm so anxious to know which scenario I'm dealing with that I come straight out and ask Garren whether he's going to wait for me or if he thinks his chances are better alone. The city light we're passing under illuminates his shock. His pupils shine like faraway stars as he says, "If I told you I wouldn't wait, would you come with me tomorrow?"

I want to say yes but I can't. "Where?" I ask.

"We should avoid the border—we're missing persons. So east or west." He shrugs. "Take your pick."

I haven't answered the original question and Garren angles himself away from me and adds, "You do know we ultimately have to go, right? What if this guy can't tell you anything on Monday? Are you going to shut down on me and go into denial? Because I swear I won't wait then. If this guy has nothing to say to you I'm not going to sit around while you call up all the hypnotherapists in the yellow pages. *This is it.*"

"I know." I nod heavily, my chin pulled close to my chest. "I know."

Garren tugs up his collar and turns back towards me. "Okay." He nods too. Then he looks at me like there's something else, something more. It's gone so quickly that I have to wonder if I imagined it.

We hop on the subway and ride it back up to Lawrence. The house on Cranbrooke Avenue is the closest thing we have to home now and as we approach it I wheel around on the sidewalk to check whether there's anyone around to see us step inside. A lone man in a red hooded jacket is ambling along in our wake and I link my arm through Garren's and pull him closer to warn him that we can't go in.

We cross the street, my arm still wrapped around Garren's like we're a couple, and slow our pace until the man's well ahead of us and Cranbrooke Avenue is empty again. Alone on the street, Garren and I make a dash for the house. Inside, we keep running, up the stairs and into the twins' room where we stare along the avenue wondering if anyone witnessed our return. It's at least twenty minutes before we begin to feel comfortable.

My stomach begins to grumble as we wait. It reminds

me that I've only had a waffle, fruit cup and movie popcorn to eat all day long. I tell Garren that I'm going downstairs to eat some instant noodles and peanut butter because if the police show up I don't want to be arrested on an empty stomach.

"Gourmet combo, instant noodles and peanut butter," he remarks, smiling for the first time tonight.

"Yeah, I might even splurge and have some crackers," I joke.

Garren moves away from the window. I can still make out his smile in the moonlight. "I'm coming with you to make sure you don't polish off the entire box."

It's a relief to be kidding around with him again. I feel the tension of the last couple days begin to invert, turning me giddy. "Just try to stop me," I say. "I'm thinking of breaking out the Kool-Aid too. Pickles. Cereal. A complete feast."

Garren laughs as we step into the hallway, each of us armed with a flashlight. "We should order pizza. Then we'll find out if anyone on this street really takes the words 'neighborhood watch' seriously."

"It could be worth it if we got to finish the pizza first." I'm grinning so wide that it seems as though my cheeks could snap like a rubber band and go boomeranging around the room.

Down in the kitchen I pull the pickles out of the fridge first. I chomp into one as Garren and I construct imaginary pizza orders. His all have pepperoni on them but he doesn't like anchovies or pineapple, which I'm fanatical about, and when I find out he doesn't like olives either I declare, "Okay, there's absolute proof we're not related because my mom, dad and I are all olive fiends."

"What about your sister?" Garren asks. He's taken out the Cheez Whiz and is smearing a stack of crackers with glowing orange.

I consider that for several seconds. Olivia loves chocolate (doesn't everyone?), scrambled eggs, pierogies, baked beans, mashed potatoes, bananas, pears and grapes, but as for olives, I can't remember one way or the other. I've supposedly known her for her entire life, yet olives have never come up. "I don't know. You'd think I would but . . ."

Garren pauses, poised to tackle another cracker. "That doesn't mean anything, you know. It's normal not to remember every single thing about someone."

"But not normal to forget whether you've done certain things or not." I explain about not knowing whether I've ever been on skates and while I'm telling Garren that, my thoughts fly to that night at the party with Seth and how his kiss felt brand-new.

Meanwhile Garren's girlfriend, Janette, lives just down this very street—could at this precise moment be sitting at home wondering why he hasn't been in touch. He's said so many times that he doesn't feel the same disconnect with his past that I do; it's impossible for me to bring up the subject again. I plug in the kettle to boil water for my noodles and lean back against the counter, finishing off another pickle.

My mouth tingles from the pickle tanginess but the

unspoken question won't disappear: *Does what he has with Janette feel more real than his relationships with his old girlfriends?* The question loops around in my head until I erupt and say the nearest thing I can. "Your girlfriend's so close. Are you tempted to go to her for help?" I don't mean to sound like I'm pushing him over there to get us more money and I immediately add, "Not that I think you *should* go to her. It just must be hard to resist."

Garren lowers himself into a chair and pops a cheesy cracker between his lips. After much noisy chewing he says, "I've thought about it but I don't want to put her in any danger. And we've only known each other a few weeks. Not long enough for me to go to her with something out of control like this." He wipes his mouth with the back of his hand, although there weren't any crumbs on him in the first place. "What about you? Is there someone you wish you could call?"

"A couple of friends I made at school but they probably wouldn't be able to help much and Henry's people could be watching them." I wish I could tell Christine what's happened to me in the past two days. She'd hardly be able to believe it but I think she'd want to help. Like I told Garren, there wouldn't be much she could do for me but she'd *want* to all the same. Derrick too, probably.

When it comes down to it the two of them feel like the only real friends I've ever had. In comparison Alison and my other Kiwi friends seem like cardboard cutouts or figments of my imagination.

I sit down at the table across from Garren and nab one of

his crackers. "I know you think my memory thing is bullshit, like, some psychological issue or something, but it's not. It's related to all of this. I don't know how yet. I just need some help figuring it out."

Garren pitches another cracker into his mouth and leans back in his chair. I watch him swallow and listen to him say, "I don't think you're crazy. Maybe your memory issues do tie in with everything else—I don't know—I guess it could make sense. I just don't want you to think seeing this guy on Monday's going to lead to some huge lightbulb moment that makes all this other stuff disappear. You heard Doctor Byrne—we have to make tracks. Put as much distance between us and this place as possible."

I'm counting on a lightbulb moment—Garren's right about that. I'm tired of living in darkness, both literally and figuratively. "We'll leave Monday no matter what," I promise for the second time. Between now and my appointment there's a day and a half to kill. I don't know what we'd do without this house. "Can we stay here that long? Do you know when the owners are due back from vacation?"

Garren says he thinks they left last weekend so we should still be all right today and tomorrow. Hearing myself refer to the family as *the owners* seems both ungrateful and odd. I feel as though I should at least know the last name of the people whose home I've shared and after I finish my noodles, I begin searching through drawers and scanning shelves, trying to find it. The company invoices we ran across yesterday referenced far too many names to be useful.

I don't think Garren really cares who the owners are but he helps me look. He's the one who finds an old MasterCard bill addressed to Paula Resnik crumpled up in the powder room garbage. So, the Resnik house, that's where we spent last night and where we'll remain until we leave for Lou Bianchi's place on Monday afternoon.

We've decided it's safest not to risk coming and going again until we have to. Everything we need is right here anyway and late into the night Garren and I retreat to the same rooms we opted for yesterday. I lie in bed, surrounded by the kids' toys, thinking about my mother. My heart refuses to believe we'll never see each other again. There's only so much I can handle at one time.

I need to know that she'll be okay and I reach out with my mind, trying to find her the way I saw the men coming for us at Henry's house. It's no use. The only things I see are memories from the last few weeks. Us making Hamburger Helper together. Her sitting on the side of my bed holding out a glass of orange juice for me.

I fall asleep thinking about her and when I wake up on Sunday most of the morning's already over. Garren and I watch TV all afternoon until the sun begins to set. It feels like a luxury and in between extremely serious discussions about where we should go (Garren thinks Vancouver, which makes good sense to me because it's about as far away as we can get without crossing a border or falling off the continent) and how we'll manage to get there (is it better to steal a succession of cars or unload a wad of cash from some unfortunate person and use it to take the train cross country and can we really be having this conversation?) we try to make ourselves feel more normal by talking about regular things like our opinions of the various music videos and TV shows we're watching. Garren likes U2 and Kate Bush and hates Madonna, Duran Duran and Wham! I tell him that my friends at school are sort of music snobs who mainly listen to new wave and that I've kind of turned into one myself. Garren says he could guess that from looking at me—not so much now because I'm wearing Paula's bank-teller clothes—but when I first came to his house. We're both sitting on the Resniks' leather couch, with our feet on the coffee table, and Garren tilts his head and adds, "Maybe it's because I've only seen you in real life with dark hair but it looks more like the real you than when you were blond in the picture."

It feels more like the real me so that's good to hear, especially from him. But after Garren says it, I can't take my eyes off him. I'm frozen. Staring at his green eyes with my heart in my mouth as Johnny Rotten hollers out the lyrics to "This Is Not a Love Song" on the TV.

I fidget as I tear my gaze away. Pretend I was thinking something else. Then I say, "It'll be dark soon. I'm going to have another look around the house and see if there's anything we missed." We'll each need to pack a bag of clothes to bring with us tomorrow and whatever food we can carry. Most of all, we need more cash or things we could sell. Paula Resnik's jewelry.

Garren lets me go and later I hear him thumping around

the house searching for buried treasure just like I am. We end up with a collection of watches, a Waterford crystal mantelpiece clock, and masses of glimmering earrings, bracelets, rings and necklaces from Paula's jewelry box (because neither of us can discern what's valuable or not). The only money left is in the twins' room and it's just piggybank change, which we leave alone. Garren says there's a carton of cigarettes under the bed in the spare room that we should be able to sell too.

I shove several of Paula's sweaters, T-shirts, socks and her longest pairs of pants into one of two matching beat-up carry-on bags (Paula and her husband must've brought more presentable ones along on their trip). I even have to steal a handful of her underwear. You know you're in a bad way when you find yourself taking someone else's underwear and I stop and sit on the bed, replaying Lou Bianchi's voice in my mind in the hope that it will catapult me into a vision that will offer a clue of what's in store for us tomorrow.

It's useless, though. There are a dozen different thoughts coursing through my brain—how my mom must be sick with worry for me, what Doctor Byrne said about the greater good, the Latham boy from my dreams, Garren's green eyes and how I feel when they look at me, the nagging fear that Henry's men are biding their time, just waiting for us to run so they can snatch us off the street and put us down like dogs or worse, and on and on and on. Worries and questions but not a single thing that comes close to qualifying as a vision.

When Garren and I come together again in the kitchen

that evening I almost lie to him. I mean to inspire a bit of hope by saying that I had a flash of something, a feeling that we're going to be okay, but then his eyes do their magic trick on me and I'm nothing but warm and flustered. Survival and everything else, for a couple of moments, take a backseat to the feelings I've been denying. "You're so . . ." My voice is a swirling whisper, a dream thing. It's not what I'd intended to say or how I meant to say it and I shake my head and leave the abandoned sentence shimmering in the candlelit kitchen like a sparkler on firecracker day.

"So *what*?" he asks, hanging on the freezer door, about to reach for the frozen hamburgers.

"So . . . familiar." I have my voice under better control at first but then it begins to twirl and swell. "I can't believe you don't know me."

Garren releases his hold on the fridge, stands with his shoulder against the wall. "It's still weird to hear you say that," he murmurs, and though we're in the middle of a conversation I feel like the kitchen couldn't get any quieter. "You're so sure of yourself that you make me feel like I should remember."

I yank open the fridge myself and grab the hamburgers, just to fill up the room with something other than what we're saying. There's too much longing inside me. Not only for him but for something he represents. Something I don't understand. A whole world of longing.

"I wish I could remember more," I say, draining my tone, clipping it into neutral syllables.

Garren stares down at the candles in the middle of the table. The light dances across his features, turning him golden. "Maybe tomorrow."

I smile, solidly back in the real world of the here and now because that's the first time Garren has sounded like there just might be a point to my session with the hypnotherapist. "Tomorrow," I echo. His words weren't the sign I was looking for but I accept them as the good omen they are. "I think so."

I absolutely do.

FOURTEEN

Even Paula Resnik's longest pants are short on me, making me look like the victim of a laundry shrinkage accident when we leave the house with our stash of clothes, jewelry, a transistor radio, both flashlights, extra batteries and a smattering of food (the rest of the peanut butter and crackers, two cans of tuna and the box of Count Chocula) early Monday afternoon. Because Paula's boots are also too small I've left them behind and am wearing my Doc Martens—if we need to run for any length of time it's important to do it in comfortable boots.

As soon as we step outside I feel separation anxiety from the house and want my Docs to sprint me straight back inside again. It's no longer a surprise to hear Winston Churchill pipe up. In his inimitable gruff voice he declares, "This is no time for ease and comfort. It is the time to dare and endure."

I march on with Garren, each of us in possession of roughly half the money we've amassed over the past few days. Yesterday we decided that maybe we were being paranoid to worry that Henry could find out we'd holed up at the Resniks' and check who we'd called from there but that it was a case of better safe than sorry. That leaves us having to do our travel research from the anonymity of a public telephone and when we reach the subway station Garren calls a bunch of bus companies and the train line. He's just hung up from his final call when he lunges for me, throwing his arms around my waist and burying his head in my shoulder.

"Janette's here," he whispers, his body crammed up against mine as if that will make him invisible.

I hold him tight the way Janette would. Close my eyes so that they won't search her out and call attention to us. Would she recognize me? She only saw me once and I was dressed so differently. I can smell Mr. Resnik's aftershave on Garren and the mint toothpaste we've both been using. We should've brought that with us too, I think.

You think the weirdest things when you're in trouble. Toothpaste. Deodorant. When the next opportunity to shower will come along. How my arms are holding Garren but I just feel numb. And then I begin to thaw and it's harder not to let go. My arms and the rest of my body are flooded with feelings of self-consciousness.

If Janette had seen him surely she would've stalked over to interrupt us by now. "I'm afraid to look," I whisper back.

Garren eases himself away from me and glances around the station. "She's gone." His shoulders relax. "She was leaving the station. She must be going home."

"Shit, that was close." I pick up my carry-on bag and sling it over my shoulder. Garren snaps up the rest of our things—his matching bag and then a canvas knapsack we found in the laundry room, which has the flashlights, cigarettes and some of the food in it.

We walk down to the platform where Garren tells me that train tickets to Vancouver are a hundred and fifty-two dollars each. He thinks we'd be stupid to catch the train in Toronto, where there are people looking for us, and that we need to get ourselves north to Parry Sound. "We can catch up with the cross-country train there," he explains. "But I think the first thing we need to do after your appointment is get out of the city. There's a commuter train that heads out to Oakville every hour. It leaves from Union Station same as the cross-country train does but the second stop on the way out of town is at the exhibition grounds. It isn't far but hopefully just distant enough from the inner hub of the city that they wouldn't look for us there."

I'm amazed by how much Garren's worked out just by spending a few short minutes on the phone. We don't have the money for the train fare and we'll have to find a way to get from Oakville to Parry Sound, but having a general plan makes me feel more secure, like we actually can do this. We'll disappear and they'll never find us.

As we speed underground towards Lou Bianchi's place, we talk about what we'll do once we reach Vancouver. Since Garren's been working at a restaurant he says he knows we'll be able to find under-the-table work in the food industry. "A lot of people I work with have been paid cash by other restaurants. I hear there's a lot of construction jobs off the books too."

Thinking out loud I say, "Housekeeping too, I bet. Child care. Different types of manual labor." I drape my arms over the carry-on bag and try to picture myself doing one of those things on the other side of the country.

"It'll be shitty in the beginning," Garren acknowledges. "Until we have enough money to buy some decent identification and move on to something better."

Something better. Something better, somewhere else. The vagueness of that puts my mind in free fall.

Garren adds that he has an international student identity card, in a fake name, which lists his age as twenty. He bought it from a guy at his school for drinking purposes (since the legal age here is nineteen) and says it might come in handy in the meantime.

"What did you want to do before all this?" he asks.

"I didn't have that figured out." I thought I'd be in school for years yet, that there'd be plenty more time to come up with the answer to that question. "What about you?"

"I don't know either. I was going to take a year or so off after graduation. That's why I was working at the restaurant, to get some traveling money together. See more of Europe and Asia."

It's funny, Garren's already spent so much of his time outside the country but it seems what he wants most is to leave again. "Maybe you still will," I tell him.

We have to take a streetcar after we get off the subway and when we arrive at Lou Bianchi's house hauling everything we own with us, I feel as though we're oozing teenage-runaway vibes. The homes in Lou's neighborhood are tiny and claustrophobic but brightly painted and welcoming. There are two wicker chairs on his porch, even though it's winter.

Lou himself answers the doorbell when I ring. I know it's him before he asks if I'm Lisa Edwards (the fake name I gave him). I also sense, as Garren and I follow Lou into the house, that he'll be able to help me remember but that it will be at a cost. I'm about to lose something and I can't see what. Only that it will make me unhappy.

Lou shows Garren into a small waiting room at the side of the house and then leads me to his office downstairs. I see a tape recorder laid out on the desk. Lou notices me eyeing it and says, "So you can play back everything you had to say while under hypnosis if you want to." He rubs the underside of his beard and adds, "You're younger than I thought."

"I'm twenty," I lie. "But I get that all the time."

Lou motions for me to sit in the lounge chair in the center of the room. As I do he hands me a release form to sign. It frees him from any guaranties or liabilities and I jot the name Lisa Edwards down on the dotted line and give the form back to him along with the forty-five-dollar fee. Lou fishes a receipt out of his top desk drawer and scrawls the date and his signature on the bottom. The entire time my stomach's fluttering. I can't stop worrying about the unhappiness I sense ahead.

Lou mentions my sister and stresses that there are no certainties when it comes to hypnotherapy but that he's going to do his best to help me. He asks my sister's name (which I give as Sarah) and whether there's any particular information or events about her that I'm hoping to remember. I tell him that I just want to remember what it was like to be with her but also what it was like to be with my parents before her death because I sense that they haven't been the same since losing her.

I hope I'm not fucking up my chances of success by leading Lou down the wrong path but I'm afraid I'll scare him away if I get anywhere near the truth. Lou explains a bit about hypnosis and does a relaxation exercise with me. He has a voice like trees rustling in a warm wind. It makes me feel floaty and calm. And then we're stepping into my subconscious, Lou Bianchi's voice guiding me into a tranquil meadow. I hear birds sing and can feel the heat of the sun on my face. Slowly, a mist begins to descend and then he's leading me backwards in time through the fog. "Back to when you were four years old and in the presence of your dear sister, Sarah," Lou intones.

I'm fully aware of my lie and why I told it, but in my current state I no longer want to hide anything from Lou and I amend, "I don't have a sister. I have a brother. His name is Latham. I think he's dead."

My words don't come as a surprise to me. It feels as though I've always known the truth.

"Tell me about your brother, Latham," Lou suggests.

I begin to cry under my breath. I promised Latham I'd never forget.

Lou's Zen voice instructs me to relax. He reminds me that I am observing the past but no longer inside it. My sorrow recedes but doesn't disappear as I listen to him say, "In a moment I'm going to count from one up to ten. When I reach ten I want you to go to a happy time with Latham. You will be fully aware of all the details that surround you—the sounds, sights, smells and whoever else is nearby. Take your time observing and when you're ready I want you to describe everything that's happening for me."

Lou begins his slow count upwards and when he reaches ten I'm like a person reborn. The first time I came into the world I was a blank slate, instinct without knowledge. That was approximately sixteen years ago. The second time, a little over a month ago, others deliberately reconstructed my consciousness, playing God. This third time I'm born complete with knowledge and an unobscured view of the truth. I feel like the first astronaut who landed on the moon, like I can see the arc of twenty-first-century human existence in a way that few people would ever believe possible.

We've come so far but fallen so fast. We're our own worst enemies and this time it really might be the end.

I stare seventy-eight years into the future and tell Lou everything.

FIFTEEN

The weather changed faster than expected. Too many trees died in the Amazon—billions and billions of them—and the planet lost its buffer against global warming. In the United States climate change denial was completely swept away by the late 2020s when the droughts grew longer and the storms more severe. There were heat waves and heavy downpours on a scale North America had never known. Drought ravaged the Southwest, resulting in the beginning of a mass migration north and away from the coasts. Eventually many coastal cities were entirely deserted due to rising sea levels. However, New York remained a symbol of national strength and flood barriers were erected to protect the city from aggressive storm surges.

In Canada too, certain regions were drying up while others were the victims of massive floods. Scientists throughout the continent began plans to divert major rivers to areas starving for rain and to construct gigantic dams to contain runoff from rain in mountains that they knew would soon stop freezing.

Near the end of the 2020s a fascist-leaning Canadian government ill-equipped to deal with the constant fires raging in the west and a host of other environmental disasters, provoked mass protests that led to enormous unrest. In the instability a national political party that sought to merge Canada with the United States rose. It was widely supported by a Canadian population who feared chaos and violence and was elected to power in 2031. Negotiations began with the United States government immediately and on October 26, 2032, a new nation—the U.N.A. (United North America)—was born.

In 2036 the center of U.N.A. government was relocated to Billings, Montana, where the climate was more moderate and its inland position was a strategic military defense advantage. Around this time automation that had begun in the industrial revolution evolved to include the ever-more-popular presence of robots in the home (as domestic servants and companions) and workplace. Within the next fifteen years the retail, manufacturing, hospitality, security and health sectors quickly came to rely on robots to fill the majority of their positions. In turn this caused acute unemployment and by the mid-2040s mammoth social welfare camps had been erected in the majority of inhabitable states. The citizens who resided in these camps were referred to by those still employed as "the Cursed." Because the residents were required to perform manual labor in the camps, the very existence of the social welfare camps caused additional unemployment. Several studies documented that once the Cursed were forced to rely on a camp for basic needs, they were unlikely ever to gain employment outside one again. By 2055 the U.N.A. unemployment rate was 36 percent in a population of 500 million.

Even with these crippling economic conditions much of the world continued to regard the U.N.A. and Northern European countries (which suffered a similar unemployment rate except Norway and Sweden where robot employment was permitted only in sectors that would endanger humans) as a safer and more prosperous place to live than their homelands. For decades now large swathes of Africa, Southern Asia, the Middle East, Southern Europe and Latin America have been ravaged by drought, torrential flooding and dangerous sea level rises, making much of their terrain uninhabitable. Hundreds of millions of environmental refugees continue to sweep across Northern Europe and the U.N.A. In response Northern Europe and the U.N.A. have bulked up their defenses with a force largely composed of robots that are commanded by human members of the military. The defense force's chief aim is to keep foreign nationals off its soil.

In the U.N.A. the robot units that patrol and guard the country's borders and surrounding oceans are popularly known as DefRos. Inland, homeland security units that constantly monitor highways, schools, government and public offices, shopping zones and other highly trafficked areas for disturbances are called SecRos. Because of their more direct dealings with citizens, these units are constructed to strongly resemble humans and are skilled in human communication as well as defense.

While several companies manufacture DefRos and SecRos alike, Coppedge-Hale Corp is the government's largest supplier. Despite the omnipresent military force, terrorist attacks on domestic soil have become more frequent. There is great anger with the West, both for causing irreparable environmental damage worldwide and its continuing hostility to eco-refugees. Several of the attacks have been against vertical farms (where the majority of crops are now raised) in urban centers, others against the Zephyr, the extensive high-speed domestic railway network that expanded as world oil supplies dwindled and air traffic became heavily restricted. The worst threats have been biological in nature as terrorists designed an array of viruses. In 2058 a fast-acting Ebola-Hanta copycat causing hemorrhagic fever was deployed at Union Station in Denver, killing 113 people within hours.

These are all well-known facts children of 2063 are free to read in textbooks about the twenty-first century, and I continue to tell Lou Bianchi, who has given up questioning me about my fake sister Sarah to focus on my unlikely tale, everything I can think of about changes someone from 1985 could barely hope to understand. I explain about the Bio-net, the network of nanites operating inside people of the future. Not everything about the time is darkness and threat—many of humanity's old illnesses have been eradicated. There is no more cancer, diabetes, Alzheimer's or AIDS. The U.N.A.'s people are strong and healthy. Even unwanted pregnancy and obesity is prevented by the Bio-net. No one goes hungry (except illegals who have somehow made it past DefRo defenses), and life expectancy is well past the age of one hundred. Much human trauma is repairable thanks to the nanites. Limbs can be regrown, damaged cells repaired, heart attacks and strokes prevented.

However, our strengths have become our weaknesses. Now the terrorists aim their threats at our Bio-nets, programming them to destroy us like they did in Denver. U.N.A. scientists quickly erect their defenses via our nanites, constantly updating their programming so that no new bioterror threat can take down many U.N.A. citizens with it.

On the Dailies broadcast each morning, the government informs us of these threats and advises us how strong in spirit all U.N.A. citizens must continue to be. If the news is especially bad the Dailies will often remind us of a dark time in U.N.A. or United States history when goodness and right prevailed. Because much of our news also comes from our allies in Northern Europe, the Dailies play many quotes from British Second World War Prime Minister Winston Churchill—mostly ones that contain the word "courage."

Directly after the Dailies and breakfast it's time for school, which the U.N.A. resurrected thirteen years ago and which runs year-round, Monday to Friday. The process of phasing physical schools out began in 2025 and continued for fifteen years before they were formally retired in 2040. For the next decade all school-age children were taught at home by EdRos and through an early version of gushi (a full-immersion virtual-reality system indistinguishable in quality from real life). Thanks to the Bio-net, gushi is now advanced enough to be experienced directly from within people's own nervous systems rather than on a screen. Entertainment, interactive fantasy games and stories, sexual experiences (commonly called "mashing"), broadcast of the Dailies and travel to far-away places occur largely in gushi. However, in the decade when gushi was used in place of real-world education many young people began to suffer from mental health issues due to the social isolation and overdependence on virtual reality.

As a result of these problems, when the government decided to return to the former school system, they looked far into the past for inspiration. All former school buildings were destroyed and Victorian-style structures erected in their place. Teachers were required to dress in clothing that wouldn't have looked out of place in that era while students wore short-sleeve gray unisex jumpsuits with a collared white shirt underneath. Physical textbooks began to be produced again and the importance of participation in sports as part of one's program of well-being was emphasized.

All students spend their seventh through eighteenth years in the U.N.A. school system. Gushi access is blocked on school property but is encouraged as harmless entertainment after hours, as long as one participates in moderation. In fact, most people's sexual lives occur almost entirely on gushi where they feel free to experiment without pain or discomfort, in complete safety where there is no limit to what is possible. "Mashing" is considered ecstasy precisely because it's only what you want it to be and *all* that you want it to be—orgies, sex with aliens or mythical creatures, acrobatic physicality that would be impossible to emulate in real life without injury.

The only time the majority of people engage in sexual relations with another live person is as part of a fertility ritual when they're ready to have children. Marriage still exists for the purpose of raising offspring but love matches are rare. Most people (of all sexual orientations) use the Service to unite them with a suitable life partner. The Service has been performing DNA and personality matches for over twenty-five years. So accustomed to gushi mashing are the majority of people that the Service has to train newly married citizens in how to have sex with each other so that no one will be harmed attempting unsafe activities during a fertility ritual. Love matches and what people now refer to as "grounded" sex is largely frowned upon in the U.N.A. and what remains of civilized society elsewhere. Despite the Bio-net's ability to shield people from sexually transmitted diseases there is a widespread distaste for the exchange of bodily fluids.

However, there are those who support *grounded* experiences of all kinds over gushi participation and believe robot employment should be heavily restricted to boost human employment numbers. The grounded movement regarded the reformation of the physical school system in 2050 as a major victory. Generally, supporters of the grounded movement also oppose the identity wiping of eco-refugees, suspected but unproven terrorists and other political dissidents. Because the government only executes proven foreign national terrorists, the government itself considers its actions against eco-refugees and others as lenient and forgiving. In reality, once their personalities are wiped and covered (W + C) with a new persona that is programmed to devoutly support the state in any way it can, these apprehended foreigners and formerly noncompliant citizens are sent to work with hazardous materials or under dangerous conditions. Often the W + C prisoners are sent to perform toxic environmental cleanup alongside robots or assist in storm evacuations and high-risk rescue operations.

The grounded movement continues to protest this treatment and promote the value of a life rooted in reality but its more radical members have on occasion overstepped the boundaries of what the government is willing to humor as civic participation and become W + C victims themselves. Though the movement contains some very eminent and powerful citizens, individual members must be circumspect in speaking of their views and stress pacifism as the only acceptable way to attain their goals. Calls for revolution are not tolerated by the U.N.A. government. Protest rallies that involve even the slightest property damage are not tolerated by the government either. The U.N.A. leaders and the governments of its allies are more powerful than they have ever been yet they also face more internal and external threats than ever before.

In 2059 a limited nuclear exchange between Pakistan and India tore holes in the world's ozone layer. The war was over water and was only one of many such wars for resources but in this case the use of nuclear arms and resulting damage to the ozone layer caused reduced crop yields and exponentially increased DNA damage worldwide. The number of eco-refugees spiked and, along with them, the threat of terrorism.

It's no wonder, in an existence as harsh as this, that people seek to disappear into gushi, a virtual world where any comfort or excitement a person desires is theirs for the taking. I come from a place and time where every citizen is implanted with a microchip containing their identification at birth. The SecRos and DefRos are capable of reading the chips from a distance of thirty feet. Citizens have been murdered for their chips or had their dead bodies mutilated for them. These stolen chips then arrive on the black market where they are implanted in someone else's arm for a price because despite the might of U.N.A. security forces, there is a continual leak of refugees and potential terrorists into U.N.A. territory.

In this future society, personal freedoms are curtailed in the name of the needs of the many. Each U.N.A. citizen must perform compulsory government service for a period of eighteen months after they turn twenty-one. The "comp" jobs are in one of three streams—homeland environmental projects, homeland security services or homeland agriculture. While young people may register a particular request for one of the three streams, such requests are often denied.

Unlike in 1985, long-term careers are no longer solely of citizens' choosing either. Aptitude tests administered in the final years of basic education (around the age of seventeen) are measured against occupations with existing or projected vacancies. Three possible occupations are suggested to each young citizen who must then narrow their options and select a single one from the three. Only the most well-connected U.N.A. citizens are at liberty to create a fourth option for themselves or reverse an earlier decision and make another choice.

It's an age of sacrifice and duty on one hand and one of constant escape to a fantasy world that knows no boundaries on the other. Even "the Cursed" are not denied access to gushi as long as they put in a full day's work in the camps. It's the U.N.A. populations' favorite pastime. The grounded movement liken gushi to a twentieth-century narcotic and maybe they're right because it's often enough to distract us from the nightly curfews, mechanized security patrols, lack of control over our own lives, the constant threat of a new war to weaken an already fragile environment or a fresh bioterror plague that will bleed our bodies dry.

I can imagine how nightmarish and unbelievable the future must sound to Lou Bianchi. I wouldn't believe it myself if someone came to me with such a bizarre story, except that I know it to be the truth. The God's honest truth, as they sometimes like to say in 1985.

One of the strangest things about it all was that I didn't consider many of the things I've explained particularly unusual while I lived them. Most of it was just background noise to my life . . . until it wasn't.

When they took Joanna I began to wake up to what was wrong with our world but it wasn't until they took Latham that I was truly wide awake. And by then it was already too late.

SIXTEEN

My father, Luca Kallas, is the vice president of Coppedge-Hale Corp, the leading manufacturer of the nation's security defense robots. That's what Garren meant when he told the SecRos, on that morning back when I was twelve and a half and full of fury and sadness, "You better be careful there—you know that's the boss's daughter." It was no dream—it was a buried memory.

That was the first day I really noticed Garren but I noticed him often after. Everybody knew his mothers (one of them an archivist and the other a prominent physicist) were members of the grounded movement and in later years I learned that he and his younger sister, Kinnari, made no secret of their own support for the movement. It seemed natural and right to them, like breathing.

My older brother, Latham, and I attended the same school as Garren and Kinnari Lowe in Billings, Montana, where the head office of Coppedge-Hale Corp was located along with the federal government. Latham and I were designer babies, like most of the children in Billings—intelligent, attractive and even-tempered. As the offspring of a wealthy and powerful parent, we had every advantage and, like so many other young children, I worshipped my father. This, too, seemed as natural and right as breathing at the time.

In those early years I never blamed my father for disappointing me. The birthdays and special occasions that he failed to attend and the times he was "too tired for children's voices" didn't make me love him any less and Latham, just sixteen months older than me, was always there to pick up the slack. I could never complain that I was lonely or had no one to play with; we were inseparable when we were children, almost as if we were twins except that Latham was worldlier and could always see through my father.

Latham and I were expected to be perfect (as custom ordered) and in the beginning my parents didn't have any major complaints but then I started to see things before they happened. Mostly they weren't things of any consequence but my mother, Leila, detested my visions and labeled my second sight unnatural. She began to slap my hands when I mentioned my visions and forbid me to speak of the things I saw to anyone. "Not even your father," she said.

"What about Latham?" I asked, because I couldn't imagine not sharing the things I'd seen with him.

My mother's lip curled as she replied, "You must never speak of it again and when you stop talking about it, the strange things will stop happening. Do you understand me?"

For years I didn't mention my second sight to Latham and denied the visions even to myself, until Joanna, the nanny and domestic servant that my parents had employed starting when I was six (during a short period of time when it became fashionable for wealthy people to hire human domestic servants rather than robots), noticed me freeze while I was accompanying her on an errand, like I'd seen a ghost. I loved Joanna and eventually I trusted her enough to explain about my visions and swear her to secrecy. Joanna called my second sight a gift but I didn't understand the visions enough for them to prove useful. Mostly they seemed random and pointless.

Once I saw my friend Elennede fall from a tree and injure her head but when it actually happened the Bio-net healed her without difficulty, rendering the vision a useless warning. I only ever saw things from the near future and they were always about myself or those close to me. My father being driven to work. Latham sassing a teacher at school. Me, meeting people I hadn't come to know yet but soon would.

It wasn't until I had a vision about the SecRos taking Joanna that I realized my gift's potential importance. I had no idea why they would come for her—Joanna was one of the kindest, gentlest people I'd ever met—but I immediately confided my vision to her.

Joanna's eyes filled with worry. "How long do you think I have?" she asked.

I told her I didn't know but even as I said it I felt the danger grow. "Not long. But why would they want you? There must be some mistake."

Joanna began to whirl around her bedroom, packing up her things. "No mistake," she told me. "I'm an illegal, Freya. I was born in Mexico and smuggled across the border in a small group along with my aunt and uncle when I was seven. The smuggler or the chip seller must have turned us in."

"But my father can help you," I said firmly. If she was only seven when she crossed the border how could she carry any responsibility for her illegal status? It wasn't right. And my father was one of the powerful men in the U.N.A. Surely this was something he could fix.

Joanna's hair billowed out behind her as she swept up more of her belongings. "It's better if I just leave. If they ask you, pretend you know nothing. Don't bother your parents with news of your vision. They don't understand."

Joanna was clutching her suitcase in her left hand, ready to flee, when my parents charged into her bedroom along with the SecRos. My father took one look at me and then refused to let me catch his eye again. I heard him ask the SecRos which detention facility they were bringing Joanna to. "Harlowtown," one of them replied. "Do you have further instructions, sir?"

"Yes, take her to Jamesview instead. On my authority."

My father turned towards Joanna. "It will be better for you there."

I thought that meant he would help her in some way but it still didn't seem enough and I interrupted, "But, Dad, why does she have to go at all? Why can't she stay here? She hasn't done anything."

My father's face grew rigid and my mother said, "Freya, let us handle this." She pointed for me to leave the room and when I tried to speak to my father about Joanna later that night my mother instructed me not to bother him and waved me away a second time.

"You know who your father is," she whispered as soon as he was out of earshot. "He can't be seen appearing to help illegals. His position makes that impossible. You need to understand that."

I didn't. I still believed he'd help Joanna in some secret way, maybe not by bringing her back to us but by making sure she was safely settled somewhere else in the U.N.A., the evidence against her lost. The next time I had a chance to speak to my father about it alone he said, "Try not to worry about her anymore, Freya. I've made sure she's in a good place." Then he winked and added, "Don't say anything to your mother about what I've told you. She'd be angry with me for months if she knew I'd stuck my neck out like that."

And so I said nothing and tried to be content with Joanna's safety, although I missed her desperately. Our new domestic, Ro (Joanna's replacement), smiled too often, which made me feel worse. Only two days later she was setting my breakfast on the table when I caught a glimpse of Joanna on the Dailies among a crowd of W + C women who were working on a chemical spill site in Minneapolis. She had that weirdly zealous look in her eyes that wiped and covered people always projected, like they were burning on the inside. Burning with a desire to do whatever would make the U.N.A. stronger. The Joanna I'd known was gone forever. They'd taken her identity from her and turned her into an instrument of the state.

My father refused to talk to me about what had happened to Joanna, saying only that he'd been betrayed. My mother sat me down in her private solarium, a place where it was forever a perfect day in May. Then she told me there were many hard truths about the world that I hadn't come to accept yet. "Your father's work comes with enormous responsibility. He must be seen to be above reproach." In a word: perfect.

I interpreted her comments as an admission of guilt. Having taken my father at his word that he'd found a good place for Joanna and later listened to him claim he'd been betrayed it seemed obvious to me that my mother was the one to betray him. She must've forced him to change his mind by reminding him of his duty to Coppedge-Hale Corp.

I hated her for that and knew I would never forgive her. She'd destroyed a person I'd loved. I was angry with my father too but assigned the lion's share of the blame to my mother. Hearing Garren say, "It's inhumane, what they do," later that same morning made my hate surge stronger, like he was giving me permission to stop feeling anything good about my mother.

The rage I felt down to the core was her fault and no one could tell me any different, although Latham tried. He said the decision about Joanna would've always been our father's to make, not our mother's, but that she'd been doing his dirty work for years when it came to us. "Because he can't stand not to feel like the good guy to you." Latham threw up his hands and added, "When are you going to see that, Freya? What does he have to do for you to open your eyes to who he really is?"

As angry as I was with my mother, I couldn't bear to argue with my brother for long. "Maybe you have the opposite blindness and forgive *her* everything too easily," I said. "Did you ever think of that? You know how she's always been about my visions. She wants us to match up with these ideals she has in her head—an ideal daughter who I'll never be."

Latham stood with his hands on his waist and said, "I've told you before, I think your visions scare her because of what they could mean for you."

Latham has his own pet theories. He'd overheard my parents discussing my second sight when it first started to manifest. My dad wanted to take me into a facility for testing but my mom said she didn't think my abilities were very strong. Then she reminded my father that the government might show too much of an interest in me if I was proven talented. My father replied, "Our enemies are multiplying. The

U.N.A. needs all the defense assistance it can get. If Freya can help, we should make that help available."

I didn't doubt that our father had said that but it didn't mean his motives were bad or that my mother wanted to protect me. "Look, we're never going to agree when it comes to them," I told Latham. "But let's not let them make us fight each other, okay?"

Latham rolled his eyes. "We're not fighting. I'm just trying to clue you in. But okay, okay. Fuck them both. I'm tired of their expectations hanging over me."

At the time my parents had high hopes for the both of us—that at least one of us would take an interest in Coppedge-Hale Corp (which with my father's influence could easily become a fourth career option) and that perhaps the other would show an aptitude for politics. This was never to be as Latham and I turned deliberately away from my parents' dreams. As he moved further into his teenage years, Latham began dealing in false transit documents, banned substances and other illegalities. His criminal dealings were low-key and he was well connected and smart enough never to be caught but people in general sensed there was something wrong about him and believed my parents had spoiled him.

I developed nasty habits of my own, at first behaving badly (causing disturbances at school, failing to show up there on various days and taking things that weren't mine) to get back at my mother and later because I'd grown used to it. My father interacted with me and Latham less and less as his disappointment with us grew but my mother was forced to continue disciplining us. Latham tried to charm his way around her, and often succeeded, but although my rage over Joanna faded slightly with time, my anger with my mother never entirely disappeared. I wasn't interested in trying to get along with her. The more she made her unhappiness with me known the more I challenged her.

Latham said I only made things harder on myself and that if I eased up on her she'd ease up on me. "Yeah, and what fun would that be?" I asked with a smirk.

But in unguarded moments I still had a soft spot for my dad. He must've sensed it because there were occasions when my father cast his disappointment aside and sided with me against the school, something he never did for Latham.

My old friendship with Elennede continued into my teenage years. Her rebellious nature made our alliance seem like fate. Elennede was the only person I confided in about my parental troubles. She was also the only one who knew how I stared at Garren Lowe, although she didn't understand my fascination with him and as a result we didn't talk about him much. I'd pass him in the halls—usually taking too long a look at him—and overhear snatches of conversations he was having with other students. Often they were devotees of the grounded movement too. They were like an unofficial school club and some people complained that they were cultlike but I never got that feeling; they were just passionate about what they believed and wanted to change things for the better.

I didn't think that everything about their way necessarily

was better (I liked gushi as much as most people) but I knew that the government W + Cs were wrong. My brother wasn't very political either and avoided most of the more activist types from school. Then, at seventeen, he surprised me and began to change, developing an interest in Kinnari Lowe. Although she brought out the best in Latham, influencing him to curtail his criminal dealings, my parents disapproved. It wasn't wildly unusual for young people to develop temporary romantic attachments to each other but Latham spoke about Kinnari as if their relationship would become something permanent, a love match.

Because she was often at our house in those days I became friendly with Kinnari, who I already knew a little from school. Since her mothers were members of the grounded movement they saw nothing wrong with Latham and Kinnari's relationship and invited our entire family along to Kinnari's sixteenth birthday party at the end of July. My father offered a work-related excuse for his absence but my mom, Latham and I agreed to attend, despite my parents' continuing unhappiness at Latham and Kinnari's pairing. I was looking forward to the party because I knew Garren would be there. He was scheduled to leave for law school at the end of summer and if I didn't speak to him soon I'd probably lose my chance entirely.

Like most of the young people in Billings, there was nothing Kinnari really needed, but Latham had told me she was a fan of old-style movies and named several she was hoping to collect in a format from the early twenty-first century known as Blu-ray Disc. They'd stopped making spectator movies altogether in 2037—by then the rising popularity of interactive gushi had made spectator movies an unlucrative business—but Garren and Kinnari were fans of many old things and their mothers had bought them each Blu-ray players for Christmas. With this in mind, I instructed my trans to drive me over to the shopping zone on the far side of town to visit an area populated with antique stores. Clean and swift, the single-person solar-powered vehicle was the most common method of local transportation, for those who could afford it.

As I neared the antique media shop I noticed that the area was somewhat dilapidated, as most people have no interest in old things and the ones who do are drawn to them despite the unattractive surroundings. Only a block from my destination I happened to spot my mother traipsing out of a dingy café with a stranger. He was holding her hand and as I whizzed by them he pulled her close and kissed her full on the lips.

I was shivering as I commanded my trans to park on the next block. I couldn't believe my mother would allow *anyone* to kiss her on the lips. I was a product of my upbringing and was disgusted to imagine that my mother might be engaging in grounded sex. It was one thing for my brother to do it; he was young and free. My mother had children and had dedicated her life to being with my father.

I selected three Blu-ray movies for Kinnari from the antique store and returned home visibly upset. Latham wanted to know what was wrong with me. I told him about the kiss and he smiled to himself a little and said, "Good for her if it's true. She should've left Dad years ago."

"I should've known you'd say that." I shook my head at him. "It's not like she's a prisoner here. You wouldn't say the same if Dad was tonguing some woman in the street, would you?"

Latham wrinkled his forehead. "Look, what they do with their own lives isn't our business, right? You should just let it go."

If it weren't for the bonfire of anger for my mother that I'd built up inside me over the years, maybe I would've been able to do that, but I was fuming with her when the three of us left for the party and snapped at everything she said in the multiperson trans my family rarely used anymore. Kinnari's mothers were kind and gracious to us when we arrived but I continued to tear strips off my mother, who had no idea why I was furious with her. It was a rare lovely day—not too hot and without a cloud in the sky—and the party was held in the Lowes' backyard garden. A large group of us were seated on the patio drinking mango juice and snacking on finger foods when my mother decided to fight back with a dispassionately delivered comment. "If you think you're embarrassing me with this behavior, Freya, you should think again. The only one you're embarrassing with this selfish display is yourself. Why don't you think of someone else for a change? This is Kinnari's birthday party. Can we focus on that for a few minutes?" She slanted her gaze away from me and sought out a connection with one of Kinnari's mothers. "And a lovely party it is, I might add. Your garden is beautiful and you've done a wonderful job with Kinnari."

My mother, the ultimate fake. She would have been happy if Kinnari never set foot in our house again but it was always about appearances with her. She must have totally lost control of herself to go as far as kissing someone on a public street (even if it was in a part of town most people she knew would never find themselves).

My bottom lip was trembling when I stared at my mother and I'm not sure what horrible thing would've burst out of my mouth if Garren Lowe hadn't, at that very moment, crouched down by my chair and said, "Freya, if you have a second there's something I want to show you." He smiled as he waited for me to answer him, his dark hair wild and wavy like it would later be in my dreams.

I'm sure my face was reddening with humiliation but Garren reflected none of my discomfort in his face. "Listen to, actually," he added. "That seventies record I was talking to you about at school the other day."

I nodded as if I knew what he was talking about and followed him from the table. "Thanks for the rescue," I said as soon as we were far enough away not to be overheard.

"You looked like you were about to twist her head off," he said. "You two really know how to push each other's buttons, huh?"

"It's not even that." I bit the inside of my cheek. "I mean,

I hate her all the time. *All the time.* But today I found a new reason." A live human band of classical musicians was playing near the back entranceway to the Lowe house and I stopped to listen to them. If my mother ever paid for a live band it would probably just be as a show of status, otherwise she'd consider Ros or holographic musicians just as good.

Garren was listening to the band too and I glanced into his green eyes and said, "I wish I had your mothers for parents. They're so cool."

A shrug stretched slowly across Garren's shoulder blades. "A lot of people think they're kooks."

"Only stupid people. And who cares what stupid people think?"

"Exactly." Garren smiled again and this one felt like it was one hundred percent genuine and just for me.

I didn't want our time together to end and I smiled back, feeling warm in the face again. "So the seventies record, does it exist?"

"I have a lot of records but I didn't have a specific one in mind," he said. There'd been a sixties and seventies music revival going on for years and China (the parts of it that were still functioning) was cashing in on it by ignoring a human cloning ban and assembling their own super-groups and artists from the spliced DNA of former rock stars. Some of the current biggest acts were female singer/songwriter Chena (a Tina Turner/Cher clone), Supreme (another female solo act who was an amalgamation of all the original members of the Supremes), and the rock band ABBA3+Elton (having failed to secure Benny Andersson's DNA, Chinese geneticists had substituted a cloned Elton John as the fourth member of the band). So far many of the Chinese acts had proven hugely successful in the short term but quickly crashed and burned, suffering addictions and mental health issues that had largely been eradicated in the U.N.A.

I was already well aware, from what I'd overheard at school and later from Kinnari, that Garren's interest was mainly in original music rather than genetically engineered copies and I said, "Play some for me then. Keep me away from my mother for a while."

We went up to Garren's room, which looked as contemporary as my own except for the contents of the wooden shelves in the corner and what I guessed must be an antique record player. I stood peering down at it, afraid to touch it.

"Don't worry, you're not going to break it," Garren told me, freeing a thin black disc from its outer cardboard sleeve. "The machine's not as fragile as it looks but the records themselves can get pretty scratchy." He handed the disc to me and pulled the glass lid of the record player open. "Here, I'll show you how to use it."

Soon I was putting on records for myself and we listened to old music by Neil Young, Patti Smith and The Band, musicians I'd barely heard of before. During "Heart of Gold" I almost broke down and told Garren about my mom and the stranger kissing but changed my mind at the last second and murmured something about the song being haunting.

I figured Garren wouldn't see the incident from my point of view, being big into the grounded movement like he was. Just then Kinnari knocked on her brother's door. She and Latham slipped into the room, joining us to listen to records, and the opportunity to be alone with Garren had passed in the blink of an eye.

SEVENTEEN

When Latham found out Hendris (the Jimi Hendrix/ Janis Joplin hybrid who critics agreed was the most talented of all the spliced musicians) was playing one final live concert in Chicago before she gave up music, he asked me to go with him and Kinnari. "You know you love Hendris," he said, and he was right. She wasn't a product like the others; she was a genuine artist. That's why she was giving up the music industry. She said no matter what her genetic roots were she was still a real live person with her own dreams and feelings and though she loved music she didn't want to feel like she owed her success to her DNA. So she was turning away from a multimillion-dollar career and towards her other great passion, painting, which she intended to do under another name.

There'd been heightened terrorist activity in the U.N.A. recently and neither my parents nor the Lowes would've allowed Latham and Kinnari to travel all the way out to

Chicago but Latham (who hadn't given up his old delinquent tricks entirely) promised he'd fix things so that they wouldn't have to know. He'd scored multiple transit documents through one of his many contacts and planned to tell our parents that he was going to do a twelve-hour volunteer stint at the social welfare camp just outside of Great Falls. All U.N.A. students were required to lodge fifty volunteer hours at a government-approved activity before graduation and my brother even had an administration officer at the camp ready to cover for him and Kinnari (and even me, if I wanted to go with them). Meanwhile they'd catch the Zeph (the nickname for the U.N.A.'s train system) to Chicago, arriving within five hours.

I was surprised that Kinnari was willing to lie to her parents and run off to Chicago behind their backs and said as much to Latham. "Are you kidding?" he said. "It's this major grounded experience—she's *dying* to go. She doesn't like lying to them, but she knows they'd never say yes. Garren said he would've come too, except he had plans he couldn't shake."

I was glad Garren couldn't make it. The temptation to go to the concert would've been unbearable otherwise and I'd had a crazy screaming match with my mother earlier that day and wasn't allowed to leave the house, except to go to school, for the next week. The last-minute Hendris concert was in only three days' time.

Latham looked downcast when I explained why I couldn't go. "*Shit*. You really should be there. Maybe we can come up with something. If you suck up to Mom for the next couple days maybe she'll forget about putting you under house arrest."

"She might forget if we were talking about *you* but if I sucked up to her it'd only make her suspicious," I said. Besides, the more alibis we tossed around the more likely they'd blow up in someone's face and take the entire trip to Chicago down with them.

"Shit," Latham repeated, shoving his fists into his pocket. "This sucks."

"Don't worry about me," I told him. "Go. Have a good time. Tell me everything when you get back." Gushi was being blocked from the event, which was billing itself as one hundred percent grounded but the odds were that someone would eventually find a way to share the experience.

Latham nodded but I could tell that if I didn't do something he was going to keep moping about me not being able to go with them. I had a flash of inspiration and convinced him we should do the next best thing—dive into the gushi experience of the 1969 Woodstock concert, which featured performances by both Jimi Hendrix and Janis Joplin. I was no expert on old music but knew of the concert because of my Hendris fandom.

Latham loved the idea and we stared inward, our Bio-nets shutting down input from our real senses as our minds jumped into as realistic an experience of that mud-soaked, drug-fueled hippy festival as you'd ever want to live through. It was epic in parts and exhausting (and even boring) in others and though it felt like it had gone on for days the experience was all over in about two hours. For days after that Latham and I peppered our conversations with each other with hippy lingo and made references to doing acid and magic mushrooms.

I didn't foresee anything unusual about the Hendris concert beforehand. The morning Latham left he was hyper like a little boy and I was jealous that I was being left behind. He hugged me goodbye and said, in the stoned-out tone we'd perfected over the past few days, "Don't let the man keep you down, man."

"Fuck the establishment," I said back. Then I raised my fingers in a peace symbol salute.

That was the last time I saw Latham as himself.

Later that night I was curled up in bed, trying to sleep, when my mind flew to him and Kinnari across the country. They were in the middle of a crowded, throbbing mass of people. Kinnari was dancing, my brother's arms wrapped around her waist, and the music was so loud that they wouldn't have been able to hear themselves think. Beads of sweat gathered on my upper lip as I felt fear spread through the crowd.

Behind Kinnari and Latham someone shouted, "Help me!"

Latham held Kinnari tighter and tried to tug her towards the stage, away from the disturbance. "Don't touch me!" a terrified male voice protested.

Chaos rampaged through the concert grounds. People

began to run and in their fear trampled others who had fallen. Everywhere there were people staggering, bleeding and raw. Then I saw a boy who couldn't be more than fourteen foaming at the mouth and tearing at the arms of an equally young girl, scratching the flesh off them. His eyes rolled back in his head and the girl was crying, trying to twist her body away from him. But he was relentless, like an animal with prey. I watched him sink his teeth into her waist, watched her fall to her knees before being swallowed up by the terror of the crowd.

Alone in my bedroom, I shook myself free of the vision and stared at the ceiling, my teeth chattering. *Latham. Kinnari.* Would they make it to safety? When would the horror I'd seen come to pass? Was there time to stop it?

I disappeared instantly into gushi to search for news about the concert. At first there was nothing but soon a journalist in New York issued a report about an unspecified disturbance at the Hendris concert in Chicago and said military forces were on the scene. I stayed awake all night waiting for another update, debating with myself about whether I should wake my parents.

Finally, the morning Dailies were broadcast and with them, the awful news that a new plague had been unleashed in Chicago last night and that the entire state was under quarantine. I thought it must have been another virus by the terrorists and I was jumping up from the kitchen table, on my way to tell my father my worries about Latham, when Latham himself stumbled into the kitchen, his skin damp and his eyes wild. I turned to run towards him and he threw out his hands in front of him and jumped back. "Don't come near me, Freya," he cried. "They . . ." His tongue was crashing over his words. "They were fucking crazy, like rabid animals. I'm not . . . I'm already not right. I shouldn't have come back here."

I cursed my vision for being too late. What was the point of having second sight if it couldn't keep my brother safe?

"I saw it on the Dailies," I told him. "How did you get away? Where's Kinnari?"

"Back with her family now. You know me; I have friends in high places. We managed to get out okay. She's in a little better shape than me but not much." Latham smiled but it only made his face look manic and sick. He motioned for me to move away and then lurched forward. "I have to get to my room. Get some things and . . . get away from here. I'm . . . just . . . so *tired*."

Latham's body jerked like he was about to fall and I stepped forward to help him.

"Stay back!" he snarled.

I stopped dead, letting him pass.

"Go to school," Latham instructed in an eerily strangled voice. "You'll make them more suspicious if you stick around."

I slipped into a kind of partial denial then, I think. I went to school where I had to scale a rock wall in gym class and listen to Elennede bait one of our more sensitive teachers, my mind constantly flitting back to Latham. *He'll be fine,* I told myself over and over. *Not like the people in Denver.* Whatever he'd been infected with couldn't have been as bad, otherwise Latham wouldn't have still been on his feet so many hours later.

Then midafternoon gushi was unblocked so that the school could receive another Dailies update. The school hardly ever unblocked gushi and everyone was immediately afraid. My fellow students listened raptly as we were informed that the origin of the new plague had been uncovered and was not the direct result of terrorist actions as was first thought.

For years the DefRos have been using the biological weapon P-47 to help defend the U.N.A.'s border with Mexico. The weapon was intended to temporarily blind and weaken those attempting illegal entry into the U.N.A. It acted as a paralyzing agent so that the illegals could be scooped up by trucks and then dumped back on their side of the border.

Now it appeared that two biological weapons, P-47 and Mossegrim (first used by the terrorists in the late 2040s but tweaked by them many times since), had converged, through direct infection, to form a brand-new threat the Dailies referred to as Toxo. While Mossegrim, even in its newer strains, could usually be cured if it was treated within forty-eight hours thanks to the ingenuity of U.N.A. scientists and the strength of our Bio-net, there was currently no cure for Toxo. Experts theorized that a small group of people who had at one point in their lives been exposed to P-47 had also recently been infected with one of the newest strains of Mossegrim. Their infection had reached a critical stage during the Hendris concert where it was now known that many more people had been infected by Toxo via blood or saliva.

The Dailies continued to explain that initial Toxo symptoms resembled the common cold. Soon fever would set in and the infected would begin to emit an odor. In later stages they would act erratically and aggressively and finally they would become blind and rabid, attacking everyone they encountered. They would remain in this hostile, feral state for an as-yet-undetermined amount of time until, it was theorized, they would die of dehydration, having lost the instinct to nourish themselves. The update closed on a quote by Mark Twain: "Courage is resistance to fear, mastery of fear—not absence of fear."

No one could concentrate after the Dailies and our teachers tried to assure us that the scientists would win in the end, that they always had and there was no reason to think that this time would be any different. My left eye wouldn't stop twitching and I couldn't get enough oxygen. I had to dig my nails sharply into my sides to remind my lungs what they were supposed to be doing. The action reminded me of how the infected boy had relentlessly torn into the girl from the Hendris concert crowd.

Was she dead now or was she infected like Latham? How long did my brother have?

As soon as I got home I sprinted up to his room. My

mother was standing in the hallway, watching him through the open door. I heard Latham howling before I reached her and froze in the hallway.

There were tears in my mother's eyes. She said, "Don't look at him, Freya."

But I couldn't help myself. I crept towards her and stared across the force field keeping my brother penned inside his bedroom. Latham stared back at me, snarling. He gnashed his teeth and lunged for me, the force field bouncing him backwards across the chair positioned in the middle of his room. His nose was crooked and bloody when he looked up again and he surged towards us a second time.

My mother clamped her fingers around my wrist and guided me along the hallway. "Was he in Chicago last night?" she asked, sounding a million miles away.

I nodded and fought the urge to storm back towards his room. Where had my brother gone? The real Latham had to be in there somewhere, lurking beyond reach of the infection.

My father arrived home shortly. I was sent to my room for the night, a precautionary force field activated there for my protection, but later I heard a scientist friend of my father's in the hall. They must have contacted him to discuss Latham. My parents let him into my room before he left and he administered a scan that showed I was clear of infection. He sounded relieved and told me that my parents were clear too.

Next, my mother came to speak to me. She said they

were waiting to see if a cure would be announced and, like my teachers, she assured me that there would likely be one soon.

I believed her, despite what had happened to Joanna, despite all the arguments we'd had over the years and despite the man I'd seen her kissing in the street. My mother loved Latham. She would do what was best for him. Protect him with everything she had.

I went to sleep believing that.

When I woke up I was still in lockdown and our domestic, Ro, had left breakfast for me. I had to watch the Dailies from my bedroom. U.N.A. president Caroline Ortega was holding a live press conference. She announced that the virulent nature of Toxo made it a real threat to national security. According to her, tens of thousands of people in Illinois had already been infected and there was not yet a cure in sight. She stressed that although the search for a cure was well under way everyone was advised to stay indoors and avoid contact with other humans. SecRo patrols would instantly be tripled and the U.N.A. was temporarily under martial law.

Then the worst news came. The president declared that Toxo posed a unique threat and required a uniquely firm response. If we weren't careful, Toxo plague could overcome the nation. To avoid this scenario all infected were to be immediately euthanized. This would prevent further spread of the virus. Anyone who'd been infected was urged to do their civic duty and turn themselves in. The SecRos would then escort them to a local SecRos holding facility where they would be painlessly euthanized. Those who did not turn themselves in would be considered at large and when apprehended by SecRos would be killed on the spot.

I threw my mouth open and started screaming frantically for my parents. I needed to know they wouldn't let the SecRos take Latham, no matter what the president had said. My father was a powerful man with powerful allies. He didn't have to publicly flout the rules, just keep Latham under lockdown until a cure was discovered.

It was hours before my father came to my door and told me that he was having Latham moved to a secure facility, not for termination but for everyone's safety, including his own. He said they had to keep Latham's body nourished until the scientists could come up with a cure. I was on the verge of crossing over into hysteria, rocking back and forth as I paced in front of the doorway, and my dad kept saying, "Look at me, look at me, Freya. I'm not lying to you."

I peered into his eyes and did what I could to quiet my mind and read Latham's future. I saw the SecRos taking him and saw him, like my father had said, safe, sleeping in a strange bed with sheets as white as sunny-day clouds.

"Freya," my dad said, "he's going to be *all right*. They're going to do everything they can for him. The biologists are working around the clock. We just need to keep him alive in the meantime."

My father explained that I was to remain in my room, where I would be safest, while they did the transfer. He said he hoped it would be accomplished soon but that SecRo units were in short supply because of the emergency.

I don't know what time it was when they took Latham but rain was pelting my window when I had my next vision. The future I'd foreseen earlier had changed. In my mind, Latham lay lifeless with two SecRos standing over him. In death his face was peaceful, unlike the last time I'd seen him.

I leapt to my feet, my body feeling that it didn't belong to me. Then I was bolting towards my bedroom door scratching at the wood and screaming for Latham. The very fact that I was having the vision meant it hadn't come to pass yet. Latham was still alive. There was a chance I could save him. I shouted for my brother's life, scraped my fingers raw.

The SecRos came for me and my mother. *Evacuation.*

The Toxo was blasting through the population like wildfire. The U.N.A. might fall.

The final memory I have of my life before is a SecRo injecting something into my arm. *Good night, Latham. Goodbye. I'm sorry I couldn't save you. I will never forget you. I'm sorry. I'm sorry. I'm sorry.*

I choke on my tears and wake up in 1985 screaming.

EIGHTEEN

don't know how I got here. The SecRos took us . . . and the next I knew I was in Sydney, Australia, in a time long before, waiting to catch a flight up to Toronto with my mother and Olivia. I don't need Doctor Byrne or any other expert to explain to me that my New Zealand memories—Olivia steering the boat in Kawakawa Bay, me necking with Shane in the backseat of his car, the sermon at my father's funeral—they're all false. A wipe and cover job. I was never that girl swimming on her father's back in Valencia.

Latham's dead. I'll never see him again.

Loss ricochets through me, a gaping bitter emptiness that I'll carry with me for the rest of my life. All I have left of my brother is his memory. Thousands of them. They flash behind my eyes as I sit up in Lou Bianchi's lounge chair, pressing my palms against my eyes to stop the tears. Latham was always there for me, ready to listen or try to make me laugh. He was there till the very end, struggling against the sickness inside him that wanted to hurt me.

Meanwhile Lou's murmuring, in his at-one-with-the-universe voice, that when he snaps his fingers I'll be wide awake and feel perfectly calm and refreshed.

"I am awake," I tell him. "I'm *awake*. I'm fine." I stop crying, as if on cue, because I don't want to freak him out. "Look, you need to do this for my friend upstairs. We're from *the same place*. He doesn't remember." The urgency in my tone probably sounds like mental illness. "I won't say anything to him about . . . you know, anything I saw to influence him before you take him back. *Please*, just try."

I rocket up from the chair before Lou can refuse and race to the waiting room where Garren's sitting back in his seat with his head resting against the wall. "What is it?" Garren asks, tensing at the sight of my wet eyes.

I feel Lou behind me. I swivel to glance back at him before replying, "You won't believe me if I tell you. Go with him and see for yourself."

Lou's lips are cemented together and his features have taken on an air of resentment. He must think I'm faking, trying to play a trick on him. "This isn't a joke," I tell Lou. "Look, we'll pay for another session. What can it hurt?"

Lou checks his watch. A sigh of irritation escapes from between his lips. "I have another client due in twenty minutes."

Garren's shaking his head, his hands cupping his elbows. "What're you doing, Freya? This wasn't part of the deal."

"Just a few minutes," I plead. "You need to see what I've seen."

"Yeah, a few minutes and another fucking forty-five dollars that we can't spare." Garren's eyes shoot over to Lou. "Sorry, no offense to you."

"None taken." Lou allows his head to roll back on his shoulders as he stares at the wall behind Garren and then shifts his focus to the collection of beat-up bags resting on his hardwood floor. Lou's eyes flicker and he sighs again, this time resignedly. "Look, if you do want to do it I'll give you a few minutes for free but it really should be what *you* want to do and not what your friend here wants."

Garren glares at me like he regrets ever walking through Lou's front door and logically I know Garren's the same person I used to stare at in the hallways, the one who rescued me that day at his sister's party when I couldn't tolerate another minute with my mom, but I can't push the two separate versions of him together in my head and make them one.

"If it's really for free . . . ," Garren qualifies at last.

Lou nods. "Just this once. And I don't have long. Let's go."

I take Garren's place in the waiting room, sitting among our things. My brain's overheating with sixteen years' worth of memories. Real ones. My father isn't dead—he hasn't even been born yet. He's the same man from my false memories but he's alive back in 2063 . . . unless they couldn't find a cure for the plague in time. It's possible that the U.N.A. could've fallen by now if the scientists couldn't stop the Toxo.

Elennede. My father. All the teachers and students from school. Are they dead and gone like Latham?

I used to think the emptiness inside me was for my father but now I know it was for my brother and I know, too, that I was wrong to hate my mother. The stress that came with my father's position warped her. The last five weeks have shown me what she would've been like under different circumstances. Kinder and warmer with only a hint of the anger she was capable of appearing on the surface.

Latham saw her more objectively than I did; she wasn't entirely blameless but everything wasn't solely her fault. My father was wrong too but it's not his fault that Latham's dead either. The entire world was wrong and I'm glad my mom doesn't remember the way we used to fight back then and that she doesn't have to remember losing Latham.

By now, maybe Henry's convinced her that I have a drug problem and have run away to live on the street. I'm sorry that my absence will cause her pain but it's better this way. She'll have a chance for happiness in 1985.

Seventy-eight years. How did they do it? Countless things people couldn't imagine in 1985 are possible seventy-eight years from now, but time travel isn't one of them.

I'm so lost in thought that I have no idea how long Garren's been gone when he trudges towards me and snaps up two of the bags from my feet without a word. He's out the front door in a flash, leaving me to run after him.

Outside I spread my fingers gently across his back as we walk on together. He must be devastated about Kinnari.

From so many years away I still feel that I failed her and my brother. I should've seen the threat before it was too late. The little ability that I have is practically useless.

Garren whips around to look at me. "I don't know what you expected but that was a complete waste of time. He didn't tell me anything that I didn't already know."

"*What?*" How can that be?

Garren thumps his carry-on bag. "He gave me your tape. You want to tell me what's on it?"

It's begun to snow and it makes it difficult to look at him head-on; I can't stop blinking for long enough to focus.

"You said I needed to see it," he reminds me. "We *stayed* for this."

He needs to know, of course, and I stare at the flecks of white gathering on the sidewalk, wishing there was someone else to tell him. There's no good or easy way to explain any of the things I remember and I begin blurting them out in between gulps of air. Garren doesn't stop walking and doesn't look at me. He waits until I've come to the very end of the story and then he draws one of his hands across his forehead and says, "You need *help*." He adjusts the carry-on bag so that the strap sits higher on his shoulder. "I know everything's fucked up and there's this crazy thing with our dads and Henry. I don't know what that's about—what the story is behind it—but it's sure as hell not *this*." He points at the sidewalk under our feet.

"You just let this guy trick you into some kind of false memory," he continues, "but it's . . . it's off-the-charts crazy, what you're saying. You need to snap out of it and get real in a hurry."

I knew that's exactly what he'd think but I can't let him brush our pasts aside. They're who we are. "It sounds crazy but it's the truth. This is why I recognized you—I knew you back there. My brother and your sister were—"

"I don't have a *sister,* Freya. *You're* the one with the sister." He cocks his head, his face flushed with frustration. "If this psycho explanation of yours makes any sense how come it doesn't explain who *she* really is?"

It does. I just didn't mention it because everything else was more important. Olivia is President Ortega's daughter. Her father was killed in a terrorist explosion in Calgary six years ago, when he was secretary of state. I've only met Caroline Ortega twice in my life, both times before she was elected president, but she must have needed someone to send Olivia back with, someone who would look after her. I explain this to Garren knowing it'll sound as mental as everything else.

"You're completely delusional," he says, his right sneaker losing traction slightly on the icy sidewalk. Regaining his balance, he slams his left foot down like he means to kill something underneath it. "We can't keep going like this. With you thinking you're someone from the future. I don't want to hear that from you again, understand? If you have to say it, I can't be around you."

"I can't stop saying it, Garren. It's the truth. I'm not going to pretend for you. The past doesn't disappear just because you don't want to hear it. Think about it—this is why so many of the facts surrounding our lives are duplicates. The scientists put them into our heads. They must have been in too big a rush with the evacuation to come up with entirely distinct cover stories." I brush stray snowflakes from my eyes. "Henry's not our grandfather—he's no one, a stranger wrapped up in the cover story. You were sent back because of the Toxo outbreak, same as I was. I don't know why things didn't come back to you the way they came back to me. Maybe we need to try again with someone else when we get to Vancouver. You have everything locked away in there, just like I did. There has to be something that will make you remember."

Once he sees it, the truth will be undeniable. His heart will know it at a glance. How could it not? It's the difference between breathable sky that stretches out in all directions and a ceiling coated in blue paint from a hardware store.

"Shit." Garren stops in his tracks. He hurls one of the bags to the ground, shrugs the other off his shoulders and stares at me, breathing hard. "This is never going to stop, is it?" He folds his hands on top of his head, his thumbs sifting through his dark hair. "I can't do this, Freya. You're going to make me crazy. Is that what you want? The two of us losing our fucking minds on the West Coast? It sounds like a good way to get caught to me. If this is the way you want to do it . . . I'm sorry, I just *can't*." Garren lowers his hands, his left at his side and his right digging into his pocket. He pulls a fifty-dollar bill out and hands it to me.

"No," I protest, knowing exactly what the gesture means. "Don't do that. We're in this together."

"I thought we were." He bends to loop his fingers around his bags. "And I hope you're going to be okay, I really do. But I need to give myself half a chance and you're . . . you're out there in your own universe."

He's the one in denial, but saying that won't change anything. I can't believe we're right back where we were last Wednesday when I showed up on his doorstep.

I slip his fifty into my pocket as he turns and walks away. I don't know how I'll do this on my own but I have no choice. After all I've been through—all I've already lost—I can't fall to pieces now. I have to keep running. Alone, if that's the way it has to be. I pull my bag close to me and head in the opposite direction.

For about thirty feet, I feel brave and resolved, like every last one of those Winston Churchill quotes they used to drill into our brains on the Dailies. I don't let myself turn back to watch Garren recede into the distance. At first my sadness for Latham is so overpowering that I can barely feel Garren's absence.

It hits soon enough.

I'm seventy-eight years from home with no one to help me. My parents must've thought they were saving me. I wasn't supposed to remember. Something went wrong.

I need more answers. I need to know what happened to the U.N.A. If time travel is possible after all, can the future be saved by returning to a moment before the outbreak? Is there ongoing communication between the past and the future? Can we leap forward the same way we came back?

My head starts to ache like it used to as questions pummel my mind.

Doctor Byrne was adamant that Garren and I had to get far away and never contact our families. He wouldn't offer us any answers last time and the odds of him talking now aren't any better. I'd get caught if I went near him or Henry anyway. There's just one other person who might know something and even if I'm right about her she probably won't help. If Garren were with me I wouldn't risk contacting her, but now I don't have much to lose and I trudge to the nearest phone booth and dial my mother's work number. When the receptionist answers I ask to speak to Nancy Bolton.

"Good afternoon," Nancy declares seconds later. "How can I help you?"

"Nancy, it's Freya." The pay phone's cold and grimy in my hand. I try not to imagine who was holding it last and what they did to it. "Don't get my mother. I don't have much time. I need to know if you can help me."

"Help you how?" she asks, sounding bewildered. "Where are you? Are you all right? The police have been looking everywhere for you."

"I don't have time for this, Nancy. I've *remembered*, okay? And I know you're not an old friend of my mother's—that you didn't meet her until just over a month ago, which means you must be working for *them*. So if you actually care whether I live or die and you know anything that can help me, I need you to tell me now."

"I do care." Nancy lowers her voice. "But there's nothing I can do for you, honey. Nothing I can tell you. I'm sorry."

My nose is running. I feel so helpless that it makes me want to destroy something. How can she call me honey and still refuse me? Rage burns through my veins.

"Unless . . . I do have some money and I'm sure that's something you need too," Nancy says.

I find my voice. "You know this isn't what my father would want. Them killing me. You know who he is, don't you?"

"I do," she says softly.

"Then you know he must've sent me back to try to save me and there's . . ." *No one for me to turn to.* I'm like any other street kid.

"This wasn't the way things were supposed to be," Nancy interrupts. "I really am sorry. Tell me when and where I can meet you so I can help you out in the only way I can. Are you still in the Toronto area?"

"Why should I trust you?" I ask.

"You shouldn't. You shouldn't trust anyone now."

Except that I need more money to get to Vancouver. I don't even know where I'll sleep tonight. Garren's gone and I have no plan B of my own. My head's throbbing so hard that I want to throw up. I'm exhausted too. I could curl up in this phone booth right now, pass out cold and not wake up until morning.

"I'm not . . . feeling well," I stammer. "I have to go." Back to the house on Cranbrooke Avenue, just for a while. Just until I can sleep off this feeling.

"*Freya.*" Nancy's tone is loud and piercing. "You give me a time and a place and I swear I'll be there. Alone."

"The Eaton Centre. Tomorrow at noon." The Yonge Street shopping center's the first public place that pops into my mind. If I'm going to meet her anywhere it should be somewhere crawling with people. And if I decide against meeting her it'll be the easiest thing in the world not to show up.

"Where in the Eaton Centre?" Nancy asks. "It's a big place."

I've never actually been there. My face is drenched with sweat and a wave of nausea grips me and shakes me. I have to get back to the house. Now.

"Is . . . is there a bookstore?" I sputter.

Nancy says there is and she'll meet me there. I hang up and hobble into the street, feverish and weak. The sickness must have something to do with remembering. Maybe the Bio-net (is it still operational inside me?) can't handle the shock to the system. I've never heard of anyone recovering their memory after a wipe, never knew it was possible.

I'm shivering and I've lost track of where I am. I need a bus or streetcar stop. Better still, a subway station. A black woman bundled up against the cold so that only her eyes and nose show between her hat and scarf scrutinizes me as I pass her on the sidewalk.

I spin to trail after her. "Excuse me. Where's the subway from here? A bus. Anything. I'm lost."

"You're *high*," the woman scolds. "Higher than a kite. No wonder you're lost, honey."

There's that word again. *Honey.* Sick as I am, I laugh bitterly.

"If you keep messing with the drugs you'll throw your life away," she continues. "You're young. You get yourself right back on that straight and narrow path and stay there."

I nod soberly, like she's reaching me, whatever it'll take for her to give me directions because I don't know how much longer I can stay on my feet.

"I know you know what I'm talking about," she says. "You can laugh about it if you want to but inside you know." The woman takes a tentative step closer to me and points down the road. "The next left at the lights will get you to the subway. About five minutes down the street. You can't miss it."

"Thank you." I'm disproportionately grateful, as though she actually is saving me from a life of drug addiction.

It's not long before I'm on the subway, sliding down into a seat near the door and shutting my eyes. The motion of the car heightens my nausea and forces my lashes open again. Next to me a man's reading the newspaper and listening to a Walkman, the Tears for Fears song "Shout" leaking out of his earphones. One moment I'm concentrating on the lyrics and trying not to throw up and the next I'm jolting awake at Chester Station. Across the aisle a different man is watching me over the top of his paperback, frowning. Maybe he thinks I'm a drug addict too.

I pull myself up and haul myself off the subway car. I've

gone too far east and need to work my way back to Bloor so I can transfer to the Yonge line. Thirty-two minutes later I arrive at Lawrence Station. For the first time I take the shorter route to Cranbrooke Avenue, straight up Yonge Street. I'm burning up and tear off my coat to carry it. The Eggo I had before leaving the house hours ago is snaking its way back up my esophagus. I can't keep it down. I stagger away from the grocery store on my left and throw up next to a fire hydrant.

My vision's blurry and my feet are clumsy. I clomp up the street like I'm wearing clown shoes. The only thing keeping me going is Latham. I don't want his death to be for nothing. I can't have been sent back in time seventy-eight years only to be captured and killed like he was. I turn onto Cranbrooke Avenue, walking faster now. On the sidewalk I skirt past a woman and little girl who might be the same people Garren and I saw from the Resniks' window the afternoon we first broke in. The woman offers her own version of the scared/disgusted look everyone's been aiming at me since I left Lou's place but her daughter smiles at me.

I smile back, my teeth sticking on my gums, and the two of them hurry by me. Once they've gone the street looks clear. I reel towards the Resniks' front door and let the house swallow me whole. I'm overjoyed to be back inside it again; the house is the closest thing I have left to an ally. I teeter in the direction of the living room and collapse onto the couch where I sleep like the dead.

NINETEEN

Later I wake up in the dark to the sound of scraping. Garren took both flashlights with him and I don't know what time it is or how long I've been out for. As I lie motionless, listening to the noise in the blackness, I realize someone must be shoveling outside. Janette's brother probably. I climb upstairs to the twins' room and risk a quick glance outside to confirm my guess. I've never seen Janette's brother but the boy pushing snow to the curb looks about the right age.

I remain upstairs until the noise has stopped, signaling that he's finished the job. Then I head back to the ground floor, light a candle and carry it into the kitchen where I drink three glasses of water in record time. The thirst aside, I feel better. Hungry even. I notice that the clock reads two minutes to nine. I must have been asleep for over four hours and I hope I'm going to be okay now that the worst is behind me. But I'm scared to eat much in case I get sick again and limit myself to applesauce from the fridge.

I have huge doubts about whether I can trust Nancy but I plan to meet her tomorrow anyway. As much as I don't want to risk being caught, I can't give up on the idea of finding out how I got here and whether she has news about my father or any of the other people left behind. If I don't take the chance I'll never know more than I do right now. Every remnant of my old life will have been washed away without a trace. There's the money too. I desperately need more. Garren and I have already been over the Resnik house with a fine-tooth comb. If I don't get extra cash from Nancy it will mean either begging or stealing to get enough money to make it to Vancouver.

I wonder if Garren's already on his way there or maybe he's changed his mind and is heading for some other place. That's a distinct possibility, considering that he thinks I'm crazy and therefore more likely to be caught and share whatever information I have about him.

I feel so lonely without him. I don't know how to think of him anymore—as the person I knew in the past or as the guy I've gotten to know in the past few days. I've felt alone before but never like this. *Me against the world.* I need to hear a friendly voice. It's a risk like everything else but I don't even try to talk myself out of it, just resolve to wait until ten o'clock to leave the house. Coming and going like I have increases the odds of being noticed by neighbors but there are less people out at night and I'll be extra careful.

I pull on Paula's boots before leaving, shove my long black hair under one of her hats. Henry's men definitely wouldn't be able to recognize me at a glance and anyway, they're probably still looking for a duo. They can't have any way of tracking us, otherwise we'd have been picked up days ago. Our microchips must have been removed before we were sent back.

The real danger is that my call might be traced and I promise myself I won't stay on the line a second over two minutes no matter what. Out on Cranbrooke Avenue, and then Yonge Street, I keep my eyes peeled for anything suspicious. The snow's stopped and the sidewalk has been partially plowed. A happy young couple are walking their dogs (one small and one large) while chewing on pizza slices. I resist the urge to ask them where the pizza came from. It smells delicious and I feel my stomach growl in protest against my caution in sticking with applesauce. Across the street, I spy a phone booth outside a lighting store and sprint over to it.

I dial Christine's number, hoping that she isn't out or if she's home, hasn't gone to sleep yet. I need to know there's someone out there who cares what happens to me, even if they don't know what I've really been through or who I really am.

The phone rings four times before Christine's dad picks up. I apologize for calling so late and give my name as Nicolette, which I know will throw Christine because she and Nicolette have probably never called each other in their lives.

"Hi," Christine says suspiciously once she's picked up the phone.

"It's not Nicolette," I say quickly. "It's *me*."

"*You*. Where are you? Do you know you're officially *missing*? The cops have been questioning everyone. I told them about the guy you were meeting a couple of days before you went missing. Did he kidnap you? What's going on? Are you okay?"

"Not really. But he didn't kidnap me. It doesn't have anything to do with him. I just . . ." My voice is beginning to crumble like a cracker. "I needed to hear a friendly voice."

"Are you coming back? Where are you? I can get my dad to come pick you up right now."

"No, no. I can't come back. I can't explain why either."

"Then I can meet you," Christine says. "Just me."

"I wish we could do that but it wouldn't be safe for you. I can't even stay on the phone long." I'm already running low on time.

"Are you going to be all right?" she asks, sounding scared for me. "Tell me what I can do."

"I don't know." There's really nothing. The unsaid words bring tears to my eyes. I fight them off, afraid that if I start crying I won't be strong enough to cut the conversation short.

"Promise me you'll call back and let me know you're okay."

"I'll try." I hope I can. Hearing Christine worry for me makes me feel like I matter.

"Did you call your mom?" she asks. "Can I tell her you called me?"

"Don't tell anyone. Promise me you won't. It could make things worse for me."

"I won't then," Christine says solemnly. "I won't tell anyone."

"Thanks. And thanks for being home tonight, Christine." I hang up without warning. Christine's someone else I'll never see again but at least I know she's still out there. I wish I could've spent more time with her and Derrick but I'll never regret remembering Latham, even though this is where it's led me.

As I exit the phone booth I notice someone else in the distance with a pizza slice in one of his hands. He's just stepped out of a door that I assume is the entrance to the pizza place. I hurry down to it, remembering Garren's joke about ordering pizza to see how seriously the residents of Cranbrooke Avenue take the concept of neighborhood watch.

I can't let myself think about Garren. It's too hard. I have enough to worry about without wondering whether he's okay and whether we'll ever run into each other again.

I buy a slice of Hawaiian pizza and a Coke and finish them both on the way back to the house. I feel more like a stranger in a strange land now that I know for a fact that I don't belong in 1985 but the past several weeks and the false memories the scientists must have given me have lent me a familiarity with the era that makes it feel less jarring than it would've otherwise.

The food is weird (so much salt, fat and chemicals) but

my body craves it anyway. Cars and factories spew pollution into the air. People throw things away like it doesn't matter what they do. It's crazy and they can't keep living like this but there are so many things about 1985 that I like. No SecRos. No terrorist plague. The freedom to do what you want and become what you want.

The people here fear nuclear war but I know that won't happen anytime soon. Or could it? Have Garren and I changed the past by coming back? How many others like us are out there—refugees from the future?

Back in the darkened Resnik house my mind runs wild trying to formulate answers to an endless sea of questions. Eventually my brain's too worn out to think beyond myself and what's going to happen to me tomorrow. I'm dying to turn on a light—or better still, the TV—but I have to settle for the kitchen radio. The noise is company. I'm afraid to go to bed because I know that when I get there it'll be impossible to avoid being overcome with loneliness and fear.

When I can't put off sleep any longer (I don't want to be late meeting Nancy tomorrow) I try the couch where I toss and turn, not because it's uncomfortable but because it's not any less lonely than being in bed. In the end I head upstairs, pull off my clothes and change into one of Mr. Resnik's T-shirts. Then I settle myself in the spare bedroom, the last place that Garren slept, as though that will somehow inspire a vision about him.

It doesn't.

I just lie there curled into a ball until the darkness takes me.

For hours I have no awareness of myself. If I dream, I don't remember it. There's nothing and no one.

It's still dark when I open my eyes again. There's a figure in the room with me, coming closer. I must be dreaming and I try to open my eyes a second time.

"I thought you'd gone," a male voice says. "I checked the kids' room first and I thought you were gone."

When I realize the voice belongs to Garren, it only confirms I'm dreaming—or having a premonition. The real Garren would be miles from Toronto by now. I was the only thing stopping him from going sooner.

"You were right," Garren continues as he looms over me. He stops and sits on the side of the bed. I feel the mattress shift under his weight. "I don't know why I couldn't remember everything before but . . ." The pain in his voice prompts me into an upright position. Even in the dark I can see that his eyes look glassy. They gleam with grief in the moonlight. "*Kinnari*. I shouldn't have let her go. There'd been so many terrorist threats lately. I should've known it was too big a risk."

This is no dream and I feel tears begin to form behind my own eyes as I think of Latham and Kinnari and the years they should've had ahead of them. "It wasn't the terrorists," I say, my voice creaking with sleep and sadness.

"I know. I remember that too." Garren grips the bedspread, his knuckles flaring. "But I could've stopped her from going to the concert. She could be here now, with us. Alive."

"I should've seen it beforehand," I tell him. "I didn't see anything until it was too late and then . . ." I don't have the words. Latham's lost forever. He would've loved this time, despite its many faults. I want him and Kinnari to be alive so much that it seems my will alone should have enough power to change history.

"It's not your fault," Garren says, tears fighting their way out of his eyes and slipping down his cheeks. "You can't control what you see."

If I hadn't spent so long denying my gift maybe I would be able to control it by now. I should've tried at least.

Garren's staring at me like he can guess my unspoken words. "It's not your fault," he repeats. "None of this is your fault."

"And not yours either," I remind him.

Garren's head bends like a broken twig. I hear him crying under his breath. Such a low, desolate sound that I can't stand it and pull myself closer to him on the bed. I fold my arms around him and feel his wet cheek against mine.

We don't talk. We just hold each other, our tears mixing until I can't cry anymore.

I kiss his cheek, my fingers creeping up the back of his neck and into his hair.

I'm glad he's here but together our sadness is overwhelming, even once my tears have begun to dry. Garren holds himself apart from me and touches my face. Slowly, he follows the curve of my cheek around my chin, like a blind man intent on discovering what I really look like.

No one's ever touched me like that.

I stare back at him like we're two other people entirely, although I've felt this way about him for so long. I lean closer and press my lips against his, our mouths closed. Mine tingles at the thought of what I've just done.

His lips are soft but cold and I wonder where he's been all this time but I don't want to break the quiet between us by asking. I open my mouth as I slide mine back against his, slip my tongue into the shared space we've created. We've never done this together either but it feels as familiar as walking, or maybe it's just Garren himself who makes it seem that way.

My body feels like a constellation, like a hundred stars glittering in the darkness. To feel so sad and so light at the same time seems like a minor miracle. I thread my fingers through Garren's and squeeze. He squeezes back. Kisses me longer and harder until I feel as though I'll burst.

I untangle myself from him just enough to tug Mr. Resnik's T-shirt over my head and let it fall to the floor. Garren sweeps his fingertips across my naked shoulders, tracing my form. Then his fingers are featherlight on my back and my waist, his eyes clinging to my breasts. I reach out to help him slip off his T-shirt. He's so perfect in the moonlight that it seems almost unfair and I touch his chest and kiss him again, my hands roaming everywhere, even the places I can't see.

I feel for the button on his jeans and snap it open. Garren yanks off his pants and cups his hands around my breasts. The way he looks at me makes me beam brighter. He runs his perfect fingers over me until I can't stand it anymore and wriggle out of the last thing I'm wearing. Garren pauses to take in the sight of me. Our mouths merge, his lips as hot as mine now. The bed creaks under our shifting weight.

We're quiet and still, Garren lying between my legs, staring into my eyes like he's waiting for something. I'm waiting too. My hands skim restlessly down his back and begin to slide off his underwear. Garren finishes the job of getting rid of them and I press one of my palms into his chest, easing him back so I can look at him the way he looked at me.

He's a minor miracle himself—the stuff that artists dream of—and I feel my throat sting and swell, too small to contain my feelings. I lunge for him on the bed, drowning him with kisses as I sit astride him. He's hard under me, would barely have to push up at all to disappear inside me. I could do it myself if I wanted to. Swallow him up the way the house swallowed me earlier.

I could . . . I could.

But then I stop to look at him and he's giving me that steadfastly quiet look again as if to ask me the question neither of us will voice out loud. I hold his gaze but somehow I can't say yes or no. I'm mute.

We freeze on the bed like a paused movie scene. Garren's the first to move again. He spreads his palm gently across my pelvis and then drops his eyes, breaking the current between us. Then he's pulling away from me, forcing me to move too. I climb off him and sit back on the bed. Garren squeezes my thigh, like a gesture of reassurance. Then he's sweeping his clothes into his arms and padding out of the room naked. With the door ajar, I hear him on the stairs.

I reach for my T-shirt and huddle under the covers, working my way through everything that just happened. Garren didn't leave town after all. He's remembered our past and we just got closer than we've ever been but I don't know what it means. My mouth, and most of the rest of my body, is still tingling.

It takes me a while to cool down and get my head together. The clock radio reads 3:07 by the time I follow Garren downstairs. He's sitting in the candlelight listening to the radio with a mug of coffee in front of him. His feet are resting on the chair across from him and when I step into the kitchen in my T-shirt, Garren's eyes flicker. He looks sad again, confused.

I lean against the counter and ask, "Are you okay?"

"Not really." He peers down at his coffee. "I'm sorry."

"Sorry for what?" I don't want to start regretting what happened upstairs and I'm beginning to wish that I'd pulled on a pair of Paula's jeans before coming to check on him.

"Sorry that I didn't believe you," he says, raising his head to look at me. "Sorry that I left you there outside Lou's house. You've been right about everything all along."

I wish he'd never left me too but it's difficult for me to blame him. The truth sounds like science fiction. Not many people would believe it.

"Where did you go after you left?" I ask. "I thought you would've been far away from here by now."

Garren's frown is weighted with guilt. "There was no one else I could go to so I went to Janette and asked if she had any money she could give me. I told her that the cops were after me but that I couldn't tell her why. She was upset that I was leaving town and convinced me to spend the night. She snuck me in after her parents went to bed." He curves his hand around his coffee mug. "I was thinking about all the things you'd said when I fell asleep. I started to dream about them but it was so detailed. Too detailed to be a dream and when I woke up I kept on remembering. Everything. My whole life until the time the SecRos took me and my mom."

"Did they explain what was happening? What they were going to do to you?" Knowing how we were sent back won't change our circumstances but I can't stop wondering about it. I'm a person out of sync with the world around me. Somehow I need to make sense of it.

"It happened fast," he says. "I think my mom may have known more but she just said we were being evacuated."

"And your other mother, do you think she's still back there?" The physicist. I wonder why she wasn't sent back with Garren too.

"She was the one who arranged to have us taken so I

guess she must be. Like your dad. Unless you think they're somewhere else?"

"Given my dad's position, he probably felt he had a responsibility to stay but I don't know, maybe he could be somewhere else." Some other time? I know Garren's not going to like this next part but he's not going to change my mind either. "I'm going to talk to someone tomorrow who might know more. A woman who's been pretending to be old friends with my mom."

"Freya."

I didn't think it was possible for Garren's frown to get any more entrenched but I've just seen it happen.

He swipes his feet off the seat across from him and leans forward in his chair, the candlelight dancing frantically across his face. "Don't go. It's too big a risk. Haven't you taken enough of them lately?"

"We need more money. And I need answers. I need to know if the U.N.A. is still standing and whether my dad's alive. Don't you want to know the same about your mother?"

"Of course I do. But you can't trust this woman. She'll want them to *take you*, just like Henry did. Obviously they didn't want us to remember and now they have a damage control plan that we've been standing in the way of."

I pull at my T-shirt, stretching it long. "This is the last chance like that I'm going to take. If it starts to feel wrong I'll change my mind at the last minute. You know, pay attention to that early-warning system of mine that went off at

Henry's. And I saw something while we were at Lou's too. I just didn't know how to interpret it."

"What did you see at Lou's?" Garren asks.

"Me, upset." I hate having to admit it to him. "And now I know it was because you'd left."

"I'm sorry." Garren shakes his head. "I wish I could take it back."

There's no taking anything back. There never is. "What about Janette? What did you say to her when you were leaving?"

"She was asleep. I didn't have to say anything." He stares at the table, plants both his palms on top of it. "You probably won't believe it but I regretted leaving you like that almost right after I did it. I came back here before I went to Janette's, in case you'd come here. I didn't know where else to look for you."

He must've come and gone before I returned this afternoon. I was lost and then fell asleep on the subway. It took me longer to get here than it normally would've.

Garren's stopped talking and he tilts his head like he's hearing something I'm not.

"What is it?" I ask.

"This song." Garren motions to the radio. "The person I thought I was liked it. But now I don't know if the real me knew it back where we're from or if it's just down to some scientist's programming." He props his elbow up on the table and rests his head wearily in his hands. "There are too many memories clashing inside my head."

I move closer to the radio and listen to the music. It makes me feel strange too. Like stepping through time has done something to us that no one else will ever understand. It's a bit like that dream feeling of falling without ever hitting bottom mixed with a nostalgia for things that haven't happened yet.

I know this song. I know it because of Garren. We listen to it on his record player seventy-eight years from now. Will it happen that way again or will the new future be different?

"Patti Smith," I note. " 'Because the Night.' You always liked this. Maybe that's why they put it back into your head."

"You remember that about the song?" Garren's skin is flushed and damp. He pushes his chair away from the table and lowers his head close to his knees. "I feel like shit. I wish I didn't drink that coffee."

"I got sick earlier too," I tell him. "It must have something to do with remembering. Maybe the Bio-net can't deal with it."

"Maybe." Garren bites his lip. "My head's killing me."

"Go to bed. Sleep it off. I was out cold for hours. But you should be fine by tomorrow."

Garren stares up at me like even moving his head is a major challenge. "I'll go up to bed in a minute. Just promise me you won't meet this woman tomorrow. It's too dangerous."

"I have to go." If I'm caught, it won't be worth it and he'll be proven right but I need the missing pieces of the puzzle and Nancy has some of them. This is my final chance.

"If you go I'm going too," Garren says stubbornly.

I know how this works. He thinks that will make me back down and do what he wants.

"Earlier today you were fine with ditching me and now we're in this together to the death?" I scowl and stare past him. Neither of us has gone anywhere near the topic of what happened between us upstairs but I still feel it in the air along with the eerie sensation from the song.

"I wasn't fine with it." Garren raises his voice. "I thought you were losing it. Having some kind of break with reality. I thought you'd get us taken, ranting like that, looking for confirmation of something that sounded impossible." He mops his brow, drives his hands into his hair. "And the worst part was that for a couple of seconds I wondered if it *could* be true, not because I remembered anything about it but because you were so convincing. I thought if I didn't get away from you I'd end up as delusional as you were."

Suddenly Garren covers his mouth and leaps up from his chair. He stomps off in the direction of the main floor bathroom and leaves me alone in the kitchen listening to "Because the Night."

Before I was sent back here I'd never been sick in my life. In the future people don't really get ill. Not in the U.N.A. anyway. The flu my mom, Olivia and I had shortly after we reached Canada must not have been a flu at all but a physical reaction to traveling through time or an aftereffect of the wipe and cover. Remembering the truth about my past this afternoon made me feel horrible all over again. Garren's in that same state now and I feel sorry for him, almost maternal, on top of all the other weird things I'm feeling.

Two minutes later he shuffles back into the kitchen and stands in front of me like a shadow of his regular self. "You win," he says. "I have to sleep. At least tell me you won't go anywhere while I'm sleeping."

"I won't. Why don't you take the master bedroom? It's probably the most comfortable." Neither of us has slept in it yet. I guess it felt like a bigger intrusion into the Resniks' lives than sleeping in any of the other rooms but I think we're both well past worrying about that now.

A very fragile-looking Garren nods at me and goes off to sleep in the master bedroom like I suggested. I return to the spare room, feeling wide awake. Despite that, soon I'm asleep, dreaming about Latham, Garren and Kinnari. We're sitting in a semicircle in Garren's old bedroom, the four of us in lounge chairs like the one I sat in at Lou Bianchi's.

A Hendris song is playing and I look over at Latham and say, "I never really forgot you, you know. You were always there . . . this feeling in my head that I couldn't explain."

"I know," Latham says. "You don't have to worry about me anymore, Freya. I'm fine."

"What about Dad?" I ask.

Latham smiles. "I thought you were going to hate him forever."

I thought so too. I meant it at the time. "I thought he was killing you. That it was his fault."

"And now you know better—that it wasn't anyone's

fault," Latham surmises. "But anyway, don't worry about him either. He'd just want you to focus on yourself now, focus on getting where you want to go."

"Does that mean you think that I shouldn't go tomorrow?" To meet Nancy, I mean, but I can see that Latham already understands that. It's so good to see him, even though I know it's only a dream. It's like there's a part of him that still exists, a part that I dragged back with me seventy-eight years in time.

"You'd know the answer to that better than I do," Latham says. "You're the one who can see things. It's not like you'd listen to me anyway, is it?"

"Maybe," I answer.

Garren's sighing from his chair, making a sour face. "No, you wouldn't."

With that I wake up in the sunlight to the sound of a door closing down the hall. *Garren.* I should check on him, make sure he's okay. I get out of bed and head for the master bedroom. The door's closed and I hesitate before grabbing the knob and twisting.

Garren's sitting up in the queen-size bed, shirtless, swigging from a tall glass of water. I stand blinking in the doorway, memories from last night in the spare room streaming through my mind.

"Hey," I say, moving slowly towards him. "How're you feeling?"

"Better," he tells me. "Thirsty."

"I was too afterwards. Let me get you another glass of water."

"Thanks." Garren holds out his freshly emptied glass.

I take it and then motion to the walk-in closet, which I disappear inside without further explanation. Paula's entire wardrobe is draped neatly on hangers and it only takes me a couple of seconds to locate a pair of her jeans to throw on. I pick out one of her sweaters too. Everything's slightly too tight, too short and overall too small on me but it's better than continuing to walk around in front of Garren in Mr. Resnik's T-shirt.

I don't take another look at Garren before leaving the room in my new clothes. Because I keenly remember the unquenchable thirst I felt yesterday, I not only refill his glass but bring him a second, both of them full to the brim with ice water.

"You're a lifesaver," Garren says when I put down both glasses on the bedside table next to him.

I smile. "That's a really 1985 thing to say."

Garren snaps up one of the glasses and drains half of it before smiling back. "Yeah, I guess it is. It's still all there in my head, those eighteen years' worth of fake memories. The scientists did a good job." He takes another sip of water. "But I remember better now. Better than last night, I mean. A lot of things were jumbled up in my head, like with the song."

"I'm glad you're feeling better." I try not to stare at him too fixedly. It'd be easier if he were wearing a shirt.

I pivot to leave the room and Garren says to my back, "Can you stay a couple of minutes?"

There are hours yet before I have to leave to meet Nancy. My bag's still packed. The only things I really have to do before I leave are shower and dry my hair.

I turn and step closer to the bed, edge my way around it and sit cross-legged on the farthest corner from Garren. "I'm still going later, you know."

"We can get the money some other way," he says.

"Maybe, but no one else is going to have the answers to my questions."

Garren sets down his water, a bottomless frown sinking into his face just like it did last night in the kitchen. "She won't tell you anything. It'll be like with Doctor Byrne all over again."

"But Doctor Byrne didn't try to take us," I remind him. "We weren't in any danger from him." I've spent a lot of time with Nancy. I can't really believe she'd want to hurt me either. She said she couldn't tell me anything but that must have been a lie. Since she knows who my father is she must know other things, like how we got back here. For all I know she might be able to get a message to my father and make them change their plans about me and Garren.

The covers are twisted around Garren's lower legs and he tugs on them as he sits back in bed. "I was serious last night. If you go, I'm coming with you."

"I made that decision for myself when you weren't around. The only person I want to risk here is me."

"Well, it's not just you anymore," he says. "We *are* in this together. I shouldn't have left you yesterday and I'm not letting you leave without me today."

"I could rush out into the street this second," I tell him. "It'd take you a minute to throw your clothes on and follow me. I could be gone in that time." I'm angrier than I thought I was. I was so happy to see Garren last night but clearly I haven't forgotten about him ditching me in the first place.

"Maybe I wouldn't bother with my clothes," Garren says, sounding angry too. "I think you'd have a rough time trying to go unnoticed with a half-naked guy chasing after you through the snow."

I suck my teeth and stare at my ankles.

"*Try me,*" Garren adds.

I raise my head to look at him. Our eyes lock. He's staring at me with an intensity that makes me wonder if he seriously wants me to do it just so he has the chance to prove himself. I stare stonily back, not giving him the opportunity, not giving him anything.

Finally he reaches for his water. Swallows what's left in his glass and moves on to the second.

Then his eyes find me again, the challenge gone from them. "Are you okay?" he asks.

"You're the one who's sick. I've been fine since last night."

"I don't mean that. I mean . . . *last night*." His tone is tentative. He focuses on my ankles like I was seconds earlier.

"Last night you were in shock," I say evenly. "We both were."

"We were," he agrees. "That doesn't mean you were okay with it . . . or not okay with it."

I don't really want to talk about this now. We have more important things to think about. But since he's brought it up I can't stop myself from asking, "Why did you stop?"

Garren pulls his knees up towards him under the sheets and folds his arms around them. "I thought . . . it was really fast. Maybe too fast for you. And I wasn't sure about the Bio-net."

"The Bio-net," I repeat. "What about it?"

Garren's green eyes won't let go of me. "I didn't know whether they'd turned parts of it off before sending us back. Like fertility controls."

That never occurred to me. It should've but it didn't. I had a period a couple of weeks ago. Maybe that means I could get pregnant like any other 1985 girl.

I look away as I say, "I think you're right—I think they're off." I adjust my posture so that it mirrors his and try to put some distance between us and the topic. "My mother and Olivia don't remember where we're really from. I can tell. The wipe and cover worked on them."

"On my mother too," Garren says. "She's mourning a person we never even knew. A stranger. Someone the scientists slotted into our memories. They treated our minds like playgrounds."

"No one should have that kind of power. They tried to erase my brother and your sister."

"Tried," Garren repeats, respect blazing in his eyes. "You were too smart for them."

I don't think it's about being smart but I bet my premonitions have something to do with it. And I'm beginning to think loss plays into the persistence of memory too. Fresh grief can't be an easy thing to write over. There was some part of me that never forgot Latham, like I told him in my dream. I only needed a push to break through. It was probably the same for Garren; it just took a little longer.

"So all that aside, is being grounded all the time everything you hoped it would be?" I ask.

Garren smiles a little. "I wouldn't say that exactly. I never pictured being back in 1985, living on instant coffee and food that tastes like it's made of plastic."

"And you probably didn't picture running for your life," I say. "Living by candlelight and wearing someone else's clothes."

"That's kinda put a damper on the fun, yeah." Garren's grin brightens. It reminds me of the one he gave me in the backyard the day of Kinnari's birthday party. "It's so different here," he continues. "No eco-refugees. No Ros policing everyone. No welfare camps—all the jobs done by real people. The people here still travel to other countries. Fly, even."

Most of the planes in the future are pieces of DefRo

weaponry, not passenger jets. The commercial airline industry is in ruins. "No gushi," I add. "No instant communication."

"The telephone," Garren points out. "And broadcast news on the TV."

The telephone. I smile automatically at the suggestion. The telephone is primitive compared to what we grew up with. You can't even see who you're talking to. And back here all the communication and entertainment devices are stationary and external. Once, ours were part of us. Now we're without. I've had over a month to get used to it but it's an odd feeling, being disconnected this way. Cut off from something that doesn't exist yet.

I reach out and curve my fingers around my toes, feeling the future stretch out ahead of me, too far to reach. "People here get sick all the time. They die from things we've cured. But they seem . . . I don't know . . . less jaded, less suspicious." Maybe because they haven't seen how things turned out.

"And they live their lives for real," Garren says. "Not spend half of them hiding in their own heads."

I release my hold on my foot to point at him. "Aha, you do love it here!"

I watch Garren's grin bloom again. "You have to admit that it has its good points." He pauses, his expression turning sheepish. "So you're not mad at me?"

I thought we'd gotten clear of the subject and it takes me several seconds to catch up and say, "For leaving yesterday, yeah. But not for what happened last night." That's the truth of it but it's not the whole truth. "Things are already complicated enough, though. I think it's better if we don't complicate them more."

Garren nods thoughtfully.

I uncross my legs and begin to get up. "I should jump in the shower and start getting ready."

Garren reaches across the bed to grab my arm. "Wait a second."

"What?" My skin begins to break out in invisible goose bumps.

"Just . . . that makes sense—we need to focus on this meeting and then on getting out of here. But I don't want you to think last night was only because of the shock." He releases my arm but my skin's still singing where he touched me.

I'm quiet. My throat's stinging like it was last night in the spare room. "For me either," I admit. "But still . . ."

"But still," he repeats, his green eyes sticking to me like Krazy Glue. "I know."

I tear my gaze away from him and head for the shower.

TWENTY

When I slip out of the bathroom twenty minutes later, Garren, in Mr. Resnik's borrowed jeans and a black shirt, intercepts me in the hall. "We have to leave early," he tells me. "There's something I want to do before this meeting, to even up our odds a little."

"What?" I ask, my wet hair piled up on my head under one of the Resniks' bath towels. We won't be coming back here again and the thought of leaving even a little sooner than expected is a mental adjustment.

"Janette's dad has a gun. No one should be home now. We can go in through the back door, just like we did here."

"You know where he keeps the gun? Maybe it's locked up." I intended to grab the sharpest knife from the kitchen and bring it with me as protection when we left but a gun would be better. I don't want to hurt anyone but if they find us and try to take us . . .

"She said he keeps it in the nightstand beside the bed,"

Garren says. "There's a lock on the drawer but how hard can that be to break?"

"She told you all that?"

"Last week before all this happened. Her grandfather gave it to her dad when they moved to the city a few years ago." Garren slouches slightly but his eyes are steely. "I hate to do this to her but those guys who showed up at Henry's had guns."

"I can't argue with that. Okay, just give me a chance to dry my hair and finish getting ready."

While I'm doing that, Garren jumps into the shower himself. Then I take a thorough look around the house, trying to return the rooms to the state we found them in as much as possible. I can imagine how creeped out the Resniks would feel if they knew strangers were sleeping here and using it as a base. With the beds made maybe they won't have to know and will just think it was a basic robbery.

I'm in the middle of drying the glasses I brought Garren earlier when he steps into the kitchen. He peeks at what's left in the fridge and cupboards and then leans against the counter. "Did you eat anything?" he asks.

"I was thinking about having the spaghetti. Do you think there's time?"

"If we're fast." Garren puts a hand to his stomach. "I'm starving."

He dives back into the cupboard for the spaghetti sauce and soon we're eating it over undercooked pasta (we're both too impatient to wait long). We do the dishes again and double-check the contents of the bags we'll be bringing with us. This time I've remembered a toothbrush, toothpaste, deodorant and soap. I take one of the bigger knives from the knife block and stuff it into my bag too.

After checking that the coast is clear, we leave by the front door, same as we always have, me back in my Doc Martens knowing they'd win a footrace against Paula's pinchy boots any day. Garren guides us east towards Janette's house at the other end of Cranbrooke Avenue. There's no car in the driveway and both her neighbors' driveways are also empty. We jump the fence into the backyard, dropping our bags over first. Garren says he wishes he'd thought to steal a set of keys when he was inside the house last night.

He kicks in the door easily enough anyway. We race through Janette's house and up to the second floor. "Money," I say suddenly. "We should check for money while we're here."

"Yeah." Regret drags at Garren's jaw. "I'll get the gun. You take whatever cash you can find."

I start in the master bedroom where he immediately goes to work on the nightstand with a hammer and screwdriver that he liberated from the Resnik house. I rifle through dresser drawers and then the closet, scanning for cash. There's a camera bag on the top shelf of the closet, next to a travel iron and hot water bottle. I pull them all down hoping to find a secret stash of twenty-dollar bills behind them.

"Bullets!" I yell to Garren. The packaging makes them

look almost like office supplies or soap for men. For a second I'm horrified.

But it could come down to us or them. I jump up and grab the ammunition.

"I've got the gun," Garren shouts back. "Let's go!"

I jam the box of bullets into my coat pocket and loop my bag back over my shoulder. We hurry into the hall where the noise of a door opening turns us both to stone. *He said no one would be home.* Garren motions back to the bedroom. I take a silent step backwards and then another. Garren follows. The floorboards groan underneath him.

He doesn't waste a moment. He surges forward, charging along the hall and downstairs with the gun in his right hand. I'm right behind him but I can't see anything yet. The foyer, downstairs hallway and living room are all empty.

Then we reach the kitchen. The woman who must be Janette's mother is standing stock-still with the telephone in her hand. Garren has frozen in front of me too. I step out from behind him, grab the telephone receiver out of her hand and hang up with a slam.

"What are you doing?" she asks in a shaky voice. "What do you want?"

Garren hesitates.

Since I've never met Janette's mother, acting the part of a criminal for her comes easier to me. "Give us your car keys. Quick." I glance at her purse on the counter. "Are they in there?"

She nods, her face a study in tension and her eyes cling-ing to the gun in Garren's hand.

"Hand them over," I command. "Any cash you have too."

She reaches cautiously for her purse, jerks the zipper open and plucks out her keys. She holds them out to me. Then the money from her wallet. I can see at a glance that it's only twenty-seven dollars.

Garren springs to life, ripping the phone from the wall and then stuffing the phone cord into one of his pockets. "Now you're going to go down to the basement and stay there until we're gone," he orders.

Janette's mother flinches. She edges past us and out of the kitchen. We follow her to a doorway. She glances back at us before reaching for the doorknob. We stand at the top of the stairs and watch her descend into the basement. Cool air wafts up to meet us.

I close the door behind her. Garren drags a kitchen chair into the hallway and jams it under the doorknob. "It won't hold her long," he says. "Let's go."

We rush out of the house. Since I'm the one with the car keys in my hand, I head for the driver's seat. They programmed me with driving memories. I should be able to do this.

I lean over to unlock the passenger door and Garren hops in next to me and tosses his bags into the backseat. I slide the key Janette's mother gave me into the ignition. Twist it and pump the gas pedal. The engine starts. So far so good. I slide into reverse, relieved that Janette's mom has an automatic.

My implanted memories of driving in New Zealand involve shifting gears but this should be easier. I back out of the driveway like I've done it a thousand times before, but once we hit Yonge Street I'm so focused on obeying traffic signals and making sure not to run anything over that I don't have any spare brain power for directions.

"Where am I going?" I ask Garren as we zip down Yonge Street.

He's busy ejecting the gun magazine. "Bullets," he prompts.

The box is jutting out of my pocket and I reach for it and then hand the box over. "Do you know what you're doing with that?"

"A little. I had a friend back in Billings who was into old weapons like this." He pauses to look over at me. "Sounds weird, I know. He took me to a shooting range once."

"I didn't know there were any shooting ranges left."

"Not many," Garren says.

I smirk. "All you grounded people are crazy for old things, huh." The car behind me honks for no reason that I can see. Garren glances up to catch me staring into my rearview mirror.

"You're doing fine," he says. "The guy's just an asshole."

"Directions," I remind him. "Where are we going?"

"It's a straight run down Yonge Street to Dundas but we should probably ditch the car somewhere and switch to the subway. Once she calls the cops they'll be looking for the car."

We dump the car a block from Eglinton Avenue, about ten feet from a NO PARKING sign. Garren has the gun down the back of his jeans and the box of bullets tucked into the satchel he's carrying on his back. We walk briskly, rather than run, in the direction of the subway so as not to call attention to ourselves. I'm ultra-conscious of the knife in my bag and the lethal weapon in Garren's possession. We're bona fide criminals now.

"That must've been really weird for you with Janette's mom," I say.

"I never met her mom before," Garren tells me, his breath visible in the air. "Just her brother, but I could see the family resemblance in her mother. She and Janette have the same eyes." I don't specifically remember Janette's eyes, just her strawberry-blond hair and that she was pretty. I watch Garren's eyebrows pull together as he adds, "Maybe we'll get lucky and she'll give a really shitty description. Otherwise, if Janette puts it all together we could be in trouble. My photo could be flashed all over the news."

"The cops were looking for us before this anyway," I point out.

"And here you still want to risk hitting this major downtown shopping mall." Garren shakes his head. "We should just leave Toronto right now. Forget meeting your mom's friend."

"I won't blame you if you do." Then I wouldn't have to worry about him.

But Garren's silence makes his decision clear.

"I've been thinking you shouldn't be with me when I meet her," I add. "Maybe just stick close enough to watch. That way, if *they're* coming you'll have an advance view."

"And cover you?" Garren suggests, like we're in a TV cop show.

"Right." I picture me and Nancy meeting surrounded by books. I concentrate hard and the layout of the store begins to take shape in my mind. Unfortunately, there's nothing beyond that. No sense of danger and no feeling of well-being or satisfaction either.

I rub my eyes as I turn towards Garren.

"Anything?" he asks. "What can you see?"

"Just the bookstore itself so far."

We descend into the subway where I imagine people are staring suspiciously our way. Garren keeps his gaze pointed at the floor space between his feet, like he's giving me room to think and hopefully see something that will help us. The bookstore, the bookstore, the bookstore. That's all I see. Shelves full of paperbacks. The sleeves of Paula Resnik's coat as I approach the magazine stand.

I break away from the vision and graze Garren's knee. "I'm still not getting much. Maybe it's too early."

"I wish you weren't going to do this," he says.

"I know. And I hope I don't regret it. But if there's more to know, I have to hear it. This could be our last chance for our entire lives."

Garren nods tiredly. "I'll be watching you. If you have a premonition about being in danger, don't wait. Get out of there right away."

We arrive at the Eaton Centre stop early and wander the nearby PATH, a network of pedestrian tunnels filled with shops and services that link various parts of the city. I wasn't aware of its existence before and Garren says he's never been down there himself but he figures we're less likely to be spotted there than wandering the mall or out on the street.

Most of the people we pass on the PATH look like office workers and pay little attention to us but I'm increasingly nervous and just want to get my meeting with Nancy over with. At seven minutes to twelve Garren and I part company across the street from the Yonge and Dundas entrance to the Eaton Centre. He whispers in my ear that he'll be right behind me.

I feel numb as I stride through the shopping center, scanning for the bookstore. Garren told me it was on the top shopping level, right in the middle of the mall. As soon as I spot it another image comes into sharp focus in my mind, one of a man my father's age. I'm walking through the mall with him, listening intently to whatever he's telling me. Nancy's nowhere to be seen.

I snap back to the present and survey the bookstore, looking for Nancy or the man from my vision. Bookstore employees aside, the only person in the store is a gray-haired lady thumbing through a slim hardcover.

As I step inside the store someone touches my back. "Freya?"

I twirl to face Nancy. She has an envelope in her hand and thrusts it towards me. "This is for you," she says. "I'm sorry it couldn't be more but I hope it will help."

I slip the envelope down into one of my front pockets. "Nancy, you have to tell me what you know. How we got here. What's happening at home. Whether the U.N.A. has fallen."

Nancy's top lip quivers. "I told you I couldn't discuss any of that. It's out of my hands."

"What about my mom? How is she? What's Henry been telling her?"

Nancy glances worriedly over her shoulder before returning her attention to me. "You can guess how she is but there's nothing you can do about it. Look, Freya, this place is too exposed. You should go now."

"The Toxo—what happened?" I can't let her disappear without a word about what's happened to the world I'm from.

"No matter how you ask, I can't say anything about any of it. I'm sorry. I really am."

I clutch her arm, feeling wild. "I'm not going to let you go until you tell me. Do you understand?"

To be thrust out of my own time and dropped down in the past without warning. Minus a brother. Minus a father. Now minus a mother too. Forced to run for my life. I deserve to know *why*. I deserve more than whatever amount of money is inside the envelope she gave me.

"I think that's a conversation you and I should have

instead," a clipped male voice declares. The man from my vision, in a gray suit and matching vest, pries my fingers from Nancy's arm. "I'll take it from here," he tells her.

"Believe me, I didn't know," Nancy says with a pained expression. "I'm sorry, Freya." She scurries away without another look. My gaze follows her out into the mall but I don't have enough time to search out Garren. I can only hope that he'll continue to remain hidden because I can't read the man's intentions yet.

"Who are you?" I demand.

"We've never met. I think we should leave the store before we attract too much attention." He motions to one of the bookstore employees who is staring at us from behind the cash register across the room with a decisive frown. "I don't think they liked the look of you grabbing Nancy."

"I'm not going anywhere until you tell me who you are," I insist.

"The police could be here in a few minutes if that's what you'd like," the man says dispassionately.

"I can't believe that's what you'd want yourself."

He smiles tepidly. "All right, Freya. If you want to play it that way, it's fine. We'll have you in the end anyway. I think you know that."

He's so sure of himself that my stomach drops. I step slowly out of the store with the man and pause in the hallway. There are too many people. Surely he wouldn't want to cause a scene.

"I'm not leaving here with you," I tell him. The words are

barely out and I'm flashing headlong into the future. Along the hallway other suited men are waiting for us, through the crowd. As I near them a shot rings out. I spin around, searching frantically for Garren. *We have to get away.*

The premonition cuts to black. I don't know how this will end.

"It's either us or the police," the man says. "We can't afford to let you go."

"Why?" I lean over the railing and stare at the bustling levels of shopping mall beneath us.

The man stands next to me, his posture stiff. "Tell me, how did you remember?"

"Why should I tell you that? Why shouldn't I just throw myself over the railing right now? That way no one gets me. Not you and not the police."

The man rests his arms on top of the railing, his chin drooping. "We're not going to kill you, Freya. You just can't continue to remember." He raises a finger and points to the left and then the right. "They're waiting for you in either direction. There's no escaping this. But I need to know everything I can about how you remembered."

"What happens if I don't tell you?" I imagine the worst torture. Broken bones and severed limbs. My blood runs cold.

"Nothing as dramatic as what you're probably thinking. But we need to do the wipe and cover again and that will be dangerous in itself. We don't have the proper equipment here to perform as thorough a job as they thought they'd done back in the U.N.A. It might be a bit rudimentary and leave you a different person than you could've been." He sounds apologetic. "If you tell me what you know about how you remembered in the first place it might help us to do a better job."

"You're going to butcher my mind." *A different person than I could've been*. That's like a death of its own. I think of the wipe-and-cover victims I've seen on the Dailies, their personalities rubbed out and replaced with devotion to the state. That's the kind of powerful result a W + C is capable of, when they can control it. Uncontrolled, it seems that anything could happen. At best, I'd forget the truth—have my brother, my father and my real past stolen from me a second time. At worst, I could come out of this a vegetable, forever damaged. And not just me . . . If they get Garren I'll never forgive myself.

But I wouldn't remember anyway. All of this would be gone.

That's what I first sensed at Henry's but had no name for—the things they would take from me. My memories and maybe more, the very essence of who I am.

I gaze down at the miniature shoppers below me, going about their business, oblivious to the decision I'm facing. It would be worth it to jump and save Garren, save the person I am now.

"You don't want to do that," the man admonishes. "It's not what we want either. We're not the bad guys, Freya. We *wanted* to help. We've helped other people like you and your family but there's a more important aim. Global survival."

"What do you mean?" I lift my head. "How is any of this possible?"

"You know about the wipe and covers," the man says quietly. "We've seen some that have taken quite a toll on young people—the neurological immaturity increases the risks—but I've only heard of one person who remembered his past after a wipe. He was a seventeen-year-old identical twin back in the U.N.A. and his twin hadn't been wiped."

"So I'm a scientific oddity." If I can keep the man talking long enough maybe another vision will stream through my mind and help me decide what to do.

The man nods pensively. "You want to share your thoughts on that?"

"How about you tell me more first. You're the only person I've come across who hasn't told me they can't talk about it."

"It's true. The others can't talk about it. It's a programmed Bio-net fail-safe. The second they begin to transmit information about the future and what we're doing here, a wipe sequence is triggered."

"Why?" I glance to the left, at the Special Forces–type duo in the distance who are probably itching to charge over here and haul me away if only I wasn't in such a public place. They're as human as I am but I know they'll do whatever they have to in order to take me, the same as the SecRos would've.

"Can you imagine the trouble it would cause in the present if it was known there were people who'd been sent back from the future living among the population? News of future environmental instability—and now the plague—could potentially be enough to significantly destabilize this society." The man looks at me from the corner of his eye. "It's the guardians' job, people like Nancy Bolton, to make sure those sent back settle in successfully. We couldn't reasonably expect that everyone who has come across time would be capable of remaining quiet about their experiences. Besides, the wipe and cover makes the adjustment easier—for most people anyway."

In the secret sliver of my mind's eye that I suspect helped me remember in the first place I see Garren and me running. Alive. Intact. Running scared through Toronto streets. There's still a chance for us. The vision proves there must be.

"What did you mean by a more important aim?" I ask, stalling. Garren must be waiting too. There are too many of them, too far apart. Five of them that I can see, including the man next to me. Even if I could get to my knife in time, there's no chance I could escape them all.

"Environmental legislation," he replies. "We waited too long last time. Global warming has been catastrophic for the entire planet. We have a chance to slow its pace. There are several other units like us in the United States, infiltrating the political system there, poised to make the changes we need that hopefully will have a profound influence on policies worldwide."

"How long has this been going on?"

"In the United States, ten years. We've had a few key people up here in Canada since then too, as support resources, but it wasn't until the nuclear exchange between Pakistan and India that a select group of very important people in the U.N.A. who were aware of the project began to wonder if life, even in the U.N.A., would soon be doomed. So we began a second phase of the project, settling a limited number of well-connected U.N.A. civilians up here in southern Ontario." The man strokes his nose and pauses. "With the plague outbreak there were requests for immediate resettlement, including that of you and your mother. I tell you all this so you know that none of this is being done with the intention of hurting you. We just have too much to protect. If this plays out the way we hope, we'll be changing history. Everyone will be better off. Even you."

Future me. The person who'll be born sixty-two years from now.

"I'd like you to try to understand, Freya. And I'd like it if we could start walking now."

I cast a look ahead of me. There are still two security types beyond us and two behind.

"You think I should understand?" I say as I take a series of snail-paced steps in the direction the man's indicating. "You think I should approve of the big picture enough that I won't blame you for what you're planning to do to me."

"I'd like that," he replies. "I realize it might not be realistic. Especially for someone your age."

I bristle at the fact that generations before me ruined the planet but that I'm expected to willingly sacrifice myself. "I could've already told someone what I know if I'd wanted to. You could let me go. I won't say anything. I'll just disappear."

"That's not going to happen, Freya, but I'm going to do everything I can to help you, I promise. I need to know anything you can tell me about remembering. It's important. Not just for you but for anyone else sent back."

"Anyone else?" I've been walking as slowly as humanly possible and now I stop entirely. "You mean they're still sending people back? The U.N.A. is still out there?"

"Some of it is."

Some. "My father?"

The man nods impatiently. "Last I heard, yes. The SecRos have helped slow the spread of Toxo but there's still no cure. The survivors have been falling back to the north, your father and President Ortega with them."

So there's still hope, even for those left behind. My heart leaps at the knowledge that my father's still alive. "Can we get back again? How did we get here?"

"Keep going, please." The man cups my elbow and guides me forward. I wrench my arm away from him but continue to walk beside him. "There's no returning to the future and you wouldn't want to be there now even if it were possible, believe me. Tell me what you know about remembering and I'll explain."

I shoot him a look of angry disbelief.

"I'm not in the habit of lying," the man says.

"I don't even know who you are," I snap.

"My name doesn't matter but I'm a *director*. There are only a handful of us on either side of the border. I came here today to make sure this was handled properly. You're important to us. I want you to know that. We want to make sure this doesn't happen to anyone else. There's also the matter of your friend Garren. Has he remembered too?"

I shake my head. "He doesn't know what's going on. I kept telling him that I felt like I knew him, even before my memories really returned. He thought I was crazy. I haven't seen him in days. He thinks this is all some diplomatic conspiracy involving the murders of our fathers. You've scared him off. He's gone."

"We'll find him too," the man says.

"But he doesn't remember. He doesn't *need* a wipe. You could just let him go. There's nothing he could tell anyone, even if he wanted to."

"So you say but you might lie for him," the man declares.

"I might but I'm not. I don't have to." The gap between us and the director's allies is shrinking. Two of them are standing in front of the Eaton's department store at the north end of the shopping mall, eyeing us up. I'm running out of time and I stop again. "I'll tell you why I think the W and C didn't work—I'm not your average person."

The director's so intent on what I'm about to say that he doesn't berate me for stopping.

"I have a kind of second sight," I admit. "Since I was very young."

"That wasn't in your file," the director says.

"It wouldn't be. I hid it from my parents. But it's the only thing I can think of that would interfere with the wipe and cover. I sensed there was something wrong from the moment I started to physically recover from the journey here. The feeling got stronger when I ran into Garren but I didn't have a real breakthrough until I went to a hypnotherapist."

The director squints, unhappiness spreading across his face and creeping into the slope of his shoulders. "Hypnotherapy shouldn't have had any impact. Your procedure was performed faster than usual because of the Toxo threat but the nanites neutralized the neurons associated with your old memories." He straightens his spine, twin lines of concentration forming between his eyebrows. "You could be right about the link with your second sight. I don't understand the nature of the relationship between the two offhand but we'll investigate that."

I keep my theory about the role grief played in remembering to myself. "You said you'd tell me how we got back here," I prompt.

"So I did. We don't have time to cover the extensive background information now. It will have to suffice for me to say that our presence here is thanks to a discovery we call the Nipigon Chute. In 2044 a U.N.A. archivist uncovered a case study about an American man named Victor Soto in an Australian mental hospital in 1963. The man claimed to have fallen out of a boat on Lake Nipigon in northwestern Ontario in 2041. His doctors performed electric shock therapy until they considered him cured and he'd come to look upon his experience as a delusion."

My head's reeling but I don't have time for awe. I need to stay focused.

"But he knew too much about the future for it to be a fiction," the director continues. "And the U.N.A. began researching Lake Nipigon itself. Eventually we learned the exact location of the phenomenon. We've still barely scratched the surface in beginning to understand it but we believe the Nipigon phenomenon is as natural as gravity. It's possible there are more of its kind on the planet—so far undetected—and that others who were intellectually ahead of their time at various points in history may have traveled through similar chutes.

"That's only theoretical as this point but one thing we do know is that the Nipigon Chute is strictly a one-way journey through time. A jump back seventy-eight years, seven months and eleven days into the past with the physical end point of the journey being a large salt lake in Western Australia, Lake Mackay. Victor Soto was lucky to have arrived in Lake Mackay after heavy rain; otherwise he would've suffocated in the salt and none of us would have been aware of the amazing opportunity nature seems to have bestowed on us."

The director tilts his head, his eyes shining with reverence. "It's incredible, isn't it? A second chance for the entire world."

It is incredible; there's no denying it. The place and time I'm from desperately needs another chance. No wonder the director wants to make sure I forget. We thought there were no more real mysteries left on earth, that the only major changes we'd see would be made through our own technologies. I'm speechless.

But if the director thinks this will be enough to make me give in and go with him, he's wrong. I want my second chance in the here and now, not reserved for some future Freya that may never be born, depending on how history is rewritten. And I want a second chance for Garren too. I want us to stand on the shores of the Pacific Ocean and be free.

"How many of us are back here?" I ask, stalling again.

"I think I've satisfied enough of your curiosity," the director replies. "We have to go, Freya."

I can't put him off a second longer. The future's only steps away and I begin walking, closing the distance between us and the security men. My mind is absolutely clear. No new visions. I can't wait anymore. I wasn't a foot nearer than this when I heard the shot in my premonition.

I leap ahead of the director, my weight on my bent left leg to the rear of me. In one fluid action I lift the knee of my right leg and whip out my right foot, kicking into the director's abdomen with the ball of my Doc Martens boot.

I've never done anything like this outside of gushi. I'm stunned that in real life the action works almost as well.

As the power behind my strike propels him backwards into the air, a single gunshot rings out. Then another. Roughly thirty feet ahead of me, both security men buckle.

One of them's taken a shot to the thigh and the other to the hand. I scan desperately for Garren as I sprint forward and to the right, towards the set of doors that will dump me onto Yonge Street with the pedestrian crowds.

The two security men in my wake have raised their weapons and are running after me. As I begin to turn again I catch sight of Garren behind me. He's pointing his gun at one of them, yelling at me to *go*.

The security guy nearest me, the one with the hand wound, is reaching for his weapon with his good hand. I careen towards him and launch my right foot solidly at his groin. He crumples to the floor, bullets flying around us. My eyes zoom back to Garren. He's almost made it.

"*Go!*" he shouts again.

I watch a bullet rip into his sleeve, midway between his elbow and shoulder. His hand flies to the point of entry but he barely slows down. Then he's with me and we're tearing out the door and onto the sidewalk, directly into the midst of a group of chanting Hare Krishnas.

Their pace slackens, a vision of halting orange confusion, but the chanting doesn't stop.

"*Hare Krishna, Hare Krishna, Krishna Krishna, Hare Hare, Hare Rama, Hare Rama, Rama Rama, Hare Hare.*"

I fight my way through a sea of orange robes, Garren next to me, doing the same. We run south to Queen Street, the sound of the bullets and the Krishna chanting ringing in my ears. I don't know how close the director's men are. I don't know where we're going. We just run and run and run, not stopping for traffic lights, not glancing over our shoulders to gauge the position of the men who are chasing us.

"In here," Garren cries, pointing at the revolving door to Simpson's department store. The store's enormous and occupies an entire city block. We race inside and weave through the shoppers, exiting again on Bay Street where my eyes land on a taxi across the street. I wave my hand like someone in danger of drowning as I shout, "Taxi! Taxi!"

The driver pulls over for us and waits. The pedestrian symbols flash a caution sign, telling us we're about to lose the right of way. Garren and I speed across the walkway. On the other side, with the taxi, I hazard a quick look back across the traffic and see the director and one of his men exiting the department store.

Our eyes lock. The director points at me as I throw myself into the cab, Garren a second behind me.

"Start moving!" Garren shouts.

"Where to?" the driver asks, eyeing us in the rearview mirror.

"South," Garren says. "We have to *hurry*."

We're cruising down Bay Street before the director and his security men have even made it across the street. I lean forward in my seat to study Garren's right arm where he was hit. He moves his left hand to cover the wound just as I open my mouth to ask how bad it is.

Garren flashes me a warning look, shifting his gaze to the driver.

I understand and stay quiet.

"If we keep going south we'll end up in the lake," the driver quips. "You want to give me a more specific destination?"

It's only then that I notice Garren doesn't have either of his bags. Mine's gone too. I don't know when I dropped it but the important thing now is Nancy's envelope. As Garren tells the driver that we want to catch up with the commuter GO train somewhere after Exhibition Station I dig into my pocket for it and peek inside at the collection of fifty-dollar bills. By my count there are twenty-two of them.

Eleven hundred dollars.

I'm not sure if Nancy was telling the truth about not knowing that she was followed today but the money will help. It will take us both all the way to Vancouver and give us something to live on while we look for work. We're still almost three thousand miles from where we want to be and seventy-eight years away from where we came from but I have the answers I was looking for and the single person in the world who I can trust is sitting next to me, injured but safe.

At this exact moment in 1985 it's the most I can hope for and I sit back in my seat and exhale for what feels like the first time since leaving Cranbrooke Avenue this morning.

TWENTY-ONE

After the taxi driver drops us off at Mimico Station, Garren disappears into the bathroom to examine his arm and I ask about the next commuter train from Toronto. The woman at the ticket counter tells me it's due in seven minutes and quotes a platform number.

I buy two tickets to Oakville and hover nervously around the men's room, hoping that our taxi driver doesn't listen to the news and doesn't suspect we had anything to do with the Eaton Centre shootings once he does inevitably hear of them. I won't be happy until we're moving again, putting miles between us and Toronto.

With two minutes to spare Garren emerges from the bathroom. I tell him that we need to get onto the platform in a hurry and hand him his ticket. "How's your arm?" I whisper as we veer towards the platform. His right sleeve is torn and wet where he must've washed the blood from it.

"The bullet barely grazed me," Garren says under his

breath. "But it's like a shaving cut—won't stop bleeding. I had to take off my socks and tie them around my arm."

I stare down at Garren's feet but his jeans are long enough to hide the fact that his feet are bare inside his shoes. I throw my arms impulsively around his waist and hug him close, overcome with relief that we're okay. His arms fold around me. We stand in a tight knot on the platform, neither of us saying a word until we hear the train's approach.

I release him and stand back, sinking my hands into my coat pockets. The train screeches into the station, Garren staring at me with his eyes full of questions. On the train to Oakville we choose the loneliest seats we can find and I tell him about the contents of the envelope and everything the director revealed to me.

"I couldn't ask about your mother still back in the U.N.A.," I say, knowing he'll be disappointed. "I told him I hadn't seen you in days, that you'd taken off somewhere on your own. But she must be with the survivors in the north." She was one of the top physicists. She'd have important connections.

"From what you've said I think she was probably one of the key people researching the chute," Garren tells me. "She was always taking trips to Ontario. She told us she couldn't talk about the project she was working on there but that must be how she had the influence to have my mom and I sent back." His eyes are dazed. *"Time travel.* It's insane. I know we're living proof of it but to think there's this thing that's natural to the planet that makes it possible, it changes everything, doesn't it? It's like when they used to think the world was flat or that the sun revolved around the earth. This is a different place than we thought it was."

That falling sensation overcomes me again. Forever falling. Never hitting solid ground. Down and down and down, tumbling weightless but dizzy.

"Everything feels different," I agree. "And the weird thing is that it's *always* been this way. We're just now catching up. It must've been so hard for your mom knowing something like that and not being able to share it."

The sudden sadness in Garren's face makes me reach for his hand. "She must be okay," I say again. "They need her."

Garren nods, his thumb running along the edge of my hand. "But they're both alone now. Both my mothers. They wouldn't have wanted that."

"They'd both want you alive. They did what they thought was best, like my parents did. No one could've known it would turn out this way."

Garren stares down the length of our near-empty car. There's an elderly couple sitting at the other end of it. The man has his eyes closed and the woman's staring dreamily out the window, although there's not much to see. Fields brimming with snow-covered weeds. Cookie-cutter subdivisions. Salty roadways.

"Maybe it'll turn out better this time," Garren says in a faraway voice. "And then it'll all have been worth it."

"You think they'll be able to change the course of U.S.

politics? Slow environmental change enough to make a real difference?" I hope so.

Garren smiles faintly. "We're going to be around to see what happens, aren't we?"

"We are." It's a strange thought. We're here for good now. Home is 1985.

"Shit, if we live long enough there might even be two versions of us kicking around for a couple of years," Garren says, his eyes coming to life.

We start tracing back our family trees, calculating which of our ancestors would be alive now, and come to the conclusion that some of our grandparents would currently be toddlers. Then we freak ourselves out with thoughts of disrupting the timeline, somehow leaving messages for our future selves.

"That must be how they communicate with 2063," Garren says. "Leave messages in newspapers or books for them to read. Bury them even."

"Near Lake Nipigon maybe. And they must have people working for them down in Australia too, dragging the people they've sent back from that salt lake in Western Australia."

"They must." Garren glances out the window and into the cold. "And I bet they send us through unconscious because there's a gap in my memory after being taken. The real memories only start up again in Sydney just before we flew back here."

"Same here. Who knows how many people they have

working for them? That's at least three different countries they have people stationed in. I bet they send us through in some kind of submarine. Otherwise, according to the director, we'd either be suffocated by the salt or, if the lake happened to be full, I guess we could drown."

It's crazy to imagine the scale of such an operation and I begin to worry that Vancouver isn't far enough away from their reach. If they want to find us so badly, what could possibly stand in their way?

I share my fears with Garren and suggest maybe we should think about leaving the continent once our trail has gone cold and we can get false identities and put our hands on enough money.

"Or go farther north," he says. "Hide out in the Yukon or the Northwest Territories." There are countless options ahead of us but I can't see which one is best. There are no hints from my second sight to help.

"But, you know, maybe once they figure out we're really not going to say anything they'll stop looking for us," Garren adds. "What happened at the Eaton Centre is the kind of visibility they wouldn't want." His hand lands on my thigh. "Obviously they didn't think you were going to be that much trouble today."

My lips twitch into a grin. "Or that you'd be there doing a James Bond impression."

We're both caught in an intensely bizarre intersection of emotions—giddy at being alive while still buried up to our necks in shock at our profound losses and the unbelievable situation we find ourselves in. I wish we had more time to sit still and process everything that's happened over the past two days. I feel like I can't get a grip on any of it and as Garren smiles back I realize I'd almost forgotten about the gun itself.

"Do you still have the gun on you?" I ask, my voice low.

"Yeah, but it's empty," he whispers. "Most of the bullets were in my bag. I dropped it when I had to start shooting. Do you think we should dump it somewhere?"

"Maybe." If the cops stop us, having it in our possession would be bad news. On the other hand, would dumping it be leaving a breadcrumb for the police or the director? And what if we find ourselves in a situation where having a gun could be the kind of threat that keeps us safe (in that case no one has to know it's not loaded).

We're still trying to decide what to do with it when we arrive in Oakville. In the station parking lot I spot a guy about my age in an Edmonton Oilers hat tapping ash from his cigarette to the pavement beneath his feet. I slow down and ask him if we're anywhere near a shopping center. Having left the bags behind there are things we need. And Garren's being stoic but I can tell by the way he's holding himself that his arm's sore. We have to get him some aspirin and real bandages.

The guy in the Oilers hat gives his cigarette another tap before raising his hand to point to the left of us. "Right across the street there, but be warned that it sucks. If you want a good mall you have to go that way." He shifts his hand to indicate the direction of the superior shopping center.

We head for the closer mall and as soon as we get inside Garren wants to make the research calls to figure out the fastest way to reach Parry Sound. It's safest to collect all the info over the phone so no one will be able to recognize us and match our faces to our travel plans. I make Garren sit down while I place the calls and commit the bus times to memory.

First, we'll catch a bus from Oakville to downtown Hamilton. The next one leaves from the station back across the street in about forty-five minutes. Hamilton's only about an hour outside of Toronto—a worrying proximity—but it's a city in its own right, one I remember Ms. Megeney referring to as Steel Town.

There are only two buses from Hamilton to Parry Sound every day—one leaves at five-thirty in the morning and the other at two in the afternoon. I plop down next to Garren and quote the information, both of us with gloomy faces because we were hoping to make it up to Parry Sound today and now we'll have to spend the night somewhere in Hamilton.

"We're lucky we have the money to do it," I say, trying to look on the bright side. "Let's go get you some aspirin."

We slip into Woolco—a discount department store—and pick out a backpack each, several changes of underwear and socks, toothbrushes, toothpaste, deodorant, a bar of soap, a hairbrush, hair dye, disposable razor blades, a couple of pairs of super-cheap jogging pants each, some tops, a sewing kit (to fix Garren's coat), aspirin, a package of large adhesive bandages, antiseptic ointment and two cans of soda. After paying for all that with Nancy's money I tell Garren I want to have a look at his arm. Ahead there's a unisex wheelchair access bathroom we could slip into and I'm worried that his injury is worse than he's letting on.

"There's no time," he says. "We have to get the bus tickets. Besides, I think it's better to leave the pressure on it for now."

The part of our Bio-net that promotes fast healing must be turned off, just like the fertility controls, otherwise Garren would already be starting to feel better. I watch him swallow three aspirin and chase them down with soda.

"Honestly, it's not that bad," he insists. "I'm just not used to anything hurting. You know how it was back there."

I do. We were surrounded by threats but cushioned by the Bio-net and gushi. In 2063 I never went a full day without disappearing into the gushi dreamworld. We were all specialists in emotionally anesthetizing ourselves and any physical pain was short-lived.

Anxiety curls under my skin as I realize all my old crutches are gone forever. I wonder, for a moment, how well someone from 1985 would adapt to life in 1907 if they were whisked seventy-eight years back in time without warning. Poor Victor Soto thinking he was insane with no one around to believe him or remind him of the world he was really from.

Garren and I return to the Oakville station where I buy

our bus tickets and the guy behind the ticket counter tries to flirt with me by asking what's so special about Hamilton that it's coaxing someone like me over there. I can't decide whether flirting back or shutting him down will make me more memorable so I don't exactly do either and mumble something about my divorced dad living in Hamilton. Our parents (like countless others in Billings) must've believed they were bestowing an advantage on us when they had the scientists make sure Garren and I were highly attractive but it makes it more difficult to blend in now.

As I hand him his ticket, Garren, who was watching my encounter with the ticket guy from a spot about twenty-five feet away, says, "I've been thinking that you should keep a low profile while I get the motel room later. If the two of us walk in together we're guaranteed more problems."

I agree and find myself half hoping it'll be a woman behind the motel check-in counter and that she'll be so transfixed by the sight of Garren that she won't care that he doesn't have a credit card or that his only identification is a (fake) student card.

On the bus, I watch Oakville fade into the distance. I've never been here before and I'll never be back. All I'll ever really know of it is the guy with the Oilers hat and the discount shopping center.

Things will be different when we get out west, I tell myself. We won't have to look over our shoulders every second. And if it still doesn't feel far enough away from the director and his people, we'll keep moving on until we find somewhere that does.

Winston Churchill said, "Sure I am of this, that you have only to endure to conquer. You have only to persevere to save yourselves." I swear his words will be running around in my head for the next fifty years at least.

I didn't have a solid plan for my life back in 2063. I'd had vague thoughts about going into arboriculture and I guess I would've opted for it as a career if it was one of three offered to me. Arborists were greatly in demand in 2063 and helping plants and things grow seemed like something tangible and positive. Eventually I'd probably have had children with whoever the Service paired me up with—that's if some other major plague or nuclear attack didn't come along.

Nothing was ever certain but any assumptions I made previously are out the window. Anything can happen now. It scares me and thrills me at the same time.

I don't want to be captured. I don't want to forget who am I or where I came from. I want to move on from this day with full knowledge behind me.

When we get off the bus in Hamilton a police car drives by us and I flinch at the sight. As much as I've lost so far there's still more to lose. Garren sees my reaction, his eyes trailing mine to the police car. Then he looks away, strokes my hair, grabs my hand and pulls me closer. I start breathing again and rest my head against his shoulder. We're okay. The cops didn't notice us.

Garren goes into the station to ask about nearby motels. I stand outside watching people pass and wondering what their stories are. For all I know some of them could be wanted by the police too. One of them—although it's less likely—might even be from 2063.

Shortly Garren returns with the news that there's a budget hotel on Main Street, within walking distance. He has a small foldout map of Hamilton in his hands and we start trekking in the cold, talking about tomorrow's bus trip to Parry Sound.

"There's no point catching the early-morning bus up there," Garren says. "The train from Toronto doesn't get to Parry Sound until after midnight anyway. If we take the two o'clock bus we'll still have hours to kill there."

Parry Sound's a really small town, from what I've heard, and we'll have to work hard at not standing out. After that it will be four whole days on the train until we reach Vancouver. Since we don't have the money to waste on a compartment there'll be four days of sitting in place and we agree that we'll have to construct background stories for ourselves in case anyone tries to make casual conversation. There, too, we'll have to be careful not to call attention to ourselves but our other option, stealing a car, would add to our list of crimes and further interest the police.

The budget hotel looks a bit like a bunker from the street but I don't care; I can't wait to get inside. I give Garren some of Nancy's money for the room, tell him I'm going to be at the medical building just down the road (because I realize I forgot to buy scissors at the Woolco) and ask him to come get me in the drugstore there once he's checked in. Truthfully, the shooting and craziness at the Eaton Centre this afternoon has made me not want to let him out of my sight for a second but that's impractical and once we're on the train tomorrow we'll be attached at the hip for four days solid.

So I go into the medical building and search out their drugstore to buy scissors like a normal person and not someone who almost had her mind butchered because she remembered that she was sent traveling through time. The director theorized that others who were intellectually ahead of their eras may have also come through chutes. If that's true, which of the world's geniuses are not geniuses after all but time travelers? Galileo? Albert Einstein? Marie Curie? Stephen Hawking? And if that really is the case, where are the other chutes? Are there any that send people forward rather than back?

It's too much to think about and once Garren shows up I'm standing in the medical building lobby just biting my lip and staring at the Indian buffet restaurant across the street. "That wasn't easy," he says tiredly. "You should've heard the bullshit I had to feed the check-in lady about coming up from the States on the bus to visit my father in the hospital up north and then getting my wallet stolen. I told her I missed the connecting bus north while reporting the robbery to the police. She still made me give her an extra fifty for a deposit. What do you want to bet the deposit gets *misplaced* overnight?"

It's worth it just to have some downtime. Garren tells me the room number, says he'll go first and that I should knock when I get there. "We sound like middle-aged people having an affair," I say.

Only if we were having an affair the first thing we'd do when I got to the room and closed the door behind me is tear off each other's clothes and the first thing that happens once I'm inside our room is that I ask Garren to show me his gunshot wound. He unbuttons his shirt, carefully eases both arms out of their sleeves and unties the socks he'd looped around his right arm. The injury is the size of a poker chip and raw and bloody. His skin is completely missing where he was hit, damaged flesh exposed to the air. Ideally he needs stitches or whatever else they do for these things in 1985 . . . I don't know. But that's not going to happen and what we need to do now is make sure it doesn't get infected.

"We should wash it again and cover it in that antiseptic ointment," I tell him. I fill the bathroom sink with warm soapy water and get Garren to bend over the sink and dunk his arm in. He winces when it hits the water and that makes me wince too. The wound starts bleeding again a little, which I hope is normal.

When he pulls his arm out of the water I press one of the bandages firmly against the oozing red to halt the bleeding. "I'm starting to think this grounded shit is overrated," he says through gritted teeth.

"I'm sorry. I'm just trying to get it to stop so we can put on the antiseptic."

"I know, I know." He takes over for me, holding the bandage in place as he sits down on the side of the tub. "It's fine." But we both wince again when I smooth on the ointment a couple of minutes later. It's been a hard day—my roughest in 1985 yet—and when Garren's fresh bandage (a new, dry one) is in place and there's nothing else I can do for him, I pull back the ugly red and orange patterned cover on my bed to expose the pillow underneath. It's soft and welcoming, despite the bedspread it'd been hiding under. I sink wearily down onto it, Garren camped out on his own double bed across from me, shut my eyes and check temporarily out of 1985.

TWENTY-TWO

The darkness smells musty and feels stifling. Like it's settling into my bones and changing me from the inside. My eyelids fight to remain open. They're heavier than they should be—I'm not in control of them, not in control of anything. My body's pinned to the bed by the weight of my fear. He shouldn't be here but he is. Standing at the end of my bed in the gloomy blackness, his body writhing with hate. The sound of bone scraping against bone assaults my ears, his teeth crushing into each other with a ferocity that I can't bear.

If I can't find the strength to fight him, Latham will kill me. My brother's foaming at the mouth, an inhuman noise twisting up through his rib cage and groaning into the air. The hair on my arms stands on end.

Even if I could move, I'll never get away clean. He'll infect me. Drag me with him into a deeper darkness, strip my sanity from me and leave me with infinite rage that exists only to spread. This is what the U.N.A. will be reduced to. A devouring hate.

Garren shouts my name in the dark. I'd forgotten he was here with me. How could I have forgotten?

I have to move, have to save him. And when he yells my name a second time I skyrocket up from dreamland and blink into the daylight.

It's not night after all. There's no Latham. No plague. Not in this place.

It's February 26, 1985, and I'm lying on a hotel bed, catching my breath and gazing blearily over at Garren on the next bed over. The room's kitschy but reasonably clean—composed of two double beds (a nightstand between them), a medium-sized TV, which I notice Garren has turned on, and a small rectangular table with chairs on either side of it. The maroon curtains are closed but daylight's streaming through them and every light fixture in the room is on; there's no shortage of light.

"Bad dream?" Garren asks. "You were whimpering in your sleep. I thought I better wake you up."

"Thanks." I sit up in bed, then pad over to the window and peel back the curtains to stare into the winter sun. "It's still early. I must not have been out long."

"About thirty minutes." Garren studies me. "You okay?"

"I will be. I just have to shake it off." I don't want to remember Latham like that. The thing I saw in my dream wasn't my brother, just my subconscious torturing me.

Garren's still looking at me, but the last thing I want to

do is talk about my nightmare. "I think I'll go cut and dye my hair," I tell him. "Might as well get it over with."

I take the scissors and box of medium-brown hair dye that I bought at Woolco into the bathroom with me. My hands haven't stopped shaking yet and when I stare into the mirror memories of how savage Latham was at the end pierce my brain. He would've torn me apart with his bare hands if it weren't for the force field restricting him to his bedroom.

I grab the scissors and ruthlessly begin lopping off my raven hair. I hack away at it until it's chin-length all round. It's still my face in the mirror but I'll be tougher to recognize at a distance. I go for the hair dye next, rubbing it liberally into what's left of my hair. My eyes burn the same as they did when Christine colored my hair for me. For a minute or two I let my tears spill behind the locked bathroom door, giving in to the terror from my dream, the tension of our close call today and the intensity with which I miss my brother. Then I stop and pull myself together like Latham would want and like I need to do to get through this.

Because of my brand-new haircut there's plenty of dye left over and I open the bathroom door and ask Garren if he wants me to color his hair too. "Good idea," he says.

Since his hair's already so short I have his head coated with dye in no time, which is a good thing because I feel strange running my hands through his hair. It was different when I hugged him earlier—instinctual joy at our survival—and different with the bandaging job because I was worried that

I'd hurt him. Now I have nothing but a pair of rubber gloves to distract me from the awareness that I'm essentially massaging Garren's head. It feels pretty intimate—like a connection back to last night in the Resniks' spare room—and I push away the feeling by making small talk. "Did they cut your hair when they sent you back or was that your idea?" I ask.

"I had it done about a week after we moved up here," he says. "It was driving me crazy—always falling in my eyes."

I liked it longer but you can see Garren's eyes better with it short like this. It seems as though there's no way to hide from them. Whenever he looks my way I feel like there's a spotlight shining on me.

We go back into the other room to wait out the thirty minutes it'll take the dye to set. On the TV a repeat of *Mork & Mindy* gives way to a commercial for the upcoming news. "Gunshots fired at Toronto's Eaton Centre," the newscaster announces. "We'll have the full story at six o'clock."

Garren and I lock eyes. We knew this was coming but it feels like a surprise anyway. There's just over forty minutes until the news and we both have our hair rinsed out in time for the report. There's no footage of the actual incident, just a police officer explaining what witnesses recounted seeing—several people running in the direction of the north end of the shopping center on the upper level, exchanging gunfire. Various witnesses said that at least two men, possibly three, were shot, and that a young woman was spotted committing multiple physical assaults. None of the parties involved remained on the scene when police arrived. Because of this, there's suspected organized crime involvement.

After the police officer is finished with his statement a reporter interviews a succession of Eaton Centre shoppers, asking them for their reaction to the incident. Most people are shocked that an outbreak of such violence would occur in a public place and worried that innocent bystanders could easily have been hurt.

Garren and I continue watching the news right to the end, in case there's anything about the robbery at Janette's house. There's not (it must not be a big enough story) and we discuss the gun again and decide to abandon it somewhere in Hamilton before we leave for Parry Sound tomorrow afternoon. Checkout time is noon and the next beds we sleep in will be somewhere in Vancouver, days from now. That's if we arrive as planned, nothing slowing us down or altering our strategy. But the future's a blank slate. Hard as I try I can't tune in to any visions. It's as though even the universe doesn't know what will become of us yet.

The sun's finished setting and our hair has dried an identical shade of brown that at first glance makes us look like fraternal twins, though the rest of our features are very different. Neither of us has eaten a bite since this morning's spaghetti and we're both starving. I suggest the Indian buffet restaurant just down the street. It looks like an obscure enough place that no one would think to look for us there.

Garren swallows another three aspirin and says he's good to go. As he's slipping on his coat I notice he's sewn up the tear in the right sleeve where the bullet punctured his coat. He must've done it while I was asleep. But it's his hair that I can't stop starting at because I'm not sure what I think of it.

"What?" Garren asks, picking up on my attention.

"Just . . . shouldn't you put on your hat too? Otherwise you could make the woman at the check-in desk suspicious. You know, a guy checks in without a credit card and the first thing he does is dye his hair."

"Right." Garren nods like he can't believe he didn't think of that himself. He fishes Mr. Resnik's black wool hat out of his coat pocket and tugs it over his head. "I can go first, if you want. Wait for you at the lights?"

"Okay. See you at the lights." I watch Garren close the door behind him and wait another two minutes before leaving the room. Down in the lobby I pass an elderly woman with long hair the color of freshly fallen snow. I've seen lots of old people since we've been back here (outside of the welfare camps, few people in the U.N.A. truly looked like senior citizens) but she's the oldest one yet. Her skin's a delicate shade of pink and deeply wrinkled but her eyes are sharp and she smells like satsuma. It's the nicest thing I've smelled all day and I automatically smile at her, which makes her smile back.

There's a warmth in her face that I didn't expect but that shouldn't surprise me. The first person who helped me and Garren was a complete stranger, the blind woman whose house we'd charged into when Henry was chasing us. I don't think the people in 2063 were any worse, deep down, than the people here but we were more distant from each other and more frightened, even when we didn't realize it.

I keep thinking of 2063 as the past but it's still out there, still happening. It's a difficult thing to comprehend.

Outside the hotel I swing right and walk towards the traffic lights. A lone figure who must be Garren is standing there in the distance and I feel relief well up inside me at the sight of him, although we've only been apart a couple of minutes. Before the events of the past few days I never would've imagined that it'd be possible to experience such a range of emotions in one day. I keep zooming back and forth between anxiety at what comes next and elation that we're alive and have made it this far.

At the restaurant we consume outrageous amounts of aloo gobi, sweet rice, tandoori chicken and lamb curry. The place has a homey cheerfulness about it that makes me feel safe, especially the music and the smells. The stress falls away from me as I allow the room to work its magic. Garren seems more at ease too and after we've invented our cover story for the train journey, we begin to talk about our 1985 experiences and our old 2063 lives.

I know Garren had been planning to become a lawyer in the U.N.A.—the kind who would concentrate on helping the illegals and the Cursed. It would be tricky for him to do something like that now, considering our status, and I ask him what he wants to do in the present.

"I haven't had much of a chance to think about it," he

says. "I think I have to really get to know the times firsthand before I make up my mind. If I was older and knew what the directors were plotting I probably would've wanted to get involved and help them rewrite history." He scoops rice into his mouth, chews and swallows. "What they want to do to us is wrong but I respect their larger aims. The West has done too much damage to the planet. If we can change it, I think we have a responsibility to try."

I do too and I ask, "So what would you do to us if you were them?"

"I don't know. But I wouldn't be able to wipe someone's memory knowing that the process could mutilate their mind. I couldn't be that ruthless." Garren pauses. "But I shot at those guys today. Potentially I could've killed someone. So maybe I'm wrong and I do have it in me." Garren sets down his fork and stares at me, his face long. "I *would've* killed them if that's what it took to keep them from taking you."

The thought seems to make him unhappy and I stop eating and remember my feeling at the shopping mall railing, how I couldn't stand the thought of them capturing him and considered throwing myself over both to save him and to die as the person I am now rather than letting myself be butchered.

"What is it?" Garren asks.

"I shouldn't have put you in that position."

"You didn't," he says. "You told me not to come."

"But if you'd listened, they would have taken me."

Garren drops his gaze and rakes his fork through his

rice. "Then I'm glad I was there. If it wasn't for you I'd still be living a lie."

It wasn't a lie exactly and he'd have been safe that way. But I think Garren's like me and given the choice would've picked the hard truth. He wouldn't want to forget his sister or his other mother any more than I'd want to forget Latham.

It's not remotely the right time for this but I can't control myself. The things I imagined I felt about him in the past, when I didn't know him well enough to really feel much at all, and the more genuine feelings that have evolved over the last few days are floating to the surface and I stare at my plate and confess, "I used to watch you sometimes . . . back then. Did you know?"

Garren releases his fork and leans across the table, lowering his head so that I can't avoid his eyes. "You did?"

"Yeah." My voice is almost a whisper. "In the halls at school. You knew that, right?"

He's quiet, thinking. Then he says, "Maybe . . . a little."

"I knew it. I knew you knew."

"Not really." He shakes his head. "I don't know what I thought." He draws one of his fingers over his lips, blinking slowly. "Maybe you should tell me what to think."

Earlier today I told him "but still" because I thought it would make things easier but I'm already wondering if I was wrong. I don't know what to say. I'm not sure what I want him to think.

Garren hesitates, opens his mouth and closes it again

before asking, "So, knowing who you really are, what do you want to do with your life now? You never said."

That's easier to talk about and I reply, "I used to think I wanted to be a tree doctor, or something like that. Help nature thrive." After what we'd done to it, nature needed all the help we could give it. When and where we're from, the list of recently extinct species is depressingly long. With the gravity of our own situation I hadn't really thought about those animals until this moment but the wonder of knowing that so many of them are still out there makes me light-headed. I think of British Columbia, where we're heading, and how the whales and dolphins are swimming off its coast this very second.

No one has seen a great whale, other than those kept in captivity, since 2034 and awe seeps into my words as I say, "I want to see the whales. We should be able to when we make it to British Columbia. They're still in the ocean now. And then, sometime, I want to go to Africa. On safari, you know? See elephants, giraffes, rhinos, all those things. They seem like mythical creatures almost. I want to see them with my own eyes, not in a zoo but in their natural habitat, just living their lives like they should be."

"That would be incredible," Garren says, sounding awed too.

"So maybe you can come with me," I say lightly.

Garren's cheeks swell with the beginnings of a smile. "I'd like that."

I don't know exactly what it is we're agreeing to in saying these things but the music playing in the background is so celebratory that I imagine I know what the singer's feeling even though I don't speak Hindi.

Garren and I begin to talk about what it would be like to see present-day New York City. Before they built the flood barriers, before the Twin Towers were bombed even. Or San Francisco, with its steep hills and cable cars, before everyone left. In the future, no one lives in the southwest anymore. The droughts drove away those who could move and killed those who couldn't. It's a wasteland. *Was a wasteland.* Not now.

I imagine walking across the Golden Gate Bridge, the Pacific Ocean on one side and the San Francisco Bay on the other. An architectural marvel framed by blue. I wish we could see it in person but the United States is too dangerous for us, according to what the director told me. Since the U.N.A.'s political operation in the U.S. is more important than the civilian one up here, their security force would be better, harder to evade.

All the same, the thought that the Golden Gate Bridge is teeming with activity makes me want to dance—that and Garren telling me he'd like to come with me to see the animals. "I feel like I'm drunk on food," I say. "Is that possible?"

"When you've eaten as much as we have."

I sip my water. "I wish we didn't have to leave here."

"The restaurant?" Garren casually scans the room. "You're easily impressed."

I smile and knock one of my knees against his under the table. "It doesn't feel like we're in trouble now. It feels like as long as we stay here we'll be fine."

Garren narrows his eyes. "Why? What do you see?"

"Nothing, absolutely nothing." But it's easier to pretend we're average people while out at dinner than it is in our hotel room.

"Maybe that's a good thing. Maybe it means there's nothing major to worry about." Garren digs into what's left of his curry.

"Maybe so." I'm spending too much time staring at him again and I plant my elbow on the table, lean into my palm and look away.

Garren asks the waiter for more water, providing us with an excuse to stay a few minutes longer but eventually we make our way back to the hotel room. Garren gives me the keys so I can go first. I sit inside our room waiting for him to knock and feel the same relief I experienced at the traffic lights earlier when I hear him rap at the door.

With the two of us safely inside I go into the bathroom to brush my teeth and change into jogging pants and a T-shirt. Then I climb into bed and wait for him to finish getting ready and turn out the lights. I'm scared to sleep but not as scared as before we went to the restaurant and tiredness quickly overwhelms me.

When I open my eyes again it's dark and I know I'm not dreaming because everything's just as it was before I went to sleep except that Garren's shouting. Not words exactly but anguished cries. I sit up in bed and say his name. "Wake up," I add. "Garren. *Garren*. Wake up."

I'm nearly as loud as he is. I have to be if I want him to hear me over his own noise. If there's anyone in the room next to us they must be cursing him.

I get out of bed and step closer to his form in the moonlight. "Garren." I touch him high on his shoulder, careful to avoid his gunshot wound. "Garren, you're dreaming."

He opens his eyes and stares at me like he doesn't remember where he is or who I am. I can literally see it all begin to come back to him, weighing down his conscious self.

"You were dreaming," I explain. "Yelling in your sleep. I was scared it could wake the people in the next room."

Garren rubs his eyes, his pupils sharpening their focus on me in the bright moonlight. "Sorry," he murmurs.

"If it wasn't you it'd probably be me. Maybe we'll just keep taking turns having nightmares from now on."

"Let's make a point of not doing that," Garren says.

"We can try. What were you dreaming?"

He exhales audibly as he sits up. "Nothing good."

"I dreamt about Latham earlier," I confess, stepping back to sit on the side of my bed. "That's what I was dreaming when you woke me up—that he was here and was going to kill me."

Garren presses his lips grimly together. "Kinnari was violent like the rest of them when they came for her. I can't imagine what it must be like in the U.N.A. now."

So many dead, I don't want to imagine. "Maybe your mother and my father eventually will be sent back here too."

"We'll never know it, but I hope so. Although that would probably mean things were even worse. A point of no return."

I'm still sitting on the side of my bed, listening to his voice in the moonlight and fighting the pull I feel towards him because he already matters too much. But it's like fighting the impulse to breathe. A person can only hold her breath for so long.

"Can we turn the radio on low?" I ask. "I don't want to go back to sleep with all these dark thoughts in my head." The clock radio's perched on the slim nightstand between our beds and Garren reaches for it and switches it on. Howard Jones is singing "Things Can Only Get Better" and I chuckle drily. It should be our theme song.

Garren echoes my laughter and I tell myself to lie back, pull the covers over me and wait for tomorrow but what if there is no tomorrow, only tonight? Our luck could run out at any time. The director and his men almost had us at the Eaton Centre. If the bullet had hit Garren in the head instead of the arm, we wouldn't be here together now. A second can change everything, sending life down a different path.

There's a lump in my throat and my voice is hushed as I say, "Garren?"

"Yeah?" His voice is quiet too, like there's a third person in the room who we don't want to hear us.

"Can I get in there with you?" I can't imagine him telling

me no but my heart's beating fast, as though it fears that possibility.

"Come here." He sounds so warm that I almost forget all the bad things in my head. They shrink as I walk towards him and feel him wrap his arms around me.

He feels warm too, warmer than me, and when I sink down onto the bed with him and tell him that, he presses his lips into my forehead and says, "You feel warm to me. Just as warm as I do."

"No, you're warmer," I argue. Then I drop my lips to his, open my mouth and kiss him like this is just the beginning.

His kiss is sweet and hungry at the same time. He pulls me on top of him and slips his fingers into my hair. "I keep forgetting you cut it," he murmurs. "Every time I look at you, it's new."

I run my hand softly over his short brown hair. "For me too."

He slides his mouth down my neck, one of his hands on the hip of my jogging pants. "Mine's not that different, is it?"

Not to someone who hasn't spent as much time staring at him as I have, maybe.

Our mouths collide again and again. We're on fire. Saying each other's names in tones we've never used before. Drinking each other in with our hands. "I can't stop thinking about you like this," I whisper, my fingers on his T-shirt, riding up under it to feel the heat from his skin.

"*Don't,*" he advises, his hands in my hair again. "I can't stop thinking about you either. Even in my sleep."

We already have so many things to worry about, like staying alive, and when I pull away a bit to look at him, I see Garren absorb the confusion in my face.

"Hey." He reaches for my hand, lacing his fingers through mine so that our two hands feel like a single entity. "Shouldn't we get to have something good in all this? Why can't we have this?"

Because it will make me even more scared to lose him. But I don't say that either. I tug his hand to my lips and kiss it. *We will have this.* I'm done fighting myself. What's the point of being here if I'm too afraid to have the things I want because it means I might lose them someday?

We lie in Garren's bed exchanging wet kisses and touching each other until he has to stop and swallow more aspirin for his arm. We both know things can't go any further, that without the Bio-net it's not safe, but for now just being together is enough. We can figure out the rest later.

When Garren comes back to bed I hook both my legs around one of his and nestle into his shoulder. He kisses my hair and says, "You asked me what I was dreaming before. I was dreaming they were taking you and that I couldn't stop them. I never want to feel like that again."

"I can't handle the thought of them taking you either." I drape my hand across the dip of Garren's waist. "I'm not letting them get near you. We won't let them take us."

"We'll be each other's own best defense system," Garren says, like it's a promise.

We will. We'll have this and protect it. No one will be

allowed to stand in our way. We'll make it out to Vancouver and live our lives on our own terms. See the whales and, from a distance, watch the people who would try to hurt us attempt to save the planet. I hope they can do it and that the world will become a different place than I knew. I hope that more for the people who come after me than for myself. Garren and I can have a lot of good years here either way. We have time.

I fall asleep with my hand resting on his chest and as far as I know, I don't dream, but I remember thinking, just before I slip away from consciousness, that Latham and Kinnari would be happy for us. If they can't be together like they should've been, it might as well be us.

TWENTY-THREE

We're happy when we wake up in his bed together, happy when Garren checks out of the hotel for us and meets me at the traffic lights. We've stuffed the gun inside the pair of socks Garren had around his arm yesterday and slide the socks into a plastic Woolco bag, which we tie at the top before dipping down a side street and tossing the bag into a large Dumpster behind a tall apartment building.

Then we go into a cheap deli, buy sandwiches and sit at a red Formica table staring at each other with infinite grins as we swallow bits of white bread. I wish I could tell Christine how the part of my story involving the déjà vu guy I'd never met turned out. Nobody but Garren will ever know the entire story. We're the ultimate secret.

"We should go get the bus tickets," Garren says, his hand on my knee.

I lean in close and kiss him. I love his mouth. I love that

he's the kind of person who has always wanted to help make the world a better place.

Garren holds my face in his hands and peers into my eyes. I never want to stop looking at him, never want him to stop looking at me. If we let ourselves, we could get trapped in this moment and miss the bus to Parry Sound.

I whisper in Garren's ear and make him smile. We get up from the table and sling our backpacks onto our spines. I can hear the radio spilling music out from behind the deli counter. Everywhere in 1985 there's music. Like a party that never stops.

"Ninety-nine dreams I have had. In every one a red balloon."

Garren impulsively grabs my hand and twirls me around.

I laugh as I spin and as I swivel back towards him something outside catches my eye. Across the street a guy with a buzz cut and sunglasses is stepping into a black car. He's wearing a nondescript gray coat and could be anyone but I know better—I know it's one of the men who came to Henry's house to take us away. I'd recognize him anywhere.

"Sit down," I say urgently. "One of them is out there right now. I don't think he saw us."

Garren deposits himself in the nearest chair, every ounce of joy draining from his face.

I sit too and watch the black car merge into traffic. It's heading east and I glance at Garren across the table and say, "He's going—he's driving off."

"Fuck." Garren plunks his good arm down on the table.

"They've trailed us from Toronto. There's no way we can risk going to the bus station now. We'll have to steal a car."

I turn away from the window and clear my mind. How many of them are out there searching for us? Where's our path to safety?

A series of conflicting images flicker inside my head. Us walking to the bus station. Almost there. But so are they. We run. Garren crumples to the ground, his head bleeding.

Us in front of the deli, only steps away from where we sit right now. A black car veers into the parking lot. Garren charges at the man with the buzz cut. Garren crumples. I struggle with the man, grab his gun. It goes off against his chest.

Us inside a car, peeling off down the road. A stranger's body lying lifeless in the street behind us.

I've never had concurrent visions before. I don't know which images to trust. My arms grip my sides as I press my eyelids together and concentrate harder. It doesn't help. The same images play over and over, as if on a loop.

"Tell me what's in your head," Garren says.

Him *dead*. Him *alive*. I can't lose him. I can't make the wrong choice.

"What?" Garren's face creases in alarm. "What do you see?"

"A lot of different things at the same time. Most of them bad." I'm crippled by fear but keep my voice strong. "Just, don't do anything yet. Give me some time."

For the future to untangle itself. Maybe we can outwait the director's security forces.

We sit hunched in our chairs, staring out the window, for at least fifteen minutes. We're not the only ones inside the deli. A trio of balding men are nursing coffees and a washed-out-looking blond woman and her burly, mustached boyfriend have begun to argue in the corner. "That's fucking unfair and you know it," the boyfriend bellows to the blond woman across the table. "Do you think you're the only one who has given up things to try to make this work?"

"Oh, I *know* I am," she retorts. "I gave up everything for you and look what it got me. You don't give a shit about making this work. You just don't want me to be with anyone else. That's all this is about for you. Keeping me to yourself so that we both go down together."

The visions start up again as I listen to the couple argue. There are more details now. I see the light go out of Garren's eyes for good as he falls. I hear myself howl in my mind, my soul rebelling against the loss.

It can't come to that. *There has to be a way out of this.*

"Follow me," I tell Garren. "We'll go by the back door."

I don't know what else to do. We have to leave sometime and in my vision we were in front of the deli, not behind it.

Garren nods. He trusts that I know what I'm doing.

We get up and shamble towards the counter. I crane my head over it and focus on the twenty-something-year-old guy behind the counter. He has a mop of overgrown red hair and a ruddy complexion to match. "Excuse me," I say, "is there a back door we can use?"

"The back door is for employees only."

"Right, I know. But my dad is out there looking for us. I just saw him across the street a few minutes ago, and if he sees me with him"—I point my thumb at Garren behind me—"he'll kill him."

The redheaded guy smirks at us like he's in on a dirty little secret. "Someone's been a *baaad* boy."

Garren's lips form a crooked grin. "I could take her old man no problem but she doesn't want us to get into it."

The redheaded guy chuckles. "Okay, I'll be the good guy here and save your asses." He saunters down to the end of the counter and lifts the latch on the waist-high door to allow us entrance. Then we follow him into the kitchen where a woman in a hairnet is stirring an enormous pot of chili. She glances at us sideways but says nothing.

"Right there," the guy drawls, his finger aiming at the exit sign. As we're leaving he says to our backs, "Be good, kids!" and wheezes with laughter.

We hustle up a side street, past brick houses, green spaces and apartment buildings, our eyes constantly scanning the surrounding area. My heart's racing but my mind is empty of visions—a single wish pounding behind my eyes, that our stealthy departure was enough to magically shuffle the variables and alter our future. We've already beaten the scenario in one of my visions. And we won't set foot near the bus station. Does that mean we're in the clear or does it just mean the director's men will get us some other way?

"Let's cut back towards the lake," I say breathlessly. "We shouldn't get too close to the station."

"We need to go back for the gun," Garren declares as we turn sharply. "It's not safe out here on the street. We have to get our hands on a car."

There were no bullets left in the gun we dropped into the Dumpster but I see what Garren means. I don't know how to hot-wire a car and I guess he doesn't either. Pointing a gun at someone is the fastest way to get their car keys.

Damn. We should've held on to it.

We continue down the street, beginning to work our way back to the apartment building where we dumped the gun. My eyes keep catching on passing black cars. I gasp a little at each one.

"We're good," Garren tells me. "*We're good.* We're good." It's like a chant almost. "We'll get the gun and get out of here."

I adjust my hair under my hat, having forgotten that since it's shorter and lighter now I have no need to hide it.

Without warning a silver car jumps onto the sidewalk ahead of us, partially blocking our path. In a flash we turn and bolt in the opposite direction. Garren's legs are longer and he's ahead of me in no time, slowing to wait for me.

"Freya!" a female voice calls. It sounds both familiar and a little frail. I immediately think of my mother. What am I going to do if they've dragged her into this?

I glance back to check, slowing to a jog. The woman's not

chasing me. I don't think she could if she tried. She's ancient. Not my mother but familiar all the same. Thin and graceful with long white hair. This must be a trick dreamt up by the director. Someone who looks harmless to reel us in.

"I'm here to help you both," the woman says from her place next to the car. "The director didn't send me but he's looking for you. Please, get in the car. It's for you. You can take it wherever you want to go."

I've stopped and am gawking at her, Garren trying to pull me along with him. "Don't listen to her," he warns. "She has to be with them."

"I know what you saw in your visions back at the deli," the white-haired woman yells. "You saw them kill him. In two different places. I'm trying to stop that."

Garren lets go of my arm. He stares wide-eyed at the old woman. It's then that I recognize her. She was in our hotel lobby last night when I left for the restaurant. The woman who smelled like satsuma and smiled back at me.

I don't understand what's happening. She could've taken us last night if she'd wanted to. She could've and she didn't.

"It's true," I tell him. "That's what I saw."

The woman waves a small envelope over her head as I cautiously approach, Garren a step behind me. "I have new ID for you too. I'm going to set it down and walk away. The ownership papers for the car are in the glove box and made out in your new names. Take the car. Take the ID. Go to Vancouver or wherever else you think you want to be but you have to go *now*."

We're so focused on what the old woman's saying that we don't see the lean man barging over from across the street until it seems as if it's already too late. I don't recognize him but he's walking with a sense of purpose that can be no coincidence.

"Are you going to shoot us all?" the old woman asks. "Don't you think that might create more problems than it will solve?"

"I'm not going to shoot anyone," the man insists. "I'm this boy's uncle. He's a runaway. So is the girl. I'm just here to bring them home."

"He's not anyone's uncle," I object.

But the white-haired woman already knows that and is striding towards the man with a stillness in her blue eyes that steals my breath. "You're not taking them," she tells him.

"Listen, it has nothing to do with you." The man retreats a step. "It's family business, okay? I'm sure you think you're helping these kids but what they need is to be back with their families."

Across the street a radio crackles and a disembodied voice demands an update. The man casts a fleeting look over his shoulder at his car as the radio continues to spit out noise. The voice could be the director's himself and I hear it ask for a description of the vehicle.

"Freya, Garren, get in the car," the woman commands, moving ever closer to the man whose job it is to steal us and make us forget forever. She's closer to him now than she is to us.

"No." The man raises his hand as we step nearer to the silver car. He reaches into his jacket for his gun and aims it at us. The woman lunges at him, one of her hands grasping for the gun as her body blocks his.

She's still shouting at us and I'm staring at her, shocked that someone so old could hold him off, even for a moment. "Freya, take Garren and go. You lost him the last time you got this far. It could happen again."

Again. My veins run cold as the truth echoes inside me.

What would I do if Garren was killed today? I'd do everything within my power to find Victor Soto in the here and now, twenty-two years after Lake Nipigon whipped him into 1963. A U.N.A. archivist discovered evidence of him, which means there must be a trail to follow. And then, once I'd reached Victor, I'd ask him for the exact location of Lake Nipigon, which would send me back seventy-eight years, seven months and eleven days in time.

Eventually, I would come back to this moment, if I lived long enough. I would do anything I could to stop them from killing Garren.

It's what I *did*. Once already. The woman in front of me is another Freya. Even as I realize it the fact seems impossible to grasp. It loops repeatedly inside my head, slipping and sliding as I tumble after it. *She is me.* The knowledge pounds between my ears as Garren tears towards the altercation.

The old woman—old Freya—is driving her fist into the man's Adam's apple. I'm running too and the gun goes off. She—I—collapse in a heap. The man gasps for breath but he still has the gun. Garren grabs for it, grappling with the man. I throw myself into the fight, hurl myself between them, the old woman lying at our feet.

When the second shot goes off I don't know what's happened—which of us has been hit—until the man sinks to his knees next to my dying old body, leaving me with the gun in my hand. My fingers are bloody but I can't feel any pain—the blood must be all his. Garren and I watch the director's man thump to the ground, blood gushing from his chest.

"We have to go," Garren cries. "Get in the car."

I drop the gun and sink to my knees next to the woman I could become. The man got her in the neck and she's bleeding badly but still alive. "It's me," I tell Garren, because I don't know if he understands that yet. "She's *me*."

I reach for her hand and squeeze. Her fingers are freezing. I can barely feel her return the pressure but her gaze is holding mine. Her stare is tender, protective. "I'm sorry," I tell her. "I'm sorry."

She begins to smile as if it's okay, as if this is how it was supposed to go all along. I guess from her point of view it was. Then she shuts her eyes and stops breathing and I know we can't stay here another second.

If we get caught now everything she did would have been for nothing.

I feel Garren's arm on my back. "I have the envelope," he says quietly. She must have dropped it when she lunged for the director's man. "Please, Freya, *let's go.*"

I get up and stumble towards the car, my face streaming with tears. She left the key in the ignition for us and Garren jumps into the driver's seat and starts the engine. I burrow into the passenger seat, feeling miles away. We all lose ourselves to something eventually, but not like this. I can't imagine what the other Freya must have gone through to get here. I thought I'd had it hard but suddenly my own difficulties feel like nothing in comparison. So much of her life must have been lived with this day in mind. The odds would've been against her from the start.

I don't know how I'd do it. But I would. I never thought of myself as weak but that kind of strength is a revelation. I would go back in time to give some newer version of me a better chance at happiness.

Only I won't have to. She did it for me and I'm filled with a gratitude so cavernous that it makes me cry harder.

Why didn't she approach me at the hotel last night? The sole reason I can imagine is that ominous visions kept her from intervening earlier. It seems that she wanted to get as close as possible to the moment that she lost Garren last time. Every step we take has the potential to change something, create a ripple that gives rise to potential new dangers from the director's men. The conflicting visions in my head made me acutely aware of that. So did Garren's gunshot wound. Having failed once, given the chance to do things over it appears that I'd walk in my own footsteps exactly until just before the crucial minute, as near as a person can come to cheating fate.

Not that I believe in fate. How could I, knowing that you can change the past? But old Freya must have reached the conclusion that she shouldn't make waves. When she saw me in the lobby she knew which path we'd ultimately choose today and knew those hours in the dark with Garren lay ahead of me too. As right as those hours felt, like something that was meant to happen, that doesn't mean they were fate either—only that some moments have a special shine to them, the quality of being the best and truest they can be.

We're out of town, on a highway to who knows where, before Garren or I say anything.

"Where are you going?" I ask. I've cried all the moisture from my voice. It sounds like sandpaper.

"North." Garren takes his eyes off the road to glance at me. "I don't know where we catch up with the Trans-Canada Highway but it's north somewhere. When we get far enough away we can ask for directions."

I nod dazedly. I don't know how long this will all take to sink in.

"It'll be days before we get to Vancouver," he continues. "At this time of year we're bound to run into some really shitty weather on the way. I see a lot of motels in our immediate future." Garren lowers his voice, his right hand landing on my thigh. "I won't ask you what you see." His individual fingers tap my jeans in quick succession, over and over until I reach across the gearshift and touch him back.

I still don't know what to say—how to put my feelings into words—and Garren just keeps talking through it. About anything. That he didn't realize how strong the sun was until we got in the car. That he's glad for the false memories because they make driving a snap. That he's not sure whether the car has snow tires but he hopes so because we have a long, long way to go. Miles to go before we sleep, he jokes.

Garren's eyes fill with something I can't describe. "But you can sleep for a while if you want," he adds.

I don't want to. I want to stay awake with him. "I can drive later," I mumble. "We can switch when you're tired."

Garren nods and touches me again. It's like we can't stop. We need to keep doing it to prove we're both still here. "Okay," he says. "Okay, good." He scratches his cheek and then retrieves the envelope from his coat pocket, handing it to me. "Have a look and see what's in there."

I tear it open. There are two sets of identification inside—driver's licenses, birth certificates and the Canadian version of Social Security cards (Social Insurance cards). I stare at the faces in the photographs, our faces. My identification is made out in the name of Holly Allen and the photo of me on the driver's license looks almost exactly like I do now. Maybe my hair's ever so slightly longer. Garren's photograph is the one I've spied on his fake student card. I guess it was the only one of him I had.

"You're Robert Clark," I tell him, clearing my throat. "You turn twenty on July twelfth."

"And who are you?"

I quote my name and new date of birth. I was eighteen as of December third.

"Holly," Garren repeats. "That's nice. Not as nice as Freya but I guess we have to get used to the new names." His eyes seek mine out and now I think I recognize most of the various emotions I see in them. Some of them were in the final look old Freya gave me. Some of them are mirror-image reflections of feelings I can't ever imagine having for anyone but Garren. The bit left over is pure admiration and I listen to Garren say, "I can't believe everything she must have done to reach us. I can't—" He cuts himself off, his eyes shining as he starts over. "*You did all this*. You saved my life."

He's going to make me start crying again. I shoot him a look that translates simultaneously as *you're welcome* and *shut up*. I only stopped unraveling a few minutes ago; I'm not ready to get that raw again.

We fall mute, both of us gazing determinedly at the road ahead until I believe I can trust my voice. "I think . . . you're more of a Robbie than a Robert."

Garren's green eyes glint wetly in the sun. "Okay." He takes a swipe at one of his eyes. "So I already have myself a nickname."

I lay my hand on his leg for what must be the fourteenth time since we started driving and try to think of something else to say that won't make either of us cry. "*Robbie*, you know, ever since I got back here those Winston Churchill quotes from the Dailies keep popping into my head."

"They were good quotes." Garren raises his chin. His voice is bold and defiant as he says, "Never, never, never give up."

Never, never, never. Winston was on to something there.

I smile for the first time since we got into the car. It feels faint but I think it will soon be stronger. "Can we drive straight through to Winnipeg?" I ask. *Miles to go before we sleep.*

It seems right to be on the road. Like as long as we're moving we'll never be caught. Never, never, never. I can't see anything but the present. No visions tugging at my mind. I hope it's a good sign, and maybe when we reach Vancouver and see the whales I'll finally believe we're safe. We're not invincible but we're definitely each other's best defense system. I've proven that.

"Of course we can," Garren says, and there's his hand on me again, again, again. "We can take turns sleeping in the backseat."

"That sounds good," I tell him, and I stare across the highway at the sea of 1985 people in their clunky old polluting vehicles. The way the light hits the bobbing jumbles of metal makes the cars look nearly pretty. They shimmer as they hurtle forward and skate across lanes. There's a pony-tailed girl with a rambunctious dog in the backseat of the Buick ahead of us, and a bearded man in a leather jacket singing along to his radio in the station wagon on our left. These are our people now. This is our time. I flick on the radio and flip through the stations, looking for the first familiar song I can find. I stop on a Depeche Mode tune and Garren smiles.

We drive on, deeper into the present, disappearing seamlessly into 1985. Just a regular teenage couple with the radio up loud, wondering what, aside from love, the world has in store for them.

ACKNOWLEDGMENTS

As always, thanks to my husband, Paddy, for being my trusty first reader and sounding board and for making me laugh when that's what I need the most.

I've been on many journeys with my editor, Shana Corey, but this is our first trip through time together. Thanks, Shana, for your patience and insight. You've made my books a greater thing on every occasion and that's some special kind of magic.

Many thanks also to our partner in crime (and fellow Billy Bragg fan), editor Amy Black, and my trusty, unflappable agent, Stephanie Thwaites.

My boundless gratitude to Nicole de las Heras for creating a cover that looks like a zillion dollars and awes me every time I look at it. Nicole, I can't thank you enough.

Finally, I'd be remiss to write a book set in 1985 and not mention music in my acknowledgments. So *enormous* thanks to the bands and artists who shaped my experience of the first half of the 1980s. It wouldn't have been a fraction as cool a time without your music in my life: ABBA, Adam Ant/Adam and the Ants, A-ha, The Alarm, Alison Moyet, Alphaville, Altered Images, Art of Noise, Asia, Banana-rama, The Bangles, The Beat, Berlin, Big Country, Billy Bragg, Billy Idol, Billy Joel, Blancmange, Blondie, Bob Dylan, Bob Marley, The Boomtown Rats, Bow Wow Wow, Bronski Beat, Bruce Springsteen, Bryan Adams, Bryan Ferry, The Cars, China Crisis, Chris de Burgh, Clannad, The Clash, Corey Hart, Culture Club, The Cure, Cyndi Lauper, David Bowie, Def Leppard, Depeche Mode, Dire Straits, Double, The Dream Academy, Duran Duran, Echo & the Bunnymen, Elton John, Elvis Costello, Eurythmics, The Fixx, Fleet-wood Mac, A Flock of Seagulls, Frankie Goes to Hollywood, General Public, Genesis, Go West, The Go-Go's, Gowan, Grace Jones, Haircut 100, Heaven 17, Honeymoon Suite, Howard Jones, The Human League, The Icicle Works, Images in Vogue, INXS, Irene Cara, J. Geils Band, Jackson Browne, The Jam, Jane Siberry, The Jesus and Mary Chain, Joan Jett, Joe Jackson, John Cougar, John Waite, Journey, Kajagoo-goo, Kate Bush, Kim Wilde, The Kinks, Kirsty MacColl, Laura Branigan, Level 42, Lionel Richie, Lloyd Cole and the Commotions, Loverboy, Luba, Madness, Madonna, Marillion, Martha and the Muffins, Men at Work, Men Without Hats, Midnight Oil, Modern English, The Motels, Naked Eyes, Nena, New Order, Nick Heyward, Nik Kershaw, Nina Hagen, Olivia Newton-John, Orchestral Manoeuvers in the Dark (OMD), The Parachute Club, Pat Benatar, Paul Hyde

and the Payola$, Paul McCartney, Paul Young, Pet Shop
Boys, Peter Gabriel, Phil Collins, Pink Floyd, Platinum
Blonde, The Police, The Pretenders, Prince, The Psychedelic
Furs, Public Image Ltd., Queen, Quiet Riot, R.E.M., The
Ramones, Rational Youth, Real Life, Red Rider, Rick Spring-
field, Romeo Void, Rough Trade, Roxy Music, Rush, Sade,
Saga, Scorpions, Scritti Politti, Sheena Easton, Sheriff, Sim-
ple Minds, Siouxsie and the Banshees, Slade, The Smiths,
Soft Cell, Spandau Ballet, The Specials, Split Enz, The
Spoons, Stephen Duffy, The Stranglers, The Style Council,
Talk Talk, Tears for Fears, Thompson Twins, 'Til Tuesday,
Tina Turner, Tom Petty and the Heartbreakers, Toto, Tri-
umph, Twisted Sister, U2, UB40, Ultravox, Van Halen, Vio-
lent Femmes, Visage, Wah!, Wang Chung, The Waterboys,
Wham!, Whitney Houston, The Who, Yazoo, and Yes.

ABOUT THE AUTHOR

C. K. Kelly Martin is the critically acclaimed author of *I Know It's Over, One Lonely Degree, The Lighter Side of Life and Death,* and *My Beating Teenage Heart.* She began writing her first novel in Dublin and currently lives in the greater Toronto area with her husband. She was sixteen years old in 1985 and continues to look back on the eighties with extreme fondness. You can visit her website and blog at ckkellymartin.com.